RY

MW01143464

The Shiva

THE SHIVA

A Novel

Michael Tregebov

VANCOUVER
NEW STAR BOOKS
2012

NEW STAR BOOKS LTD.
107 — 3477 Commercial Street
Vancouver, BC V5N 4E8   CANADA
1574 Gulf Road, #1517
Point Roberts, WA 98281   USA

www.NewStarBooks.com
info@NewStarBooks.com

The Shiva is a work of fiction, a product of the writer's imagination. Any resemblance by any character to any person, living or dead, is entirely coincidental.

Copyright Michael Tregebov 2012. All rights reserved. No part of this work may be reproduced, stored in a retrieval system or transmitted, in any form or by any means, without the prior written consent of the publisher or a licence from the Canadian Copyright Licensing Agency (Access Copyright).

The publisher acknowledges the financial support of the Canada Council, the Government of Canada through the Book Publishing Industry Development Program, the British Columbia Arts Council, and the Government of British Columbia through the Book Publishing Tax Credit.

Cataloguing information for this book is available from Library and Archives Canada, www.collectionscanada.gc.ca.

Cover design: Clint Hutzulak / Rayola.com
Cover photograph: DElight
Printed and bound in Canada by Imprimerie Gauvin, Gatineau, QC
Printed on 100% post-consumer recycled paper.
First printing, July 2012

For Pablo and Jason

Oisgeflikt und aheim geshikt.

I

– Crap.

– Eisenteeth?

– Crap.

– I told you.

– Why didn't you remind me at home?

– I did.

Who's Eisenteeth? thought Mooney, standing in a rut of slush. It was Sammy and his wife Anna. Why are they waiting for Eisenteeth?

– We're late, said Sammy.

– We can't go in without Eisenteeth, said Anna.

– I'll just cover my mouth.

– You're not going in there like that.

– Stop *mintering* me.

– I'm not *mintering* you. I'm just saying.

Mooney tried to remember if he knew an Eisenteeth. He knew an Eisenberg, and an Eisenholt, and an Eisenberg, but no Eisenteeth.

– We're late, said Sammy.

– So we'll be a bit later. We've probably missed the ceremony.

– People will see us here.

– Everyone's inside.

– Eisenteeth's coming, said Anna.

Mooney looked around but saw no one coming. But he did see this:

Anna extracted Sammy's uppers from her purse wrapped loosely in a hanky.

– Here, hold these.

Then she drew out his Xalatan eye drops and handed them to

him. Sammy stood there, his uppers in his left hand and his eye drops in his right.

– How should we start?

– With the teeth, he said.

– Aw, Christ.

Sammy inserted his uppers halfway and then his wife pushed them in with her knuckles, an operation he was incapable of completing on his own. He ran his tongue over his teeth. Then Anna took the eye drops and administered one drop to each eye. Sammy blinked rapidly.

– Stand still, said Anna.

– It hurts.

– It doesn't hurt. Are you alright.

– I'm tearing, said Sammy.

– Wipe your eyes.

– I'll be okay.

– Wipe your eyes.

– Stop *mintering* me. It's late.

– I'm not. I've finished *mintering* you.

– What's this?

– This is the *postmintering*.

– OK. Let's just go in already. Eisenteeth made it, said Sammy.

– You'd better pray that I live one day longer than you, that's all I know.

– Oh, Mooney, I didn't notice you, said Sammy.

– Hi, Sammy.

– What's it going to be, Mooney?

– Same-old, same-old. And you?

– Ach, he said, wagging his hand, as if telling someone to leave.

– Hi, Anna.

– *Mazel tov*, Mooney. Your brother Dave must be very proud.

– Who's Eisenteeth? Mooney asked them.

– Eyes and teeth. Sammy said, pointing to his running eyes and then his uppers. Eyes and teeth.

He recognized the Xalatan dispenser that Sammy was just now pocketing.

– Give me that, you'll lose it, said Anna.

– It's late.

Sammy opened one of the massive doors to the synagogue.

– Coming in, Mooney?

– I'm coming.

– How come you're not inside already?

– Can't stand the blood.

– What's in the bag?

– Bagels for the bride.

– You're bringing bagels to a *briss*?

And then they were swallowed up.

In a worn, sere overcoat, Mooney had trundled across the slushy pavements of a late winter's morning snowfall and arrived at the synagogue complex, snowflakes twinkling on his whisk-broom eyelashes, carrying a brown paper bag with bagels from Sun's bakery. Besides being squeamish, the reason he had arrived late was that he had to make a stop at the drugstore to refill his prescription of Xalatan, which his doctor had prescribed a few months ago for his glaucoma. 'Kiss those thin eyelashes good-bye,' the pharmacist had said on his first purchase of the drug. 'With this you're going to be accused of curling them.' Then he added:

– You're a bit young for glaucoma.

– There's more glaucoma among young people than is commonly thought. Especially in African Americans.

– Not your case.

– In mine it's hereditary. My father had it.

The pharmacist had handed Mooney the package in a plastic bag. Mooney opened his wallet, fingered the few grimy tens and tried to pay the man.

– You pay going out.

On the sidewalk again, he was cast adrift. Wasting time. The synagogue beckoned.

Once inside, his untied shoelaces were soaking wet. Look at my shoes, he said to himself. I can't tie my laces properly. But his shoes were still on because they had been bought for him, a size too small. He held the sodden laces and miraculously he remembered how to tie a knot.

He stood before the carpeted vestibule, which was big enough to ride a bike across. Drawn to the empty main chapel first, he touched the benches appointed in blue velvet. He found it *senza* comfort. Was that the word for it? Comfortless? How did he know the Italian expression for what he wanted to say? Did he know Italian? Of course, he did. The electroshocks had frazzled his memory, but he hadn't lost it. It was just as if someone had ransacked the filing cabinets in his head and jumbled up all the folders.

He had expected the chapel to comfort him. But there was no comfort there. The very size and brassiness of the two humongous menorahs pressed on his sternum.

And now he was now sitting around a table set with pink carnations in one of the overheated basement salons. He unknotted his tie in the torrid heat, taking in the humming of cheerful voices, trying to focus on a group of several young people, Richie Michaels' girls, and then the cousins, to various degrees of consanguinity, of the mother and father of the tragic main character of the ceremony, who was now sequestered with his mother and father and grandmother, recovering from the first of the many shocks that would be coming his way.

Life, right from the start, was for the shits, Mooney thought. He was glad he had missed the ceremony.

They had sat him at the kids' table, which was lavishly laid with hard-boiled eggs, cheese blintzes, herring, smoked salmon, hot fish, whipped cream cheese, potato pancakes, knishes, defrosted strawberries, bagels, and iced vodka and assorted beverages. His stomach was beginning to grumble pleasantly.

From time to time their server came by, scowled, and dumped fresh chunks of hot fish. After a week of bad food at home, the sight of the spread, the tablecloths and candles made him shiver with pleasure. But how did he get there? He had just been in the chapel.

The 'cousins' were boys and girls in their late teens and early twenties. They had their cell phones on the table and they giggled, when they weren't laughing. And they needed nothing in particular to make them laugh. All it took was a message from someone: they'd say the name of the caller and they would all break up.

All the girls wore bangs, some to the right, some to the left, and, it seemed, two bras judging from the number of straps on their shoulders. And when one giggled, they all giggled. Why did they sit him at the kids' table? But it was going to be a fun table, he thought, despite the ferocious temperature of the room. It's the old people, he thought, they liked the heat up.

One of the boy cousins sitting next to him, hairy as a boar, Mooney thought, was wearing a T-shirt sporting the slogan 'Got Home?'.

– What does that mean? Mooney asked, shooting his cuffs from the sleeves of his shiny brown suit. Hey you, I'm talking to you.

The young man chuckled.

– Me?

– Yes, you. What does 'Got Home?' mean. Mooney blinked at him.

– It invites you to make *aliyah*.

– To Israel?

– Where else?

Parched, Mooney took a drink of the iced vodka that was on the table. It was so cold it scalded his throat and he felt his thick eyelashes fill with water. It was something he had not had for a long time, but he recognized it as something he knew well. But it was different, like a miracle that you could swallow. He wiped his eyes with his immaculate napkin and then drained the shot glass.

– What's your name?

– Jerry.

– I hear there are a lot of poor people in Israel, Jerry. Why would anyone want to go there?

– Myth. That's a myth. They're worse off here than in Israel.

– Who?

– The poor.

– I'm not sure I follow you, Jerry.

– Look, one out of every five Jews lives on the poverty line in America. One in seven below it. For example, in the US, in Chicago, there are two hundred and seventy-five thousand Jews, and one in five is poor. In NYC, one-quarter of the Jewish population live on or under the poverty line, with families of four earning less than twenty thousand a year. That's three hundred and forty-eight thousand Jews living below the US Federal Poverty Line, in New York alone.

– That's less than five thousand a year per head? said Mooney.

– Do the math.

– I did.

– The New York food bank last year gave away four and a half million pounds of kosher food to community food programs.

– What kind of kosher food? That'd include the blintz?

The boar-boy looked at Mooney suspiciously. It was hard to tell if Mooney was pulling his leg or not. But Mooney's expression was pure, almost beatific. And with the others at the table listening, Jerry didn't want to look like a fool, but he didn't want to come off mean either.

– I think there'd be some blintzes.

– A little kreplach action, too, Jerry?

– I'd say that, too. I'd say there'd be some kreplach. Maybe a knish or two.

– But I can see there are no knishes at this table.

The girls at the table giggled, all except one, Rachel, a pretty girl, with large, square front teeth all seemingly filed to the same length, her lips just about covering them. The girl next to her explained the other meaning of knish.

– It's like nebbish, but for a girl.

– What's a nebbish?

– Someone who's dull and boring.

– By the way, asked Mooney, why do they use nebbish for a man and knish for a woman? Anyone?

He drew a blank.

– Because you can go down on a nebbish but you have to eat a knish.

All the kids screamed, except Rachel.

– Getting back to our discussion, Mooney said to his companion, the other kids now listening attentively, let's say you knew a Jew on welfare pulling in less than a thousand a month.

– Living alone?

– Like a prophet.

– He would be one of the poorest Jews in America, said Jerry.

– Well, that's me, said Mooney.

– What do you mean?

– That's me. I'm the poorest Jew in America. Should I move to Israel?

– You're not really what they're looking for there.

– Too old? Or too poor?

– You'd be a burden on the Jewish state.

– But there would be other poor people there, right?

– There are some poor people there. But the highest rate of Jewish poverty in the world, believe it or not, is in Brooklyn, maybe Montreal coming second.

– What about here?

– Probably the same as everywhere else. One out of five.

– Could you pass me the boiled bagels? Mooney asked him.

– All bagels are boiled. That's why they're bagels.

– So a bagel's a bagel?

– That's right. They're all bagels.

– A bagel's a bagel, you're saying, right?

Jerry paused for a moment thinking about how to get out of the conversation. He finally just turned away from Mooney to talk to a cousin on his left.

After this affront, Mooney buttered his bagel and munched, followed by some pickled herring, which he chewed slowly, and then imbibed the vodka. He nudged his neighbour again. The other kids stopped talking.

– So a bagel's a bagel?

– Yes!

– Jerry, you know there are basically two kinds of bagels. You do know that?

– I don't really care.

– There's the Montreal bagel, which is the sweetest and chewiest bagel because it's boiled in honey-water and baked in a wood oven. It's made with malt and egg but no salt.

– I know what's in a bagel.

– So can you tell me what's in a New York bagel?

– The same thing.

– No. In the New York bagel there's no egg, and it's boiled in tap water and baked in an ordinary oven. Voilà, it's crustier and puffier than the Montreal bagel.

– But they're both boiled! insisted Jerry.

Rachel asked:

– What kind of bagels are these?

– These are Montreal bagels, said Mooney.

– And these?

– The ones in that basket are New York bagels. What's your name, sweetheart?

– Rachel.

– That's a lovely name, Rachel. How old are you, dear?

– Nineteen.

– Is that not a beautiful thing? Do you know what Rachel means in Hebrew?

– No.

– Do you, Jerry? Do you?

– No.

– It means 'ewe'.

– Oh.

– Now, Rachel, sweetheart, take one bagel from each basket and compare the crusts, Rachel. Just compare them.

Rachel picked up a bagel from each basket and tasted each one.

– He's right. This one's crustier. Rachel giggled, then went demure. That'd be the New York bagel?

– Are you studying, Rachel?

– I'm in pre-law.

– Pre-law. Isn't that fantastic. Everyone should study the law. It's the basis of civilization.

– But they're both boiled! interrupted Jerry. There's no such thing as fried bagels!

– Yes, said Mooney, there are no fried bagels, but there are *bialys*.

– What are *bialys*?

– *Bialys* are not boiled. The word comes from a city in Poland, Bialystok. Like the bagel, the *bialys* is also made with a chewy yeast dough. And it almost has the shape of a bagel, but the hole isn't necessarily punched all the way through — that way you can fill it with onions or *muhn* — poppy-seed.

– I know what *muhn* is.

– But if the hole were punched through, would it not be an unboiled bagel, Jerry?

– I've never had a *bialys*.

– The *bialys* came to America at the same time as the bagel.

Why do you think the bagel did so well, Jerry?

– Beats me.

– Would I be able to eat *bialys* in Israel?

The boar-boy didn't know what to say, or why he was even having this conversation, and Mooney didn't want to embarrass him with silence in front of the others at the table, who had been observing them. So he said:

– Could you pass me the herring, Jerry?

– Sure.

– You're a good kid. How old are you, Jerry?

– Twenty.

Mooney speared himself a morsel of herring rolled around a pickled baby onion and waved it a bit in the air with his fork. Jerry watched Mooney and thought that he had finally been liberated, and turned away to talk to his cousin again.

– So, would I be able to eat *bialys* in Israel, Jerry?

– Well, you could certainly eat bagels.

– So you recommend the Israeli bagel.

– The Israeli bagel, like the Israeli orange, is the best in the world bar none.

The boy on Mooney's right snickered. Jerry sneered at him.

– Should we, as a nation, be proud of our bagels?

– We invented the bagel, for fuck's sake, said Jerry.

– What about the Russian *booblik*? Did we invent that?

– I've never heard of the *booblik*.

– You had never heard of the *bialys* either, which is really an unboiled bagel, although you said all bagels are boiled?

– I stand corrected. And no, I've never heard of the *booblik*.

– Which came first: the bagel or the *booblik*, Jerry?

– I just told you I don't know what a *booblik* is.

The boy on Mooney's right was relishing this. Mooney cocked his head to smile at him but then turned it back on Jerry.

– Isn't it warm in here?

– No.

– Do you know where the *booblik* came from?

– I don't know that either. How could I? I don't know what a *booblik* is.

– The *booblik* came from Krakow, Poland, or maybe even Germany.

The pretty Rachel, with the astonishing teeth, asked:

– What is a *booblik*?

– You're such a sweetheart, Rachel. You seem like the type of girl who has lived all her life with a *baba* at home, not in a home. The *booblik* is like a bagel, but it's bigger and more compact, too dense in fact for a sandwich. It must be dunked.

– In what? asked the girl.

– Tea or coffee, sweetheart.

– So, it's more of a pastry than a bagel? said the girl, intelligently.

– But in the bagel family, wouldn't you say, Jerry?

– I don't even want to be having this conversation. What's your point, anyway?

– The point is, Jerry, I think you might have to retract your statement that the Jews invented the bagel.

– We did!

– And the *bialys* and the *booblik*? Look, bagel, *bialys*, *booblik*, whatever, Jerry, the truth is Eastern Europe has always had a strange relationship with its dough. Twisting and boiling it, or not. I don't think the Jews invented the bagel — and you might be shocked to learn who did. And boiled dough might just go back to the Byzantines.

– A bagel's a bagel! said the boar-boy, exasperated, making angled karate chops at his bagel with both hands. And *bagel* is a Jewish word.

– I'm not sure I'd agree with your etymology, Jerry.

Again the boy on Mooney's right snickered. Mooney detected this boy had an animus where Jerry was concerned.

– What are you saying? that the bagel isn't Jewish? There's nothing more Jewish than a bagel.

Mooney picked up one of the Montreal bagels and held it in front of his eye as if it were a telescope and said:

– The first *booblik*-bagel or bagel-*booblik*, they say, was boiled and baked in Vienna, in the shape of a stirrup. It was 1683.

– You know the date of the invention of the bagel?

– No, of the word *bagel*. And I even know the time.

– You know the exact time the bagel was invented?

– Picture this: The Turks led by Merzifonlu Kara Mustafa, Visir of the Ottoman Empire during the reign of Mehmed IV, had just been defeated at the Battle of Vienna, as you know, by an outflanking cavalry charge led by a Jan Sobieski, King of the Polish-Lithuanian Commonwealth. Down the hill he led his hussars at five in the afternoon on September 12, 1683, dashing the Turkish lines and putting the enemy to flight. At 5:30 PM, Sobieski, the 'Saviour of Vienna', as the Pope called him, the 'Lion of Lechistan', as the Turks called him, pulled his boots out of their stirrups and strode into the jaima of Kara Mustafa to discuss terms. And what's the German word for stirrup, Jerry?

– I don't know.

– *Steigbügel*, hence *beigl* in Yiddish and then eventually transliterated into 'bagel' in English. September 12, 1683 at 5:30 PM.

The kids at the table smiled, except Jerry, who looked at Mooney's angelic face, and began with the karate chops.

– It's just a bagel! Jerry said, and added even more karate chops to his bagel.

– But now, when you think of a bagel, the most Jewish thing you know, you must now think of a Pole, a Mr. Jan III Sobieski and his stirrups.

– It's just a bagel!

– Just a bagel? And stop with the karate.

He held Jerry's hand to stop him from chopping at the bagel.

– When a Jewish woman gave birth in Poland in the eighteenth century, what were you supposed to give her? Anyone? Rachel?

– A bagel? said Rachel.

– That's right, sweetheart, said Mooney. And why a bagel, Jerry? Anyone? Rachel?

– Because her legs were in stirrups during birth? said Rachel.

– Thanks, but I'll do the colour, Rachel, said Mooney.

– Don't be so ridiculous, Rachel, said Jerry.

– You would give her a bagel, said Mooney, to celebrate the edict of Jan Sobieski that revoked the ban on Jewish baking in Poland. That's why I brought my brother's daughter-in-law these.

Mooney held up a brown paper bag of bagels from Sun's bakery.

– You brought bagels to a *briss*? asked Jerry.

– You see, the bagel is practically a universal talismanic substance. A multicultural object par excellence.

Then he set the bag down on his lap and speared another piece of herring and, by placing it on his thickly buttered boiled bagel, turned the surface of the bagel a marbley blue and took a bite. He then poured himself another shot of vodka, which was still cold, and because he was still parched. Everyone went back to their eating and private conversations. He heard someone ask Rachel 'what she was doing for fun this afternoon'.

Mooney, chewing slowly, wondered how he knew all this about the bagel. And Jan Sobieski and his cavalry charge against the Turks. It just came out, so his memory was intact, but just *farmisht*. He nudged his neighbour, interrupting his conversation with Rachel.

– Don't you find it warm in here?

– No.

– Don't turn away. I'm talking to you.

– What?

– I wanted to ask you how many poor people are there in Israel? Five percent of the population? Ten percent? Twenty percent? And just how poor are they?

– Who are you?

– I'm Mooney Kaufman. I'm the great-uncle of the *briss*ee. So, where were we, Jerry? Jewish poverty in Israel?

– I'll start talking about Jewish poverty there when we start talking about poverty here.

– We've already talked about Jewish poverty here.

– Poverty in Israel is nothing like the poverty here, believe me.

– Really? said Mooney.

– There are things there that are more important than money.

– For instance?

– Spirituality.

– Does it not cost money to be a member of this fine synagogue?

– Or love.

– If I go to a hooker she'll charge me fifty dollars. Even one horrendously fat or horrendously thin. And if you want a partouse, then you're looking at, what, a hundred twenty-five an hour? And that's your *de minimis*.

– That's not the kind of love I had in mind.

– A guy your age, I'm sure it's the only kind of love you have in mind.

– Love of country, of your people, or for a child.

– How much do you think it costs to circumcise a child? I'd say five hundred dollars for a decent trim, maybe less for what they call a 'French cut'.

– What's a French cut?

– Half a circumcision, leaving a bit of the foreskin so as not to cut back on pleasure. Thoughtful parents.

– Gross, said Rachel.

– And let's say four thousand for the *kiddush* — and that's my *de minimis*. And how much do you think it cost your parents to raise you to the age of eighteen, not counting the T-shirt?

– How much?

– I'm asking you, Jerry.

– I don't know.

– Guess.

– Can't say.

– Rachel?

– You mean allowance?

– I'm talking room and board, the accumulated per diems of eighteen years, excluding loss of opportunity and *lucro cesante*. Anyone? I'd say — *grosso modo* — two hundred thousand.

– Big bucks.

– Almost a student loan.

– So what else is free that doesn't cost money? asked Mooney.

– Your health?

– Ha!

– With medicare, you can see any doctor you want.

– Even Dr. Smirnoff?

– Who?

– Dr. Smirnoff.

Mooney made him clink glasses. The girls giggled. He had the others pour themselves healthy shots, raise them, and toast Dr. Smirnoff.

– To Dr. Smirnoff.

– To Dr. Smirnoff.

They all drank.

– That one didn't count.

– You didn't look each other in the eyes when you toasted.

The vodka flowed again.

– To the bagel!

– To bagels!

He was going to get these kids seriously drunk.

Two toasts later, Mooney rose. He was drunk, and he felt like he was walking on a rowboat. He cautiously shuffled to a long table with the coffee and pastry and stood in line. The table had been meticulously set, with a long single white damask cloth and more carnations, lines of cups and saucers arranged as straight as soldiers, several elegant thermoses polished to the sheen of surgical instruments, alongside his mother's antique silver samovar for tea. Dave always took it to events like these.

Why did *he* get the samovar? That was irksome.

And there were equally burnished creamers and sugar bowls bursting with gourmet sugars and pink sachets of chemical sweeteners. There were cheesecakes and tortes, a magnificent sponge cake, *mandelbrot*, honey-cake, and *rugelach*, and frosted nothings, which he had liked as a kid.

I am the poorest Jew in America, Mooney thought, looking at the plenty. And at my age. Even the youngsters here are richer than me. That T-shirt probably cost more money that what I've got in my pocket after paying the pharmacist. He crunched a *rugelach*, the cheese dough so unmistakable.

He took his coffee cup and saucer and shuffled back to the table and set the saucer down carefully beside his plate without spilling, and without sitting down he sipped from the cup.

He leered at his venal brother Dave, who had once made a million dollars in a single day, rumour had it. They had still not exchanged a word, not even a hello-how-are-you, since Mooney arrived. With his mental powers he willed Dave to look at him.

Dave glanced back over his shoulder and saw Mooney sipping his coffee. He hadn't been sure Mooney would come. Why had he invited him? Grief comes from goodness, he thought. Mooney disturbed his peace of mind, almost as much as that swift ritual mutilation of his grandson he had just witnessed. He was all smiles of relief now, but there had been a moment when the knife was lifted off the table . . .

... and now that cunt Mooney. For a second they looked at each other. Dave waited for a nod, but nothing came out of his brother's face. What a sucker punch.

His brother might cause trouble, as he did at his son's wedding years ago, drunk on his vodka, before he was hospitalised. He nodded again to Mooney and numbly waited to see whether Mooney would nod back or cause a scene. Nothing. Another sucker punch.

Mooney sipped his coffee and stared into Dave's nod. He had wished his wish. His mental powers had made Dave look at him and he snubbed him good. Tinkering with his teaspoon, he treated Dave to a large serving of Silence, as was always the case at these public family affairs where his invitation was compulsory, while to a private do there was never an invite, never a call, by far the bigger snub. Oh, how cruelty begins at home.

His presence was a sign to the community of his brother's generosity for including the family derelict. But Mooney's answer to that was Silence, and to spit on his brother's Money, which he made in speculation, first at home and now around the world: buying up slum housing, so the standard slur against Dave went.

Dave and his varnished nails, surrounded by genuflecting friends. But they were satisfied looking, Dave's friends, and they all seemed to fit. And the most satisfied looking of all was Dave. His fortune would go on increasing, even after death, thought Mooney, which was a really depressing thought.

Mooney couldn't see Candy though, or his son and daughter-in-law, or the little *briss*ee. They must have gone off on a family huddle to calm the kid. Fucking barbarians.

After waiting for the nod that never came from his brother, Dave turned and re-engaged his small group of guests. He was really irked. Mooney had got under his skin, again. And he cursed himself for having invited him.

Mooney sat down again. He poured himself a shot of vodka, which he drank in one gulp, still parched. The vodka tears soaked his eyelashes. For a moment no one noticed him, and for that it was like being back in the insane asylum, but with much better food, and without the hounding of the nurses to get him out of bed. And now his belly was full. A great nosh. In his welfare apartment now it was always a choice between hunger and bad food, but this was great food, even if he did feel like a moocher. He broke off some bagel, chewed and swallowed.

– Do they serve breakfast like this every Sunday? posing the question not to Jerry, but to the other young man on the other side of him, who had taken relish in certain parts of his conversation with Jerry.

– After services. Even though this is a private affair, the real Jews get that table over there. At the back.

– The *shnorrer* table, said the girl beside Rachel.

The kids giggled and pointed to the table with the real Jews.

– That's the *shnorrer* table? asked Mooney. For the moochers?

– That's what they call it, Rachel said. I think it's mean.

– So can anyone come in and eat here every Sunday?

– You have to participate in the service.

– How long is the service now?

– Several hours, I think.

– They get here at sunrise. Bummer.

The *shnorrer* table. Now that was an expression. It brought back the old disgust he felt when he had first heard it uttered. Still, if he just sat through a service, he could eat here on Sundays, maybe even take home leftovers.

– What's your name? Do I know you?

– Michael.

– You must be Susie Birnbaum's boy?

– That's right.

– What are you studying, Michael?

– Physics.

– That's great, Michael. Do you know what your name means in Hebrew?

– No.

– *Micha* in Hebrew means 'as' or 'like', and –*el* means God. Like-God.

Unlike the young Jerry, this Michael had very short hair, which was peroxided yellow, and he was shaved up to his eyeballs. He wore a red Rage Against The Machine T-shirt that had a silk-screen of a confident *el Che* in short hair and burns without the beret.

– And you? Are you thinking of making *aliyah*?

– Me?

Everyone at the table laughed.

– Michael's a self-hater, said Jerry.

– Sometimes he hates the fact he was born a Jew, someone said.

– Actually, sometimes I hate the fact that I was born altogether. And some of you.

The kids giggled.

– He hates himself because Rachel dumped him, said the girl on Rachel's right. On his birthday.

Both Rachel and Michael blushed. Everyone else screamed with laughter. Between screams darts of commentary flew.

– I didn't know it was his birthday!

– Yes, you did.

– I forgot.

– You like so did know.

– Nobody breaks up with anyone on their birthday.

– Rachel did.

– Would you please stop, please?

– Now she's going out with Jerry, one of the other cousins reported.

– It happened a long time ago, said Rachel.

– Three weeks!

– But he's still so in love with you, Rachel.

– He so isn't, said Rachel.

– Yes, he is. Look at him.

Michael's face was bright red. Mooney poured himself and Michael a shot of vodka and they drank, which eased the tension.

– Have you ever been to Israel? Mooney asked, checking to see if Jerry was listening.

– Once. Years ago. On my bar-mitzvah trip.

– Did you enjoy yourself?

– It opened my eyes.

– What more can you expect from travelling? Mooney said philosophically, to Michael.

– Yes, what more.

– Would you ever think of going back?

Everyone at the table turned to look, waiting on Michael's answer.
   – Me?
   – Yes, you.
   – He's a self-hater. Why would he go back? asked Jerry.
   – I'm asking Michael. Michael?
   – I'd rather not answer that question.
   – His mother's here, one of the cousins said.
   – You don't have to answer me.
   – I can't answer you.
   – Answer him, said Jerry.
   – He can't answer you, said Rachel. He's promised his mother he would never discuss the subject in public.
   – What subject?
   – The thing.
   – What thing?
   – The thing. The thing he can't talk about.
   – Is that so, Michael?
   – She has a bad heart.
   – I don't think she'd hear you.
   – There are certain things you just can't discuss in public, Michael said.
   – We're amongst friends, said Mooney. This is private. Would you, Michael?
   – Would I what?
   – Would you go back to Israel? Would you, Michael?
   – I told you, I can't talk about it.
   – About what?
   – About Israel if my mother's around. Or if there are Jews in the room.
This broke everyone up. One of the Michaels girls pissed herself laughing.
   – Imagine there were no Jews in the room.
   – It's a fucking *briss.*
   – Just between you and me.
Jerry strained forward while the table held its collective breath. Michael blushed, about to talk. Mooney felt the ferocious heat. Michael's silence was a black hole that seemed to suck in the *kid-*

dush din. Jerry narrowed his eyes as Michael opened his mouth with restrained passion.

– I can't watch this, Rachel said. I'm covering my eyes.

– The only way I'd go back to Israel, Michael said, staring at Jerry, would be in a Hezbollah minivan.

– He said it! one of the cousins screamed.

The table broke up with laughter. Michael's blush was now violet.

– What kind of Jew are you? said Jerry.

– Go tell his mother, someone snorted.

– The best kind. The moral minority.

– If we are not for ourselves, said Jerry.

– Ourselves? Who are we, anyway? The Jewish identity is just an invention. An invention of Christians and nineteenth-century German Zionists.

– Here we go.

– We Ashkenazim are descended from Khazars!

– You're the *chazzer*!

– The Khazars were a Turkic people, Mongolians who loved to ride horses and plunder villages, who founded the first Kaganate and were converted to Judaism by Abrahamic Byzantines in the eighth and ninth century. Read Shlomo Sand.

– Read the Torah.

– We Ashkenazi Jews were never in Israel! It's not our homeland. We're Mongols.

All the kids broke up.

– You're the mongoloid! Or at least your brother is!

This didn't get such a laugh.

– And you're an asshole.

– And you're such a bullshitter.

– We're really Khazars.

– Bullshit, bullshit, said Jerry.

– The Khazars/Jews were later pushed out by the Kievan Rus and eventually pushed west by the Mongol Golden Horde into Germany, where we began to speak middle-high German, which we call Yiddish.

– Bullshit, bullshit.

– If we have to return somewhere it would be to some place

between the Black Sea and the Caspian Sea. The Pontic Steppe.
To Kazakhstan or maybe all the way back to Mongolia.
– Bullshit, bullshit.
– We never came from Israel. The only people with real Jewish
DNA are the Palestinians.
– Bullshit, bullshit.
– So you see, I'm not the self-hating Jew, you're the self-hating
Khazar who is in denial about being a Khazar. You're the self-
hater, Jerry.
Everyone was in stitches but Jerry, who stood up.
– Me? Because I don't ride a horse? You're such a bullshitter.
– Read Shlomo Sand.
– Bullshitter.
– And stop calling me a bullshitter.
Michael stood up, too.
– You are one. You are a bullshitter.
– Stop calling me a bullshitter, he said, leaning across Mooney,
poking Jerry in the chest twice with his shot glass, once for *bull*
and once for *shitter*.
Jerry didn't like being poked in the chest.
– Don't poke me.
– Why don't you make *aliyah* to Kazakhstan? Just leave Pales-
tine to the Palestinians and the Israelis. What's it your business?
You're just a Khazar in denial. He poked Jerry in the chest again
with his shot glass.
– You're the *chazzer*.
– Don't call me a *chazzer*.
– You prefer *bullshitter*? And stop poking me.
– Poking's just a start, you piece of crap.
Mooney waved his napkin limply like a flag of truce, and checked
to see if his brother Dave had noticed the commotion. His brother
Dave did notice, interrupted his schmoozing and shot an irritated
glance at him. This glance he returned with a nod.
He had created this mischief, Mooney realized.
– Stop poking me, said Jerry.
– What if I don't?
Jerry threw what was left of his coffee at Michael, which
missed him but drenched the girl sitting beside him. Michael
laughed and so Jerry threw the empty cup, which hit Michael

flush on the nose bone, from which blood flowed like the Nile. Michael wiped his nose, which kept bleeding, and threw his cup and contents wildly, hitting the kid beside Rachel on the forehead, who reacted by hoisting himself up by pushing down on the table board, which upended. Plates and cutlery were catapulted into the air and crashed onto other tables, even as far as the *shnorrer* table.

The two boys started to brawl, but not before Jerry got in a good punch. A tooth flew and they fell to the floor. Dave rushed over livid, collared Mooney and dragged him to the back of the room by the *shnorrer* table, leaving parents and kids to sort out the fight.

– Well, it's obvious you shouldn't have sat me at the kids' table. Why didn't you sit me with your rich friends? You should have sat me at least with the divorced wives.

– I should have sat you at the *schnorrer*'s table.

The *shnorrer* table took offence. Dave pulled Mooney even farther to the back of the room.

– I shouldn't even have invited you.

– Why is the heat up so high?

– And you weren't supposed to come.

– I brought your daughter-in-law bagels. For good luck.

– Leave the bagels and fuck off out of here.

– Actually, I came because I wanted to talk to you.

– About what?

– About the only thing you know anything about.

– I'm not giving you any more money.

– I need my money.

– Your eyelashes are so thick, he said to Mooney.

– It's the Xalatan. I'm taking it for the glaucoma.

– You don't have glaucoma.

– Yes, I do.

– You're too young to have glaucoma.

– I was diagnosed.

– This was supposed to be a happy day for me.

He had to do it now. Ask his brother. In a minute it would be too late.

– I need money, said Mooney. I need the money you stole from me.

– I didn't steal money from you. I've been giving you money for years.

– Dad says you did.

– Dad's been dead for twenty years.

– He came to me in a dream. Told me what you did. He told me you stole my part of the inheritance.

– The fuck I did, Hamlet.

– He told me you stole my part of the inheritance.

– You're nuts.

– You did it.

– Did what?

– Stole the inheritance.

– Why would I do that?

– You tell me.

– That would be admitting I did it. And I didn't. How much money do you need?

– You mean how much do I want?

– Ok, how much do you want?

– Three million dollars.

– Right, three million dollars.

– The money you stole from me.

– I didn't steal any money from you. I've been giving you money for years.

– You stole it.

– This is ridiculous. I have to get back to my guests.

– They're all leaving.

– Thanks to you.

Dave looked at Mooney. Suddenly it hit him that he would always have the same brother for the rest of his life.

– I'm living on welfare. You don't know what that's like.

– I know enough about it not to want to live on welfare.

– You don't know what it's like!

– What's it like?

– It's like —

– Don't answer. Just fuck off out of here.

– It's like being seated at the *shnorrer* table for eternity, said Mooney. Tell me, by what right are you keeping my money? The right of theft?

– The inheritance was settled years ago. You blew yours.

– Hey, that kid lost a tooth.

– Look, Ma's coming over. Don't upset her.

He hadn't noticed she was even there, and now she was hobbling over, brushing cake crumbs off her bosoms. The doctors at the hospital had told her not to get too close to Mooney, that she was somehow an impediment to his recovery. Them and their two-bit psychology.

– Ma.

– Mooney.

– I thought you weren't supposed to talk to me.

– I'll talk to who I want. Smartass doctors. Someday they'll learn.

– Ma, what have you done to your hair?

– I had it permed.

– It looks awful, said Dave.

– Dave, let go of your brother.

– Thank you.

– You, I don't like the way you look. Are you sick?

It dawned on them then that Dave had had Mooney in a headlock since they arrived at the *schnorrer* table.

– I don't want you two fighting. He's sick, Dave.

– It's always about him, isn't it?

– Before I die I want you two to get along.

– You're not going to die, said Mooney.

– Is it that bad? Mrs. Kaufman asked.

– What?

– My perm.

– You look great, Ma, said Mooney.

– You look like a woman who plays bingo at a Ukrainian church, said Dave.

Mrs. Kaufman didn't find that funny.

– I want you both to come for supper tomorrow.

– Can I bring my dog?

– No dogs and no wives. You're eating my heart out, you two.

– I'm busy tomorrow, said Dave.

– You'll be there.

– The fuck I will.

– And you too, Mooney.

– What are you making?
– I was thinking delicatessen. Dave, you pick it up.
– The fuck I will.
– No fat on the corned beef.
– You've got crumbs on your front, Ma, said Dave.
– I have?
– I can't make it tomorrow night, said Dave.
– Lean corned beef.
– You should brush off the crumbs, Ma.
– What crumbs?
– On your front.
– Have I got crumbs, Mooney?
– Yes, but they're invisible, he replied.

The fridge was buzzing extra loud. And that kid had lost a tooth. And you could hardly see the crumbs. What the fuck.

Wasn't it strange what happened at Dave's grandkid's *briss*? He felt guilty about it now. Tempers raged. A tooth was lost. As usual, after returning home, Mooney played with Meaghan, his dog, to deflect the bad thoughts.

The play was initiated by the dog, a mongrel with stumpy legs and a black and brown coat that felt oily smooth if you stroked it one way and bristly if you stroked it the other. A real shedder, too. There wasn't a surface in the apartment that wasn't covered in dog hair. The dog frightened easily; her own farts scared her so badly she'd jump three feet in the air.

Meaghan, as always, came up to him with her squeaky toy bagel and pushed it against his shins, making it honk. Having Meaghan and that toy bagel was like living with Harpo Marx.

Mooney tried to pull the bagel from the dog's mouth and after a brief tug-of-war, the dog got the better of him and tore off with her squeaky toy, knocking over empty milk cartons, teapots and vases, raising balls of dust with Mooney in pursuit, which was the normal protocol. This lasted for five minutes, with the dog finally loping off victorious and collapsing with a heave of air under the coffee table where Mooney couldn't get at her, chomping victoriously on her squeaky toy, making it honk till it wheezed.

How he loved that dog. Meaghan had been part of his therapy at the mental hospital. He wept out of gratitude when the staff let him keep it. Electroshock, strapped to gurneys, and pets. 2007 and there was still electroshock. Go know.

Luckily there was a young bull-necked doctor, Carl, who gave him some other therapies. Once he was submerged in warm salt water with huge belts of seaweed flapping around. The seaweed stunk and felt gooey. Submerged up to his neck, with seaweed covering his hair like a babushka, he had a chat with Carl. It was Carl who told him he had to latch onto something when he got out. Had to solve his problems with his brother.

He had stopped his doctoral studies when Dave made his first million. The sibling competitive urge drove him into business too, to try to outdo Dave, but all his ventures were *asch in porach.*

And he had to solve his problems with his ex-wife, Naomi. Resolve all conflicts, Carl said. And he had to properly mourn his father, which he couldn't do because he was out of the country. Shit like that. And the list went on.

No matter how disgusting the smell of the warm seaweed and the feel of lying in hot jello, it beat the electroshock to shit. And little by little he began to enjoy his chats with Carl, and taking care of the dog. His goal had been for Meaghan to learn to play fetch, but they only ended up playing keep-away as the dog was either too retarded or too clever to learn to drop the toy once she retrieved it.

He strained to pull off his first shoe, going at the laces that were still wet from the melted snow, and were now in a knot that had shrunk. He stood and braced the sole of one shoe against the heel of the other to lever his foot out. This only caused him to scuff the back of the heel. He would have to lie down on the sofa in his wet shoes. Okay.

He did that for a while but it was too uncomfortable. He wanted to remove his shoes but he was too tired. Then he remembered he had to fight the fatigue, that his fatigue was just depression and that action could cure depression. He had to latch on to the little things, too.

The slothful in Dante were worse off in hell than those who did evil, he remembered, because evil at least had its glory. So he should do something about the wet shoes. Get up, at least, cut the laces or something.

But no, he would just lie there in wet shoes for a while longer. There was no sound but his breath against the chesterfield, his eyes staring down at the specks of fluff and dog hair on the floor. He thought about taking out the electric broom and vacuuming the broadloom, but it would make a lot of noise, and it hardly worked anyway now. But he could try to take his wet shoes off. That was doable.

His fingernails were too bitten-down to undo the knot, so he finally fetched scissors and snipped the laces, like a trainer removing his boxer's gloves after a fight. When he pulled off his shoes and socks he saw that his feet were red with cold.

Mooney lay down on the sofa again barefoot and stared at Meaghan, whose chin was now resting on his foot. He imagined Meaghan's dying, which flooded him with infinite sadness. He imagined Meaghan's last day on Earth: he would try to stimulate her with the squeaky toy but Meaghan would not respond. He'd tempt her with a wiener, or corned beef, but Meaghan would just lay there, her chin on the floor. He knew then it would be time to take her to the vet and have her put down. And then he would be at the vet's, with the vet administering the sedative until Meaghan fell asleep. He would nestle his cheek by Meaghan's ear and whisper to her something sweet, probably her name, before the vet gave her the shot to make her heart stop. The sadness ran deep. This was all inevitable, even now when Meaghan was still full of vitality. Life is for the shits, and it's over far too quickly.

Barefoot he padded to the kitchen and boiled two eggs and put two slices of bread in the toaster. His bare feet felt so cold he could hardly feel them as he made his way over the undulating kitchen linoleum. He could put on house slippers, but they were in the bedroom, and all he could think of was Meaghan's death. That would be so sad.

But these were just the sort of thoughts that Mooney had to avoid. Thoughts, neurotic thoughts that dragged him down into Thanatos. It was no way to live. It clouded his thinking, which now had to be goal-oriented. Those eggs had to be boiled. The bread had to toast. And coffee would be made. There would be supper.

He ran the hot eggs under the tap, then peeled them, cut them in half and salted them. He put them on a plate with the toast and poured the coffee. Fabulous presentation, he thought.

He had been admitted to the mental hospital with a depression as big as a horse. He had lost his goals, they told him. After weeks of electroshock he came up with one.

He would become rich. He couldn't be the poorest Jew in the

city, in America. His plan was to get some money out of his brother any way he could, and with that money, build up tremendous equity. He would not touch this capital, only build it up. He had no idea how to spend it anyway. He just wanted to watch it accumulate, although he would spend some of it on houses, furnishings and cars. Einstein said that the most powerful force on Earth was compound interest, and Mooney wanted to feel that powerful force.

One night in the hospital his father came to him and told him that Dave had kept all the inheritance to himself. Armed with this revelation and his new goal he willed himself sane, which stopped the electroshocks. They released him and Meaghan.

Since then he continued to fantasize in his welfare apartment about becoming wealthy, not just dwelling on how he had lost everything: first his money, then his wife. He was seeking the master formula for getting rich.

He thought about inventing something, but people were always stealing other people's inventions. That left crime and financial speculation. You could get rich from crime. For crime you just needed to be ruthless, which he was not. And crime seemed like an awful lot of work.

That left financial speculation, which some people don't consider crime, because it is worse than crime. But to get rich from financial speculation you needed a stake, and specialized knowledge. So that left crime. Which was out. So that left financial speculation. There was a patient at the insane asylum who had been in finance, and he made it sound easy, although nerve-wracking enough to get you institutionalized.

– You need nerves of steel, Mooney, he had told him. You need balls. You need to be able to face the day when you could lose everything and still eat.

Mooney knew what it was like to lose everything, his entire inheritance, in fact. And several times over.

The last time he had lost all his money was not an easy one for him. But the fact that the money was gone was not his first worry. His real concern was facing his wife, and so he was not forthright with her. With such painful news to tell there was no way he could just blurt out that he had lost the business.

He had arrived home that day as usual. Naomi had placed moist roses in the thick glass vase on the dining room table. They sat down on either side of the roses. Since it was only a week before their trip to Cuba, he told her that there had been a hurricane that had wiped out their hotel's beach and that he had had to cancel the trip. She posed Cancun as an alternative. This caught him off guard. He said that it was too late to make a reservation for Cancun and that their refund would take weeks to come through. So, just charge it, she said. They were using the card too much, he said. The holidays would be fun in the snow. It's 30 below, she said. With the wind chill, he said. They could build snow forts with her nephews, the twins. Just charge it, she repeated. Can't, he said. We're maxed out. What about the business card? That's maxed out, too. Everything's maxed out. Besides, I've lost the business, he said.

And she had thought they were thriving.

The fall in fortune led to a shunning from their friends that Naomi could not take. She was either snubbed wherever she went, or, as in many instances, thought she was being snubbed. In the end Naomi was to evaporate as the money had. But other things went first.

The cable was first to go. Then the cell phones and the cleaning service, followed by the SUVs, which were replaced by a used clunker with a sticky doors and a patched-over bullet hole in the roof. Then the house. They moved into an apartment. They could only afford to go out for Chinese once a week, and they bought their clothes in something of a panic when the season's sales came on.

But then they stopped clothes-shopping as the last of their savings were mopped up by an expensive transmission job on the clunker.

At first Naomi did not complain. But one day the toilet overflowed and the superintendent wouldn't come. Naomi had to use the plunger and clean up the puddle herself. When Mooney came home after a day out looking for work, she was sitting under the bare light at the kitchen table, her prettiness fading.

– My mother's *goya* had a better life than me, Naomi said, totally distraught.

– She was off the boat.

– True, she was, and she cleaned other people's toilets, but she hadn't come down in the world.

Talking about her mother's *goya* was a strange way to begin a conversation about how she was going to leave him, but still, she had to start somewhere.

– I said my mother's *goya* had a better life than me.

– I heard you.

– You know, I once entertained seventeen women from National Council in our living room!

– I know, my mother wouldn't come. She never got over that.

– Hadassah women are so proud.

– So?

– So Larry Brickman has asked me to marry him.

– Have you been seeing Larry Brickman? Not Larry Brickman! Please not Larry Brickman!

Why did it have to be him! Larry Prickman.

– Why did it have to be him! Have you slept with him?

– He's been over a few times.

– He was in my house?

– You lost the house. This is an apartment.

– Whatever. Has he been in the apartment?

– He stopped by. But I never let him in.

– You said 'over'. That means he was inside.

– I meant he came to the door.

– Why didn't you say that? Why didn't you say he 'came to the door'?

– So I said 'over', but I didn't mean he came in. I didn't let him in. I was too ashamed to let him in and see this dump.

– So, it's my fault this place isn't nice enough for you to have affairs in?

– I can't answer that, Mooney.

– It was a rhetorical question.

– It was mean.

– He's always sniffing around you at parties.

– No, he isn't, because we don't go to parties anymore.

– So you wish we could go to parties so he could sniff around you?

– I can't answer that either.

– It was rhetorical.

– It was mean.

– Larry Brickman never invites us to his parties anymore. He had that do three months ago, his father's second bar mitzvah — could there be anything more ridiculous? — and it was just to put on a show, you know, to gloat — and he didn't invite us, did he? He wouldn't have snubbed us if he respected us.

– Who says he respects 'us'? He respects me. It would be awkward for him to invite us.

– We used to laugh about him.

– You used to laugh about him.

– We called him Larry Prickman.

– You called him Larry Prickman.

– But you laughed.

– At how infantile you were.

– He was a real prick.

– Super-size.

– Great.

– I know, he's a cheat and a liar in business, but he's nice.

– Like a dog, he was always sniffing around you.

– Don't be crude. Anyway, he's divorcing his wife.

– It'll be his second divorce.

– He can afford it.

– Is that supposed to hurt?

– I'm just saying he can afford it. He could afford six divorces.

– I suppose you'll be one of them.

– Let's stop arguing.

– Who's arguing?

– They don't have sex anymore — she has an ovarian cyst.

– Oh, I thought he would have the ovarian cyst.

– They can't have vaginal intercourse.

– Well then he can do to her what he does to everyone else.

– I asked you not to be crude. And anyway, he doesn't have a taste for that sort of thing.

– How do you know what he has a taste for?

– Do you want me to answer that?

– Yes, and why don't you shoot me out of a cannon while you're at it?

– I can answer it if you want.

– Too much information.

– He says he can take care of me.

– Of you, too?

– Of me, too.

– He's got that kind of money?

– And how. Just with what he spends on his father's independent living in Palm Springs you could buy a new car every month. I just can't live like this, Mooney. I don't know who I am anymore. I don't recognize myself in this apartment, in these clothes. I love you, but it isn't enough. I don't want to hurt you more than anything else in the world, but Larry Brickman can give me back my self-respect. Wouldn't you like to get that back?

Mooney took a moment to reflect.

– Me get back your self-respect?

– No, your self-respect.

– I wouldn't know what to do with it anymore.

– Well, I would.

– What? What would you do with your self-respect back?

– I would just hold on to it and cherish it.

– So leaving me and marrying a *chazzer* like Larry Brickman would get you back your self-respect?

– The truth is that I love somebody else. Why should I feel guilty about this, this is crazy.

– You'll feel guilty about this for the rest of your life.

– It'll go away.

– Stay with me, you're making a big mistake.

– I've made up my mind.

– Stay with me, please.

– Don't.

After she moved out of the apartment and into Larry Brickman's new house, sans the second wife, which was so far south that it made the south end seemed like the north end, Mooney found himself staring for hours at a scuff mark on the living room wall that Naomi had made the last time they made love and she had kept her shoes on. Mooney eventually had knelt down and kept staring at it for several hours, crying so hard he thought his lungs would tear.

Kissing the fucking scuff mark, now that was a symptom. So was his vision on the coldest, windiest winter's day of a drunk

wearing just a Blue Jays jersey flying across Main Street. Monog-
amous by nature, he still loved Naomi. She had satisfied him in
every way that another person can satisfy someone.

They had met during one summer when they were teenagers. It
was summer love and she was summer in person. Her skin was
toasted to perfection. She was tall, filled out sweaters beautifully,
and had the kind of knees and ankles that attracted him, though
no waist, no hips and no rear end, as his mother pointed out,
but she had rich black hair with a cowlick in front. Charming
motions when she walked, and a graceful swimmer, yet so shy
that she felt stark naked in a bathing suit. It was not just another
summer of boiling glands. They actually talked, for an entire day,
sitting on the beach, their backs leaning against the fence of the
Silverbergs' cottage. Their first kiss lasted twenty-seven minutes.
He remembered that his lips fell asleep. And his tongue was raw
from scraping her palate. Then he went home and watched *All in
the Family*.

Falling in love was easy and he thought it would always be like
that. There was nothing better than suffering from that crush.

That same night he came down with an ear infection. She vis-
ited him every day. She never understood why she fell in love with
him, she used to say, perhaps it was the ear infection. He couldn't
explain it either, their love, but there it was, so plain to see, like a
fish served with the head attached: honest, innocent love, looking
them both in the eye.

Lying on the chesterfield at the cottage, his ear stuffed with cotton batting, Mooney decided a solid bond had been formed that
would last their whole lives, and he asked Naomi to go steady.
For the whole week she hesitated about whether to accept it or
not. She was only sixteen. She knew then that if she agreed to
go steady with him that she would never be able to shake him
loose. What made her decide to say yes she didn't know. But the
moment arrived and she said yes. If she had said no she could date
other boys, some of whom she found very attractive, and who had
already expressed an interest in her, like Larry Brickman. But she
had said yes.

Her mother had made a face when she told her. They were the
richer family, from the south end, and he was from the north end,
and she understood maturely her mother's moue of distaste when

she heard his name, but it only propelled her towards him. She was leaving the lake at the end of the summer holidays, and it would have been easy not to get in touch with him back in the city.

He hesitated about phoning her in September. There was the memory of their leaning against the Silverbergs' fence, but, oddly, he couldn't remember what her face was like exactly. It was Naomi who took the initiative. One night when her parents were out of town she called him up and invited him over. They watched TV with the sound off for a while and didn't say a word to each other. Not a word. She lifted off her sweater and folded it. They walked up the stairs, her naked from her skirt up. They made love in her bedroom.

Afterwards they raided an immaculate refrigerator stocked with Chinese food cartons and delicatessen meats and kreplach and *kischka* and cantaloupes and honeydews and soft drinks. So unlike the Spartan fridge at his house.

She wasn't sure she loved him. Fatefully, her uncertainty went deep. Could she ever love anyone? She knew she was selfish, although he never saw it. That bit of self-knowledge had been inculcated in her by her mother. And being selfish, she realized that she would never really love anyone, if not him. This filled her with the fear of an infinite loneliness, and the only reasonable way to fight that was to love Mooney. Odd name. The night was revelatory.

At any rate, Naomi was gone now. There were times he wanted her back so badly that he had the equivalent of phantom pains for her from which amputees suffer.

He hadn't even touched the plate of boiled eggs and toast and the coffee was completely cold when the phone rang.

– Mooney, this is your mother.

– Ma?

– Come for supper. Dave's coming too. Just the three of us.

– Can I bring the dog?

– You can't bring a dog into a Jewish house, you know that.

3

– This is quite a mess, said Dave, turning on the tap in the kitchen sink, sudsing up the hot water generously.

– The *goya* didn't come on Friday.

– How come?

– She has her own agenda.

– Can her.

– Can't. She's sick. She has *tsouris*. More than you can imagine. And her children have *tsouris*.

– Everyone has *tsouris*.

– So.

– So they've still got to go to work. Just can her.

– That's what the *goyim* would do.

– The *goyim* are right.

– We're better than that. We're better than them.

– Just can her. She's only a cleaning lady.

– I can tell you've never cleaned a house. Lifting, moving, vacuuming, wiping, washing. It's not like work for you, with your martini lunches.

– Ma, this isn't the fifties, nobody has martini lunches. Just can her and get someone else.

– She's a native person.

– Who cares?

– You can't fire a native person. They were here first.

– You need real help. This place is a mess.

– Stop complaining.

– I'm not complaining. I'm just saying.

– You're not just saying, you're complaining, no, you're criticizing.

– You don't understand.

– It's you who doesn't understand. I can't fire her for being native.

– I'm not saying that.

– What are you saying?

– I'm saying to fire her for not showing up. Not for being native.

– That's what I said from the beginning. I can't fire her because she's native.

– You said that already.

– I'm just repeating what I always say.

– You should fire her for not coming to work.

– She has *tsouris*.

– And her children have *tsouris*, I'm sure.

– That's right. And that's even worse than your own *tsouris*, believe you me, I know. This business with Mooney is killing me.

– I don't want to hear about Mooney. And you can't live like this. I'll find you someone else.

– You found me her.

– I'll find you someone else besides her. You can keep her, but get someone else too.

– I don't want someone else. She knows where everything is. She's nimble. She doesn't make noise when she vacuums.

– Oh, she makes noise, alright. You just don't hear it.

– What?

– Nothing.

– Stop mumbling.

– Alright.

– She does a perfect job.

– When she comes she does a perfect job.

– That's what I'm saying. I can't fire her for doing a perfect job. Or for being native. So what are we going to do with Mooney?

– We're not going to do anything with Mooney.

– You have to help him out.

– Everything is *asch in porach* with him.

– It's not *asch in porach*. He's had bad luck.

– He just needs to grow up himself. You're *intershtipping* again.

– He needs our help.

— Don't *intershtip* me in Mooney's shit.

— You're not going to change my opinion. And I'm not *inter-shipping*. I'm worried.

— Don't worry so much.

— A real mother is never free.

— Christ.

— What's going to become of him?

— Just let him work things out.

— He's on welfare.

— I know.

— So does the whole city.

— Who cares?

— This city talks. And I don't want people talking about us. I want to see him settled.

— Nobody gives a shit about us, Ma. Or about anyone, really.

— That's not true. This city talks. Just help him out. One more time. I want to see him settled before I die.

— He's 46, Ma. How's he going to get independent, how's he going to change if we're always bailing him out? The doctors were right to keep us away from him.

— They know from nothing.

— He is what he is already. He's not going to change.

— He is going to change.

— He's a gambler. And he's a lousy gambler. He's irresponsible. He never finishes anything he starts.

— It was that Naomi. She hurt him. She had no rear end. And she has a losing personality.

— What are you talking about?

— You know.

— She did what she had to do. And you liked Naomi.

— She's a *kurveh*.

— She's not a slut.

— Don't contradict me just because you think you're the *shtut balabost*.

— I'm not the *shtut balabost*. And she's not a *kurveh*.

— Why are you defending her?

— I'm not defending her. But she's not a slut.

— She was a little *kurveh* without a rear end. Half the city talked about her.

– That's true, but that didn't make her a *kurveh*. She just got tired of Mooney.

– She married him.

Sometimes when he argued with his mother it felt like there was a glass marble inside his head rolling over a smooth surface to one ear, and just as it felt it would finally roll out, the surface tipped and it went to the other ear. It was almost like pain, but worse. And he felt relieved when the doorbell rang, even though he knew it was Mooney. What really irked him was how everything revolved around Mooney.

Mooney rang the bell again and waited. Dave came to the door and let him in.

It had been a long time since he had been home. He knew right away he was going to act sullen.

– Don't bring that dog into the house.

– I can't leave her outside.

– You're not bringing that dog inside.

– You'll love her.

– You can't have a dog in a Jewish house.

– Meaghan's a good dog.

– Does she have her period?

– No.

– If she has her period, she's out. What kind of a name is Meaghan?

– It comes from the Welsh, Megan, but originally from the Greek name Margaret, which meant 'pearl'.

The three of them hadn't been together for years, and Mrs. Kaufman was very excited, enough to allow Meaghan to stay. She was 'on the firing line', she said, and the last thing she wanted before she died was to see her boys reconciled.

She had spread the delicatessen supper on the kitchen table. Dave had picked up corned beef, more fatty than lean, rye bread, ribs, coleslaw and *kishka*. They began eating with concentration, and it was Mrs. Kaufman who broke the silence.

– I tried to keep the family together.

– I know, Ma, said Mooney.

– I'm still trying.

– I know.

– That's easy for you to say, but I'm so lonely. Alone like a stone. *Alein vie ein stein.*

– Where's the platter I bought you? asked Dave.

– What platter?

– The silver platter.

– We don't need to use silver.

– But where is it?

– I don't know. I think I left it at the Weinsteins' do.

– So it's at the Weinsteins?

– No. I think someone took it by mistake.

– So you lost it?

– I lost more when your father died. *Er liegt in drerdt. In drerdt.*

– Don't be maudlin.

– What?

– Nothing.

– Stop mumbling.

– Alright.

– I lost a lot more when your father died than a platter.

– That's beside the point.

– It's only a platter. Your father was a human being.

– I know that. But that platter cost money.

– It was silver.

– Solid silver.

– You should see the flowers Mooney sent me. I don't know how much he paid for them.

Dave made a mental note to send his mother flowers. She liked Mooney's fucking flowers more than his fucking silver tray.

– I'm on the firing line. Do you know what that's like?

– We're all going to die, said Dave.

– Don't say that.

– I'm going to die, Mooney's going to die, everyone's going to die.

– Don't say that. I didn't have kids for them to die.

– But we will.

– Stop already.

Dave just wanted to eat and to get out of there, so he had better check these stupid arguments with her. Communication was not smooth with his mother. It had never been. She irritated him, always had.

– I'm irritating you.

– No, Ma.

– I can see that look you get, Dave, when you think I'm irritating.

– You're not irritating.

– If I am, you tell me.

– You're not.

It was wonderful to have her two sons alone with her, but not under the circumstances. Family, in which she put so much stock, had always fallen short of expectations.

– You have me *in goless*, you two. *In goless.*

– Why you two? What have I done?

– You're the oldest; it's up to you to be generous.

– He hates me.

– He doesn't hate you and I'm on the firing line.

– He hates me and you're not on the firing line.

Here comes the shakedown, thought Dave.

– He doesn't hate you. He's the son of your dead father.

– Drama queen.

– What?

– Nothing.

– Stop muttering.

– I said you could have just said father.

– That's what I said.

– No, you said 'dead father'.

– He is dead, for your information.

– I know he's dead.

– And Mooney's your kid brother. He needs help.

– So I have to help him?

– I'm not saying must.

– What are you saying?

– It's not a must.

– What is it? A should?

– I'm not saying it's a must, that's all. But he needs help. He had a nervous breakdown.

– I don't have to help him.

– I'm not saying it's a must. It's an up-to-you.

– Is it a should?

– It's a should. It's an up-to-you. That's not a must. He needs help.

– So, it is a should.

– Okay, it's a should.

– He buggered up my grandson's *briss*.

– I'm sure it was not intentional.

– It was intentional alright.

– I had a premonition the other day, she said.

– What kind of premonition?

– Of my death.

Here's the shakedown.

– Everybody has those, Ma.

– This was a very clear sign.

– You don't need a sign. It's going to happen, anyway, said Dave. We're all going to die. That's why *yortsyt* candle companies have inventories. It's a sure thing. The manufacturers have already planned their production for next year. They've made procurements, depreciated the machinery. They're good to go.

– And so are we, said Mooney.

– Shut up, Mooney.

– I don't want to die. I don't want you to die.

– It's not up to us.

– That's what I mean, she said.

– Where did you have your premonition of death? asked Mooney.

– You're such a suck, Mooney.

– You *sha*. In the parking lot of the Bay.

– I thought I told you to stop driving, said Dave.

– I went for lunch with Bella Barsky.

– I thought you weren't talking to Bella Barsky? You said she snubbed you at *shlikhes*.

– It turns out it wasn't me she snubbed.

Mooney laughed.

– You said it was a snub that made you feel like you had never been snubbed before, said Dave.

– A snub heard around the world, said Mooney.

– Shut up, Mooney.

– It was a snub alright, but it wasn't me she snubbed.

– You said the biggest snub from the biggest snubber in the south end she gave you.

– She wasn't the snubbee, said Mooney.

– Who was then?

– What's it matter? Let me finish my story before I forget.

– You're not going to forget. Ma. Tell the story.

– I forgot.

She started to sulk.

– Ma, just tell the story.

– Now? You wouldn't let me finish before.

– Just finish.

– I don't like interruptions. I forget what I'm going to say.

– I won't interrupt.

– I'm not going to tell you.

– Tell it.

– You tell it.

– I wasn't there, said Dave. Just tell the story. God you're so fucking proud.

– You interrupt and I'm proud!

– I won't interrupt. You went to lunch with Bélla Barsky. The parking lot at the Bay.

– We were having tea in the Regina Room —

– I thought you said you were at the Bay.

– Stop interrupting, it makes me forget — and this *pritztah* from National Council walks by. What's-her-name. Clara Mass. The one with the horse gums. And she was blonde for a change. I knew her when she didn't have a pot to *pish* in. Until she married Morry Mass. Getting pregnant by him was her only accomplishment. She stops and asks me about Mooney right in front of Bella Barsky. Things got hairy right from the start.

– So?

– So it was very mean. She's mean.

– Maybe she's just retarded.

– She knew what she was saying.

– Maybe she was just interested.

– My foot.

– What did you say to her?

– What am I going to say? I said he was on his feet. That he had been recapitalized.

– Where did you learn that word?

Mooney found this hilarious. Suddenly he wasn't so sullen and the corned beef got tastier. He went to the fridge to look for hot mustard.

– I'm not a bank, Ma, said Mooney holding the fridge door open.

– And he's not on his feet! said Dave. And where did you learn that word?

– I read it. Where do you learn a word? Reading.

– Reading what?

– I'm not half the idiot you think I am.

– Lay off her, Dave, said Mooney, returning to the table.

– You're such a suck, Mooney. And, Ma, he's not on his feet.

– I'm not going to tell Clara Mass that. She always snubs me.

– Always?

– She thinks I'm a *grineh*. Just because your father had that hotel on Main Street. He didn't even want that hotel.

– Why did he buy it?

– For you two.

– What else did you tell her?

– That you two had set up a new business.

– Why did you tell her that?

– It just came to me.

– Evidently, muttered Dave.

– Just like that.

– It's a lie, said Dave.

– It's not a lie. It just isn't true yet.

– Then it's a lie.

– That's up to you. You're going to have to help him out or you'll make me look like a liar. And I'm no liar.

– You just lied to Clara Mass in front of Bella Barsky. Two witnesses. And now your own confession, said Dave.

– Good intentions don't make you a liar. It's in the Torah.

– That's not in the Torah.

– It's not lying when you have good intentions. Or when it's going to happen anyway.

– Yes, it is. You're still lying.

– Dave, just lay off her.

– Shut up, Mooney. You're such a fucking suckhole.

– I didn't lie to hurt anyone.

– But you lied. To what's-her-name.

– Clara Mass.

– Shut up, alright, Mooney.

– It's a free country.

– Then leave me alone.

– Don't say shut up to your brother. Besides, Clara Mass is National Council, you can lie to them whenever you want. You can't trust them.

– I have a reputation. I can't have people going around thinking I'm setting up a business with Mooney.

– She has a grandson, one of those idiots with the *peyis*.

– Who?

– Clara Mass.

– So?

– He wears his tallis in the street. With the *tsitsis* hanging out. The entire city talks about him. And one of those flashy knit yarmulkes.

– What's that got to do with anything?

– She goes around badmouthing Mooney. Do I ask her about her grandson with the *payis*? Do I?

– No, said Mooney.

– I don't ask her about him, do I? I know it would embarrass her, so I don't go asking her about him in front of other people. The *shandah* of having a grandson who's religious like that; twirls his *payis* all day.

– Really? went Mooney.

– He twirls his *payis*. First clockwise, then counter-clockwise.

– I know the kid's uncle, Dave said. They call him Javeh. They call the kid Javeh too.

– What kind of name is that?

– The name of God.

– But I didn't ask her about her grandson. I'm a lady. Hadassah women are ladies. Not like those National Council *pritztahs*. They're giving Sophie Reiss such a hard time at the Home. Them and their presidium! They think they own the place. Made up of the National Council *pritztahs*.

– What presidium? What are you talking about?

– Sophie says they run the place. They kvetch the staff to death. Hard-working people who clean their crap. They're complainers.

– Unheard of! cracked Mooney.

– Shut up, Mooney.

– The presidium, they snub the Hadassah women.

– There's no presidium at the home. It's run by a board.

– Sophie Reiss gets more kindness from the *goyim* there.

– What's the mix? asked Mooney.

– About fifty-fifty. But you're not putting me in there, said Mrs. Kaufman.

– I didn't say I would!

– Don't get defensive, Dave.

– I never said I'd put you in a home.

– We'll take care of you, said Mooney.

– You can't even take care of yourself! said Dave.

– And then I had the premonition of death in the parking lot. Like a feeling I was going to die.

Mooney laughed and Dave, feeling bitter, began to gather the dishes.

– Maybe he's not finished yet?

– Are you finished, Mooney?

– Just about.

– Sit, Dave.

Dave sat down.

– Keep the family together. That's what your father said, she said. It's on my conscience. After all these years, it's still on my conscience. 'Family is everything,' he used to say.

– He was right about that, said Dave.

– What are you talking about? said Mooney. You were one of those kids who went around wishing you lived in someone else's family.

– No, I didn't.

– You were ashamed of our car even. Is there any more coleslaw?

– Dave, pass your brother the coleslaw.

– Creamed?

– No, the regular.

– There's only creamed.

– You know I like the regular.

– I forgot. Next time you pick it up.

Dave fumed. He couldn't believe how his brother and mother got under his skin. There was a something between Mooney and his mother that wasn't there with him. A void-filling something.

– You ordered the stuff.

– I just gave the guy the list.

– Don't argue, you two.

They sat silently watching Mooney chew his coleslaw for a few minutes.

– This is what I like, the mother said.

– The regular?

– Seeing you two together. The three of us. Helping each other.

– I don't see him helping me, said Dave.

– He's had bad luck, she said. I want you to be good to each other.

– This corned beef is a bit fatty.

– I ordered the lean, said Dave.

– The fuck you did.

Dave felt the blood rushing through his head. Bugger it, the fatty corned beef was going to dictate the tone of the scene now.

– I think I ordered the lean, he said, trying to stay calm.

– You know you didn't.

– Just be good to each other.

– I ordered the lean.

– You don't really want me to make a comeback, do you, said Mooney.

– What comeback? If you've never made it, you can't make a comeback. You lived like a loser.

– You'd die if I made real money like you.

– Not going to happen.

– Why can't I make money?

– You know nothing about money.

– I grew up around the talk of money.

– Stop it, you two. One more word about money and I'll get hysterical.

– You are hysterical, said Dave.

– Be good to each other. That's all your father wanted.

– That and money, Dave said.

– What?

– Money. But not the kind of money you spend, the kind you keep in the bank. We lived like *shleppers* and he had tons of money in the bank.

– Which you inherited, she said.

– Which we both inherited.

– You're lucky your father came before you, Dave, she said.

– How could it have been otherwise.

– He slaved so you could have that money. That's all he wanted.

– You said all he wanted was to keep the family together, said Dave.

– He wanted that too. More corned beef, Mooney?

– Ma. Enough.

– He wanted you to love each other.

– Enough. And I'm not talking about the corned beef. Ma, he's dead, you have to accept that.

– Death is never acceptable.

– Where's the Maalox?

They had never been good to each other. Or at least Dave had never been good to Mooney. Or that's how Mooney saw it. Truth to tell, Mooney had never been especially good to Dave, either.

In spite of his knack for making money, Dave was insanely jealous of Mooney, for Mooney had many friends while he had one, a nerd with leukemia, and where Mooney found school so easy and breezed through it with high marks, he had to slug it out with tutors and, sometimes, out-and-out cheating. He had to pay kids to write some of his papers at university, and in the end he just dropped out and went into business, where he thrived, made friends, and got rich.

Actually, he had always felt delighted — consciously unconsciously, actually — when things went badly for Mooney, and that's the way it would always be. Cain slew Abel, and that was that. You didn't need a reason for it. If he gave Mooney a hand in the past, it was always with resentment, since he knew his mother never appreciated his effort, and he yearned for her acknowledgement that he was the better son. But he could never wring that out of her.

Dave also resented the fact that life in the family revolved around Mooney, when, against all logic, Mooney quit university just before getting his doctorate and tried to imitate Dave's business success, but failed, in business after business. Mooney became the weakest link that required so much pampering. What are we going to do about Mooney? was the family mantra. It seemed they loved him more, which hurt, and all everyone could think of was what to do about Mooney, how to help Mooney, how to bail out Mooney. Fucking Mooney.

Somewhere things went awry for Mooney. Suddenly everything he did ended in failure. He was not suited for business as he never stuck to anything long enough to make a go of it. The judges in bankruptcy court were on a first-name basis with him.

Dave, for all his achievements, was never the centre of attention of the family, and that stuck in his craw: and that was the way Dave saw things, it wasn't true, but that's how he saw it, and the way we see things is more real than the things we see.

– Ma, it's getting late. The dog needs to be walked.

– Which reminds me, I think you should move back home, Mooney. I can't tell my friends you're living in the north end.

– Don't tell them, said Dave.

– Can I bring the dog?

– No.

– Then I'm not moving back home.

– Ma, he's forty-six years old. You're not going to tell your friends Mooney's living at home.

– I won't tell them that. I just won't have to say he's living in the north end.

– Ma, I've got to go, too, said Dave.

– So go.

Was it possible, Dave thought, to get more irritated?

– I want you to help your brother out. When you promise me that, you can go.

– He doesn't acknowledge me as a brother, said Mooney.

– I don't have a brother.

– You have a brother, Mrs. Kaufman said to Dave.

– He doesn't want a brother, said Mooney.

– Not true. I want a brother who's dignified! Not someone

who crashes a *briss*. Not someone who hangs out with Suddy Joffe.

– I can't stand that Suddy Joffe! said Mrs. Kaufman. I remember him and his brother Duddy when they lived on Manitoba Avenue. With the *farshmarkteh* noses.

– That was over seventy years ago.

– Anyway, I didn't crash your *briss*. I was invited.

– I meant breaks up a *briss*. You embarrassed me in front of my friends.

– He didn't mean it, said Mrs. Kaufman.

– He meant it alright.

– And you embarrassed me sitting me at the kids' table. You almost made me sit at the *shnorrer* table.

– But I didn't, did I?

– You didn't sit me where you should sit a brother.

– I don't have a brother.

– But you have a brother. Here he is.

– I have no brother.

– You have a brother, and he needs your help. Help him, if only for me. Not to make me into a liar.

– You're such an *intershtipper*.

Yes, here it was. Here was the real shakedown.

– Promise me you'll meet to talk about this money business, she said.

If he promised this, he could go home. He reflected a moment on the difference between family and friends, how both categories irked you, but at least your friends were entertaining.

– I promise, if I can go home.

– When?

– Next week.

– Do it tomorrow, his mother said. I'm on *shpilkes*.

– I'm busy tomorrow.

– Do it tomorrow. You're breaking my heart. The two of you.

– Ma, don't cry.

– *Alein vie a stein.*

– Ma, don't say that.

– I need some tea. I'm dry.

4

They met the next day in a large, frilly if somewhat decayed restaurant that Mooney loathed. There were thick medieval escutcheons on the walls and plaster-of-Paris busts of Roman emperors and puce curtains covering black stucco walls. There were also pictures of football players and one of Liberace.

His brother brought him to this place to gloat, Mooney thought.

They were sat at a plush booth with a maroon tablecloth at the back of the room. The waiter, Gary, was decrepit; he had been there for ages, and was almost in slumber when they arrived. He looked like Lenin, and had small hands and a dainty marigold beard. He would have to serve their food and pour their drinks, yet it seemed he barely had enough strength to carry himself erect.

– Did you know I was the poorest Jew in the city, in the country, even in America?

– I wouldn't be surprised. Just take a look at yourself, said Dave.

– The last few years haven't been easy for me.

– Why the fuck don't they take our drinks orders?

– I said that the last few years haven't been easy for me.

Dave craned his neck to look for Gary and swivelled it back around.

– There are two things you can't do in life, said Dave: make a waiter look at you when he doesn't want to and kiss your own ass.

– I said the last few years haven't been easy for me.

– I heard you the first time. Look, I'd like to help you, Mooney.

But you go through life expecting to be comped. And you're forty-six .

– I know. I have to latch on to something. Before it's too late. Just give me my share of the inheritance.

– Don't start up again.

– You owe me money.

– I'm not going to give you three million dollars.

– Why not?

– What could you do with three million dollars? You can't even remember where you park your car.

– I don't have a car. Just give me my money and I'll get a car. You've got it to give, haven't you?

– Yes, but not to give away. I'm not bailing you out again, and certainly not with three million dollars.

– Dad said you kept the inheritance.

– Dad's dead. How could he have told you that?

– He came to me in a dream.

– Dreams are just dreams. They don't actually happen. That's why they call them dreams.

– Just give me my money.

– Stop with the bullshit already.

– It's not bullshit.

– What would you do with it?

– Invest it.

– What do you know about investing?

– As much as anybody else.

– Which is zilch.

– I need three million dollars.

– You need medication. Let's order.

– You're not taking me seriously.

– That's the problem. I am. The other day you really scared me at the *briss*.

– Nice do.

– Until you arrived.

– I was invited.

– But you spoiled it. You made me think of Suddy Joffe. Remember that day, in the synagogue on Yom Kippur. The people had been sitting all day. They were hungry and tired. But

Suddy, he had to be hungrier than everyone else. And just, just as the *chazzan* was about to open his mouth to sing yet another song about how mighty almighty God is, Suddy shouts, 'Let my people go! We're starving!'

– He was removed by the bouncers.

– They weren't bouncers. They were shamuses.

– Ma was furious.

– That little performance of yours at the *briss* made me think of Suddy Joffe. How you'll end up like Suddy Joffe.

– I've made progress.

– They let you go, that's all.

– I am making progress. I have a goal now. I have a dog.

– The last thing you need.

– He's good to me.

– He's just a dog.

– She. She's just a dog.

– She's just a dog.

– That's what people without dogs say.

– Here comes the waiter. I hope by now he has a goal.

In a slow saunter, his back curved, head out like tortoise, Gary came over to take their wine order. Dave called him by name:

– I'm looking to try a wine from a valley in Catalonia near the Priorat, Gary. But not the Priorat itself. Do you know where the Priorat is, Gary?

– Monsieur Dave, I know where the Priorat is. Everyone does. But I don't know all the valleys near the Priorat. Could you give me a hint?

– That's all I've heard.

– It's not enough.

– It's not a very big valley.

– Why don't you just order a Priorat? Monsieur Dave. You won't be disappointed. The wine from a valley near the Priorat is probably similar to wine from the Priorat.

– Alright. Alright.

– Any Priorat in particular? Monsieur Dave.

– Anything in a French barrel?

Mooney shuddered with embarrassment at his brother's ostentation, but he wanted his money.

– We have a Clos de l'Obac. A blend of Syrah, Merlot, Garnacha, Cabernet Sauvignon, and, if I'm not mistaken, Cariñena grapes, from a French barrel.

– Do you have anything from the Bellvís estates?

– I have something that was twelve months in new French oak.

– Hand-harvested?

– Monsieur Dave, you cannot machine-harvest in the Priorat. The hills are too steep, the terraces too narrow.

– You are very cultured, Gary.

– Thank you, Monsieur Dave.

Mooney rolled his eyes at this banter.

– So that's what you're recommending?

– I'm not recommending anything. I'm here to serve. You're the decider, Monsieur Dave.

– I'll let you decide, Gary.

– I'll bring the Clos de l'Obac. Two hundred French oak barrels.

– Is that because it's the easiest Priorat to reach in the cellar?

– That has nothing to do with it, Monsieur Dave.

– Any year in particular, Gary?

– 2001?

– You're not just trying to dump your surplus.

– We've had this wine for years. If we had wanted to dump it, we would have dumped it long ago.

The waiter slouched off without another word.

– This meal is going to cost you hundreds of dollars.

– The wine alone with run us over a thousand. But it's my birthday. I'm forty-eight.

– Holy shit. I forgot.

– And Candy and Danny are in Palm Springs.

– Sorry, I forgot.

– I can't remember when your birthday is either. Can you drink wine with your medication?

– I'm off it. I decided that if I wanted to get better I had to take my mental health into my own hands.

– What have you been living off of?

– I get a welfare cheque each month.

– How much do you get?

– You don't want to know.

– What happened to you, Mooney?

– Things fell apart.

– I know that. You shouldn't have gone into business. You were a linguist. You should have stayed at the university. Don't you remember, all day at home it was Chomsky this and Chomsky that, and I could barely get a passing grade in Home Ec.

– I know.

– But you were a lousy businessman.

– I took my shot.

– Shots.

– And lost. I lost everything. Naomi.

– And the poker didn't help.

– I'd say you were right there, Dave.

– Don't turn around. Do you remember Bernie Cohen, one of Dad's poker buddies?

– Him I remember. Wasn't he the guy whose brother committed suicide?

– Benny Cohen?

– Benny Cohen. He hung himself in the bathroom, said Dave.

– Hanged. He hanged himself.

– You always have to trump me.

– It's hanged. Hung is for laundry.

– Don't turn around.

– I'm not.

– I remember the mafia were after Benny. Don't turn around. You once played poker with him and his brother before his brother *hanged* himself?

– I have no memory of that.

– That's amazing. It was the worst bad beat in the city's history. Don't turn around.

The waiter returned and uncorked the bottle with huffs and puffs, then splashed some of the Clos de l'Obac in Dave's glass. Dave checked out the colour against the lamp, smelled the bouquet, sipped, swilled noisily, practically gargled, as he had been taught, to bring the aromas up through the nasal passages. Then he swallowed, and with a nod, had the waiter fill his glass full, then Mooney's.

– You know, my memory is not gone, it's just jumbled. You
know I'm on welfare. Did I say I was on welfare.

– You said that.

– I have a dog called Meaghan that they gave me in the hospital. I lost the business, they told me.

– Not the first time.

– Of course, you know about that. You could have helped
me.

– I did.

– But not enough.

– The business was going down, Mooney. You don't throw
good money after bad.

– I did.

– Until it was all gone.

– Now I mostly lie on the chesterfield with the dog, watching
TV.

– I thought you said your life hasn't been easy.

– Not like yours.

– Do you think my life has been easy? asked Dave.

– Easier than mine, I'm sure.

– Let me tell you something then, and then you can tell me if
my life has been easy. Every Friday evening I go to a prostitute
who berates me, ties me down and urinates on my genitals. This
little act of humiliation costs me five hundred bucks. And last
year it was four hundred fifty bucks.

– Where does she do this to you?

– On a bed.

– No, I mean where?

– At her place.

– Does she use a rubber sheet?

– What do you mean?

– I mean it would ruin the mattress.

– I never thought of it.

– Why do you do it?

– It's the only way I can get an erection. So now, you tell me if
you think my life has been easy.

– You've given me pause, Dave.

– And don't think I don't know what everyone calls me behind
my back. Do you know what everyone calls me?

– Should I know?

– If you could remember, you'd know.

– I think I do remember. They used to call you a scumbag when you were a kid, Mooney said.

– And I might have been a scumbag, but you used to be a suck. At home, you know, with the family, you were a suck. That's how I thought of you, as a suck. A real suckhole.

– But you were a scumbag.

– No, that's just what they called me.

– And?

– But do you know what they call me now? All those people behind you. Don't turn around. Take a drink of your wine. What's the matter? You don't like it?

– It's fine.

– Do you know what they call me now?

– I imagine they still call you a scumbag.

– Now they call me a *royal* scumbag.

– Knighthood.

– Even young people in business, even people who are scumbags themselves, and I mean *real* scumbags, they call me a *royal* scumbag.

– They differentiate?

– To the *real* scumbags I am a *royal* scumbag.

– So there are scumbags, real scumbags and royal scumbags.

– And I am a *royal* scumbag.

– The Prince of Scumbags.

– Like I said, a *royal* scumbag.

– What's a scumbag?

– Someone who doesn't return your phone calls.

– And a real scumbag?

– Someone who doesn't call you.

– And a royal scumbag?

– Someone who bankrupts his suppliers. Here's a typical conversation that any of these people behind you could be having right now: Don't turn around. Do you know Davey Kaufman, they ask? Oh, Mooney Kaufman's brother? The one they had to institutionalize? He's right behind you. Oh, yeah, right, I hear he's a royal scumbag. They don't even have to know me in person and they call me that. You can go up to any of those people at these tables, they'll concur.

– That you're a royal scumbag.

– That I'm *called* a royal scumbag. But this is the worrying part: before, it bothered me. I used to care. But now I'm indifferent.

– Are you a royal scumbag, Dave? asked Mooney. Are you?

– I've done things in business that if Dad came back to life and found out about them, he wouldn't stop throwing up.

– What's her name?

– Who?

– Your dominatrix.

– She's not a dominatrix.

– Sounds like she's a dominatrix.

– She's a fucking prostitute. Let's not gentrify what goes on between the sheets.

– Rubber sheets.

– Stop trumping me. You're the one asking me for money.

– So?

– Charlotte. Her name's Charlotte.

– Is that her real name?

– I don't know her real name. I call her Charlotte. And you know what? I think she really hates what she does to me.

– Isn't that part of the act?

– What?

– Her hating it?

– No, she's supposed to be hating me, not the act itself; she's supposed to enjoy humiliating me. She's supposed to fake like she's enjoying her fantasies of domination.

– You mean your fantasies of domination.

– Whatever. That's what she's getting paid for.

– Maybe she doesn't have fantasies of domination.

– Of course she doesn't. She's not sick. I'm the one who's sick. But she's supposed to make me think she enjoys it. That's what I'm paying her for. I don't have the slightest idea what she's really thinking. I could care less.

– So what you're saying is that she doesn't fake it well?

– What I'm saying is that she should just be faking it better.

– But aren't fantasies fake to begin with?

– Shut up and drink the wine. They'll think we're sipping because I don't want to shell out for a second bottle.

– You said you didn't care what they thought of you.

– Stop trumping me.

Mooney took the tiniest of sips to irritate Dave.

– Do you know how much this one bottle costs?

– Don't care. You can deduct it from what you owe me.

– I don't owe you anything. You owe me. And I'm not giving you three million dollars.

– Yes, you are.

– What do you think of the wine?

– It's fine.

– Stop sipping. Take a big gulp.

Mooney took a big gulp and the taste exploded in his mouth. It was like nothing he had ever tasted before. He took a second, even bigger gulp and shut his eyes. When he opened them a mist seeped into the restaurant, paralysing the other diners, along with the waiter and busboys in their labours. Beyond the table, reality became a tableau.

– Incredible, eh? Isn't this an incredible wine?

– I've had drugs administered intravenously that were less effective, said Mooney.

– And it's perfectly legal. Look, this business with Charlotte, my dominatrix, it's sick, isn't it?

– I thought you said she was just a prostitute.

– Do you always have to trump me?

– Alright, it sounds sick.

– I never know if one day she'll just . . .

– Do more than pee on you?

– No. No. No. She wouldn't do that. I mean disappear. Change jobs. Or retire.

– So?

– Well, she has a sub for when she's sick. I guess her sub would just take over the job.

– You're thinking out loud, Dave.

– But it's not the same with her substitute.

– I thought you said Charlotte wasn't that good.

– You should see her substitute in action. A total nebbish.

– I'm hungry, Dave.

– Let's order. Where's the waiter?

– That's your department.

– You know, I'm not that that crazy about this wine. Don't you find it slaty? The soil is too quartzy in the Priorat sometimes. Too rich. That's why I wanted that wine from a valley near the Priorat.

– Too bad you couldn't remember the name.

– Don't you find it too slaty?

– I have no idea what you're talking about.

– Not too chic?

– I don't know what you mean by too chic. How can anything be too chic with you?

– No, I mean, too creamy, too oily. It needs food.

– So do I.

– You know it's easier to kiss your own ass than get a waiter to look at you when he doesn't want to.

– You always say that, Dave.

– Even if he's staring right at you, he's not really looking at you.

– At the hospital we stood in line at the cafeteria.

– That would be a blessing. Someone should open up a high-end restaurant where you get served right away, like in a cafeteria. Here he comes.

Gary came over taking cautious steps.

– Alright. Let's talk about the lamb, Dave said, with no trace of irritation.

– Oh, the lamb, said Gary, shaking his head.

– Did I ever tell you about the time I lived on lamb for a month in Afghanistan? said Mooney.

– Probably.

– Believe me, it just came to me out of the blue. I tell you, I have reverse Alzheimer's. Did I ever tell you about it?

– Once. And that was enough. Look, I'm trying to order.

– I don't really remember it much. I know it happened. But the memory of it — I can't really distinguish it as an experience from something I may have just read about. Do you ever get that feeling?

– I thought you said you were hungry?

– I should go back again.

– Afghanistan has changed a lot since then, Mooney. Believe me.

– Has it?

– You can't just traipse around like you did thirty years ago learning Afghan like when you were a student hippie. Anyway, I'm trying to order.

– Afghan is not a language. They speak Dari, which is really Persian, or Pashto in the south, then there's Uzbek and Turkmen in the north, along with thirty other languages and dialects. Was I a hippie?

– What weren't you?

The waiter cleared his throat.

– Monsieur Dave, I don't think I'd go with the lamb.

– I thought the lamb would go nicely with this wine.

– You should have thought about the food before you ordered the wine, Monsieur Dave.

– How bad can the lamb be?

– The only lamb we have is from New Zealand; far too muttony, with a uriney taste, if I might add. Although there are customers who like that.

– Don't you have any Spanish lamb?

– We haven't had Spanish lamb since Christmas.

– What about the veal?

– Chop or shank?

– I want the shank.

– Why not go with the veal marsala?

– Is the veal milk-fed?

– Sorry, grain-fed. We haven't had milk-fed veal since Christmas.

– The veal marsala will cook up quickly, said Dave, and I am famished.

– You're thinking out loud again, said Mooney.

– Fuck off, Mooney. Listen, Gary, we'll go with the veal marsala. And a *boniet* for an appetizer?

– A bun-yet, you mean.

– A bun-yet. But go easy on the parsley. I'm not a cow. Can you eat anchovies, Mooney?

– I can.

– So, the bun-yet and a risotto with the veal.

– Will you need some champagne to clean the palate between courses?

– A non-vintage. I don't want any of your so-called vintage champagnes now or ever again.

– How about a rosé champagne?

– Are you making a recommendation?

– I'm just trying to move the conversation along. You're the decider, Monsieur Dave.

– What did I have last time?

– I think you had the Billecart.

– Oh, yes, the Bile-Cart!

– You always make fun of the Billecart. Very unjust, Monsieur Dave.

The waiter disappeared, tactfully, as usual. Mooney felt a prickle of heat, for it was getting warm, either from the wine or a generous hand on the thermostat.

– The Billecart has the tiniest bubbles, said Dave, almost weeping with good cheer.

– Like the song?

– It is a couple's champagne.

The waiter sent a boy over with the *boniet* and hot crusts of bread.

– Your *boniet*, the boy said.

– Bun-yet.

– Bun-yet.

Mooney swallowed the first morsel, then another and another, racing Dave to finish. Immediately thereafter the waiter brought the rosé champagne to clear the palate before serving the risotto and the veal.

– Brace yourself for this, said Dave to Mooney.

– I will.

The waiter gently released the cork, tilted the bottle at a 45-degree angle so as not to lose a single globule, and poured.

– Excellent, Dave said after tasting, enjoying a velvet belch.

– Some burp.

– The flavour comes on the burp. Try this.

Mooney first sipped the rosé champagne, then took a good slurp, a thin foam blistering the roof of his mouth in its moment of glory before being swallowed. It was so cold that it seemed every bubble had been packed individually in dry ice.

– Let me tell you about when I first tasted this. I was —

– Do you think I could order a vodka, too?

Dave's head swivelled and the boy appeared instantly.

– Could you bring us a bottle of vodka?

– Make it cold, said Mooney. Smirnoff.

– No, make it Grey Goose.

The boy disappeared. Dave settled back into the booth.

– I first tasted the Bile-Cart maybe ten years ago. I had met this little sidebar before Candy left me the first time. You do remember my wife Candy, don't you?

– They showed me family pictures in the hospital. I even think she came to visit me once.

– Candy?

– I think so.

– That's a surprise. She's usually in Palm Springs. She's there now. With her mother. They're inseparable, along with my SILK.

– What's a SILK?

– A Son I'd Love to Kill. He can't get enough of his mother. And she can't get enough of hers.

– I don't think you ever came to the hospital.

– They told me you were out of it, at first. Wouldn't do any good. So I never bothered. And then they told me and Ma to stay away from you. Something to do with your therapy. Like we were the enemy. Such bullshit.

– Candy came.

– Well, she's always in Palm Springs now.

– What about your sidebar?

– That was back when I didn't need someone to pee on me to get an erection. Who knows how all that happened? Candy's looks were going and I just didn't feel like having sex with her. Plain and *poshit*. After she noticed I was ignoring her, she would come straight at me, right out of the shower.

– What's wrong with that?

– Didn't give me enough time to think of somebody else.

– You're such a scumbag.

– Anyways, about my sidebar. I called her my Mouse, well, because she reminded me of a mouse, not physically actually, because she was quite blonde and a bit horsey, in the hips,

actually. I had no idea what hit me, actually. She was a fantasy
for a while and we had quite an affair. Candy, my hamster wife
knew all about it.

– How do you figure hamster wife.?

– Always on the treadmill. Anyways, because I was so smitten
I couldn't keep it a secret. Candy was actually pretty annoyed
when I told her, and she left me; but then she came back and
decided to indulge me. Let me keep the Mouse.

– What's with the Mouse moniker? I thought you said she was
horsey.

– It was really in the way she scratched at my chest when we
cuddled.

– Irritating.

– I give you that, but pleasing. It made me want to hit her.
Now there's someone I'd like to fuck. Don't turn around.

– Who is it?

– Phyllis Bertelsman. She just came in with her husband. Don't
turn around. Sit perfectly still. I wouldn't mind turning her
around. Of course, I'd have to get in line. That tush.

– When did you get like this?

– I've always been like this.

– I don't remember you like this.

– You don't remember anything.

– I actually do, it's just that my memories aren't in order.

– You keep saying that.

The boy came round with the vodka and a shot glass and
poured. Mooney drank down the shot.

– But that's not what I wanted to tell you about her. But are
you beginning to form a mental picture of her?

– Phyllis Bertelsman?

– No, my Mouse.

– A mouse that looked like a horse, to distract you from your
hamster wife?

– Sometimes she was my mouse and sometimes my horse.

– You're a zoophile.

– I'm a fucking sex addict. I would lie awake at night beside
Candy and think of her.

– Of who? Of your mouse or hamster?

– Of my Mouse. She was quite sophisticated, you know. She had impeccable manners. She never discussed money in bed, unlike Candy.

– Could I order some hot tea? asked Mooney. I feel a bit of a cold coming on.

Dave ordered a pot of boiling water, which the boy brought in a Danish silver teapot, setting it down alongside a riveted cup and saucer, a tea bag, lemon wedges on a side dish and silver tongs. The table was getting quite cluttered.

– After the initial infatuation, the more I got to know the Mouse the more I realized that what I thought was initially great sex was really just me pumping and priming until we were both pretty exhausted. I began leaving her bed pretty baffled, because I was doubting that I was bringing her to orgasm. I found myself thinking about how to dump her, and the when and the where. I also realized she had no compassion for anyone, and no imagination. My fantasy had become a nightmare. But for some reason, when she asked me, I moved in with her. I packed some bags one day and Candy said, where are *you* going? And I said I would be living away from home for a while. And I moved in with the Mouse. Couldn't say no. Someone about who all I thought about was how to leave them. My nightmare. At that time in my life I was really making good money, and I mean good money, and it seemed I could do anything, take on any challenge, defy any rule, because no matter what happened I was making money. And not just good money, actually, big money. I could even move in with someone else, which annoyed Candy to no end, with someone who I now fantasized about leaving. Can you picture that?

– I can picture it, said Mooney. A scumbag move.

– I knew I was acting like a scumbag, but I didn't care. Do you know that feeling? Not caring? A complete detachment from caring about anything and yet totally a part of life, of the community. I sat up on the *bima* beside the Rabbi. That's the kind of money I had. I was roasted even. But the idea of leaving her, and going back to Candy, was never absent from my thoughts. But I was full of energy. I felt, what's the word? — you're good with words — what's the word I'm looking for?

– Expectant.

– That's the word! Expectant! There I was with my Mouse,

with her claws cuddling me. And I felt expectant that tremendous things were going to happen to me.

Dave wasn't finished, but he thought it was a pretty good story so far and that it was worthy of a hefty pause. He scooped up some of the *boniet* and laid it thickly on his hot bread and then took a big bite. The pleasure rose to his cheeks. He motioned to Mooney to eat.

– This is an Italian dish.

– I didn't know that.

– Life is good, Mooney.

Dave began lathering another slice of hot bread with the *boniet.*

– Too much parsley?

– I wouldn't know, Dave.

– You know, months later, when I went back to Candy, I walk in and you know what I noticed when she came down to greet me?

– What did you notice?

– She had had the marble polished while I was gone. But really rubbed it down. And she had also had a boob job. I was quite shocked about it.

– Her new tits?

– No, the marble. And I was pissed off. I should have felt something else, though. I mean I was the one who had walked out and left her. I should have felt something else. What's the word?

– Contrition?

– Contrition. But I didn't feel . . .

– Contrite.

– . . . contrite. I felt indignant. She had no right to polish the marble so viciously. Sand it down like that. And you know what I said to her, just off the top of my head?

– What?

– The first thing I said?

– No. What?

– What did you do to the marble?

– What happened to the Mouse?

– Ah. The Mouse. The whiney Mouse. Well, I could have got rid of her by, what's that called when you move somebody from one office to another.

– Secondment.

– Just at that time she had taken to shoplifting. First, little bottles of perfume and makeup jars, then underwear, bras and panties.

– I know what underwear is.

– Then dresses, and finally a fur coat. Once with me in the store. It was very embarrassing.

– I could see how it might have been.

– So I decided to . . .

– Second her.

– . . . se-*cónd* her. She liked to put on airs about her being good at languages. So I sent her to Montreal. I only wished she had had a more uplifting hobby.

– Like backgammon?

– For example.

– The world's oldest game, said Mooney. Invented in Mesopotamia.

– You were there once, weren't you?

– No, I was just in Afghanistan.

– Isn't that in Mesopotamia?

– No.

– Didn't you walk across Afghanistan? With Harvey Persky? Didn't you almost die in the desert there? Ma was worried sick about you. She was hysterical. We couldn't calm her down. She would stay up at night waiting for you to phone.

– I was in the Registan Desert between Helmand and Kandahar.

– I thought you didn't remember anything.

– I do. But not in the right order. It had/has these beautiful reddish hills with lovely ridges. Me and Harvey Persky ran out of water and some nomads saved us. But I read that in 1998 the drought wiped the nomads out, or forced them into refugee camps.

– Drought in a desert. They could have seen it coming.

– Registan means country of sand in Persian.

– Did you learn Persian?

– I did. The Chol, that's what the locals, the Baluchis and Pashtuns, called the place. The Chol, which just means desert. But it's a plateau actually.

– I could never understand why you went to Afghanistan. Odd: the first twenty-five years of your life you spend trying to kill yourself, and the last twenty-five years trying to survive. I almost died there.

– Actually, it was Dad who died when you were there. You missed the funeral. The *shiva*. The unveiling even.

– I don't want to talk about that.

– Why didn't you come home?

– I don't want to talk about that.

– You missed the fucking funeral.

– Change the subject.

– Alright, tell me this. Why did you go in the first place?

– To learn languages. I was studying linguistics.

– You were so ambitious. Always had to be on the fucking Dean's List.

– And you couldn't compete with that.

– Dad wanted me to study; he was in business so we wouldn't have to go into business. You know, with all your honours, you made me want to drop out of university. I was even at the registrar's office, filling out the forms to drop out. Fucking Dean's List.

– Then Ma stopped you.

– She showed up there, screaming like the mother in *Psycho*.

– There is no mother in *Psycho*.

– Stop trumping me.

– You're so trumpable, Dave.

– Now that was embarrassing.

– I can see that.

– You did see that.

– I did. And I dropped out anyway. But let me get back to my Mouse, before I forget the rest of the story. I get penis shrink just thinking about it. Love is war, Mooney.

– Is it?

– Yeah, it is. So after months of living with the Mouse and several shoplifting charges down the road, I finally *secónded* her to Montreal. Unable to get over me she fell into a severe depression.

– Melancholia.

– Whatever.

– What kind of melancholy are we talking about? A dysthymia?

– What's dysthymia?

– A pretty low-grade depression. That's what I first had. You don't want to do anything really. No energy. Not knowing what's fun, what's not. Not really caring.

– Something like that. But it got worse. Go know. Anyway, she throws herself off the balcony of her high-rise.

– Killing herself?

– And how. So I've got to go to Montreal, meet up with her family, and make the arrangements, well not me personally, I have somebody at the Montreal office for making arrangements like that, but I do have to go there.

– I like Montreal.

– I like it too. Never had a bad time there. And at the funeral parlour I meet her family. Sisters, brothers, mother, father. I wasn't prepared for that. They are polite to me. She had never said a bad word about me to them. Not one. Her father, I remember, had this shock of wavy gray hair. It seemed as if he had been to the hairdresser. He was missing half of his right index finger. He shakes my hand and it seems as if he's bringing me a message from Mouse.

The waiter arrived with the veal and the risotto and removed the empty *boniet* dish. The risotto was served onto their plates and glasses refilled with red wine, vodka and champagne. Dave sawed his meat and chewed earnestly. The wine was gone, so more was ordered. They ate up the veal and the risotto, drank half the bottle of the second wine, and then Dave sat back and decided to take a bit of a break.

– Life is good — as long as it's good. But all this chewing. My jaw is tired.

– I want my money, Dave. I want the money from the inheritance. Dad told me all about that.

– He told you that in a dream, Mooney.

– Well, I thought so at first.

– You were dreaming, Mooney.

– But the dream was so real; I thought it was his ghost. He told me you stole my part of the inheritance.

– You're mental.

– Then he realized he was dead and left.

– You were dreaming.

– But first he told me that you had swindled me out of my part of the inheritance. Did you? Did you swindle me, Dave?

– No, I didn't.

– I was so sure. The dream was so real.

– You lost your inheritance yourself. You were no business-man, Mooney. And a shitty poker player. Don't turn around. The Minskys are leaving. I said don't turn around. They didn't even have dessert. I heard he blew the business. Grandfather, father working like a dog to build it up over the Depression years and then he blows it. *Asch in porach.*

– Or snorts it.

– See that, nobody even talks to him.

– I can't see anything if I can't turn around.

– When you're on your way down, nobody will even talk to you.

– You're telling me?

– You think I don't feel bad for Minsky, or you? I feel plenty bad. Look, it's like when a beggar asks you for a dollar and you tell him to fuck off.

– I don't.

– You give him the dollar?

– Every time.

– Well, most people don't. Otherwise everybody would be out begging. We know that in the back of our mind. Now I don't give him the dollar, but not because I don't feel bad. I do. I actually want to give him the dollar. I'm dying to give him a buck or two. Even a five.

– So why don't you just give him the dollar?

– The only explanation I can come up with is it embarrasses me. I could help Minsky, you know. I'd love to help Minsky. He was a great guy. Funny, generous. Everybody loved him. A great curler. But now that he's gone bankrupt, it would be embar-rassing to associate with him. I can't explain it. I'd like nothing better than to go up to him right now and ask him how he is. But what's he going to say? That he feels like shit? That they've repossessed his cottage and boat? That he's royally fucked? That this is his last meal in a fancy restaurant? He'd be embarrassed and I'd be embarrassed.

– Why don't you just help him out?

– The guy owes eighteen million dollars to his creditors. I can't help him out. He's finished: *ois geshikt und aheim geflikt*, as Dad used to say coming home from the races.

– Dad hated to lose.

– Who doesn't? He used to buy us Popsicles and Revels and we'd sit on the stoop and eat them.

– I remember that. On the stoop of the duplex.

– I hated that duplex. There was nothing more embarrassing than telling the other kids that we lived in a duplex. We had to walk up the stairs from our own front door. You know, Dad was making good money, but we lived in a fucking duplex and he drove that shitty car.

– Dad lived beneath his means.

– He was a stingy fucker.

– He saved the money for us.

– What for? You just blew yours. And I would have got rich anyway.

– We had that cottage at the beach. I loved that cottage.

– With a biffy. Everybody knew that.

– I liked the duplex. I liked the tenants downstairs. The Hechts. The older brother used to babysit us. We'd play Monopoly. You always won.

– I cheated. I used to help Dad put up the storm windows. You always got out of it. I hated that duplex. Have you seen the old street lately? You'd think you were in a war zone. Empty lots where houses used to be. Some just burned-out shells. There used to be some pretty nice houses on it.

– I live in that neighbourhood now.

– I can't understand that.

– To get welfare I have to live where they send me.

– The Silverbergs used to live at the end of that street.

– You know I went to his *shiva*.

– Silverberg's?

– That's right. Strangest thing happened though. These three Indians came in the house with ashes on their heads.

– What kind of Indians?

– Indians from India. They had read an announcement of his death, which mentioned that there would be a *shiva* at his manse. Now, as fate would have it, Silverberg died in February.

– So?

– Well February–March coincides with the 'dark month', which is the month that the Mahakal Shiva, the Destroyer, appeared as Lingam, on the fourth day of Magha. It was the Night of Shivaratri, when they celebrate Shiva's orgasm inside Parvati.

– One of the three tenors?

– Not Pavarotti, Parvati. According to the Vedas, Shiva appears as Lingam.

– Why?

– To make mankind aware of the presence of Eternal Time.

– And he ejaculates inside Parvati?

– At midnight. At the apogee of the celebration.

– What were the Indians doing at Silverberg's *shiva*?

– Sitting on the floor and drinking his scotch.

– I mean why were they there?

– They were sure they were at a celebration of the Shivaratri. The fact that the pillows had been removed from the chesterfields, well they were sure it was the Shivaratri. And these particular followers of Shiva had special powers.

– What kind of powers?

– Well, they could lift things with their penises.

– What kinds of things?

– One of them lifted an Inuit soapstone sculpture of a walrus and hunter.

– With his dick?

– Tied from a string.

– You're such a bullshitter, Mooney.

– After that they called them a cab and kicked them out. They walked over the snow to the cab barefoot.

– They realized their error, I suppose.

– But not before they had some very good scotch.

– What were you doing at Silverberg's *shiva*?

– I also came for the scotch. You know Shiva has three eyes.

– How do you know all this?

– I remember it. I can't remember where I park though.

– You don't have a car.

– I take cabs.

– You and everybody on welfare are always taking cabs.

– We take cabs because we can't afford a car.

– You could take the bus.

– It's thirty below half the year. If it's any consolation to you, a cab is a terrible form of transport.

– Why?

– The meter. You don't know how you suffer when you've got so little money in your pocket and the meter clicks. I want my money, Dave. I have to latch on to something in my life. Time is running out.

– You don't need money. You know things. Go back to university. Finish your degree. Teach or something.

– I'm too old for that. I'm 46. I need money now.

– It's people like me who need money.

– Don't patronize me.

– I'm not patronizing you.

– Just give me my money.

– I'm not giving you three million dollars. Don't look but they just wheeled in Mrs. Lakovetsky. She's all doped up. Now that's depressing.

– I'm turning around.

– Don't.

– I liked Mrs. Lakovetsky.

– Don't turn around.

– They're finished, too.

– The Lakovetskys?

– This is the last time you'll see them in a place like this, believe you me.

– The Lakovetskys?

– Yes, the Lakovetskys. There are people here who wouldn't even talk to me when I was a kid. They'd snub me as soon as look at me! Now they'd die to get a call from me. Just for the friendly feeling. It's easy going up but hard coming down. There are people who used to donate whole forests to Israel who can't afford to plant an elm tree in their backyard now. And they think they can hide it from these people. You know, there was a time when ten million net worth would get you a seat beside the Rabbi on the *bima*, on a Saturday morning, even on the high holidays. But now you need at least fifty million, net. Fucking Lakovetsky, he'll be kicked off the *bima*, believe you me. You know the last time I saw him, I was over at his house, he was sitting on this chair, he said it was a Frank Lloyd Wright chair . . .

– He was famous for his Frank Lloyd Wright *chaise longue*. It wasn't a chair.

– The thing ran him at least five thousand dollars, which everyone knew. He had this habit of making fun of himself and his five-thousand-dollar chair, but the purpose wasn't just to make fun of himself, but actually to point out to everyone that he *had* a five-thousand-dollar chair.

– What did he tell you?

– He said, Dave, I don't know at this exact moment whether this chair still belongs to me. And he thinks he can hide it from these people. They know everything that goes on in your life. Everything.

– But nobody gives a shit.

– Not true. They do. They do give a shit. And everyone gives a shit that everyone else gives a shit. No escaping these people. Unless you're a goy or you don't count.

– Then why do you stay here?

– Where else am I going to live?

– Why not Toronto? It would be better for your business.

– Oh sure, Toronto. Just the name makes me want to puke.

– I like Toronto.

– Because nobody knows you there. You know, I can't even breathe in Toronto. I start choking as soon as I get off the plane. It has to be about the most stultifying city on the continent, and there are quite a few stultifying cities on this continent. But as stultifying cities go, Toronto takes the cake. It has that putrid cesspool they call a lake, full of so much shit, like the people there. At least here the rivers flow, the shit flows, but Toronto is built overlooking a cesspool, which nobody can see, by the way. Its only attraction, and you can't see it.

– If it's a cesspool, why would anyone want to see it?

– And the rent is five times more a square foot. Why should I pay that for a city I can't even breathe in? Life is for the shits, no matter where you live, but in Toronto, I just can't breathe. Especially in summer. It's a swamp. But you know what the worst part is?

– What?

– The people. The Torontonians. They're so incredibly full of
themselves, and just because they live in Toronto. I admit I have
a good self-image, but it's not because of where I live. But you
take any Torontonian, the clumsiest klutz, the most boring nebbish, the unluckiest *schlemiel*, the scumbags and royal scumbags, and they think they are king shits because they are from
Toronto. They are dying for you to ask them where they are
from. When you meet them here, at the out-of-town-guests table
at a wedding or bar-mitzvah, their eyes say, ask me where I'm
from. Come on, ask me where I'm from. I never give them that
satisfaction. Do you see anyone here with that look in their eyes?
They want to *avoid* being asked where they are from. Their eyes
say: don't ask me where I'm from, please, don't ask me where I'm
from. The cowards. If someone is a success here, then they're a
success. They're shit-proud of themselves because of what they
have achieved, of how they have bested their business rivals, of
what they own, of their homes, of who they've fucked, of what
their kids have achieved, but not because they were born here
or live here. But in Toronto, the biggest shit runs around proud
as crap because he's a Torontonian. No, I could never live there.
Unless they got rid of all the Torontonians and replaced them
with Hindus or Pakistanis or Iranians or Chinese, anything but
Torontonians. Life is possibly as shitty as it can get no matter
where you live, but if I had to live in Toronto I would commit
suicide. In fact, you could bury me by the fence before I'd move
to Toronto.

– Alive?

– Fuck you. But yes. As punishment for breaking my own rule.
I've done a lot of shitty things in my life, but at least I haven't
stooped so low as to move to Toronto. You know what else dis-
tinguishes this city from Toronto? Two things: its sophistication
and its love of family. The people here are more sophisticated
than in Toronto and they love their families.

– I think they love their families in Toronto, too.

– Cruelty begins at home there.

– Unlike here.

– Funny hearing you talk about love of family.

– So, how's the kid?

– Carl's alright. You were at the *briss*.

– I didn't even see him.

– Candy had him sequestered with the baby and his wife. Can't stand that *pritztah* he's married to, but, still, at least she's Jewish. We lucked out there. But he can't stand me. He can't stand my touch even. And he's always with his mother. I don't know why he got married.

– I want my money, Dave.

– I don't have your money. The inheritance was square.

– Then loan me some.

– You're just going to lose it. Everything is *asch in porach* with you.

– I need it. I'll invest it more wisely.

– It's not going to happen, Mooney.

– I can start over.

– You're sick.

– I'm better.

– I am dying to help you. But it's against every principle I hold dear.

– I never had you down for a man of principle.

– What would you do with the money?

– Invest it.

– How? Another restaurant?

– In the stock market.

Dave winced in pain, as if he had been run through the eye with a shish-kebab skewer.

– What do you know about the stock market?

– I met a guy in the hospital who was an investor. He said it was easy.

Dave thought that was a laugh.

– He said it was easy, did he? Most people lose their fucking shirt in the stock market.

– This guy had made a fortune.

– And you believed him?

– You have stocks, don't you?

– I have a big chunk of my equity in stocks, yes, but I have a broker who tells me what to do.

– The guy made it sound easy.

– Some guy who was institutionalized. Is he going to help you?

– No, him they're not letting out.

– What did he do?

– He ate someone's ear at a hockey game. But he knew the market.

– Look, I'll give you some money, so Ma will stop *mintering* me, but don't invest it yourself. Contact my broker. I'll transfer fifty thousand dollars into an account in your name. What's your bank?

– I don't have a bank.

– Well open an account. At the Royal Bank. That way the transfer will be free for me. My broker will help you out. We'll see how you do. If you can make the investment grow, I'll give you more. Let's see how you do. If you don't blow it, I'll know if I can trust you with more. The Dow is so solid right now, you can't lose. But no casinos. No poker games.

– No casinos.

– No poker games.

– No poker games.

– No hanging around with those yokels at the casino, either; it embarrasses me. Especially with that Richie Pearl. He's an activist.

– He's a fucking communist, Dave. And anyway, he's dead.

– Sorry.

– I don't want you seeing those others guys, either. Especially Suddy Joffe.

– Dad's old buddy. Cousin actually.

– You're not supposed to tell people he's a cousin.

– Everybody knows.

– Ma doesn't like it. She thinks it's a secret.

– Why can't I see Suddy Joffe?

– Just don't hang out with Suddy Joffe.

– What's wrong with Suddy? He was always at the house. You used to like Suddy.

– No. You liked Suddy.

– You liked him, too.

– I didn't like Suddy.

– Ma didn't like Suddy.

– Dad did. So did I.

– Why do like Suddy?

– He has a big heart.

– And those other guys. Suddy's friends. They're almost in their eighties.

– They're okay.

– Just stop hanging around with those guys. It says something about you.

– I'm sure.

– And it says something about me, too. Hey, you know who I bumped into the other day?

– Who?

– Your ex-wife. She's working now.

– Where's she working?

– I think on Broadway.

– I wonder if she and Larry are happy.

– Stay away from her, too, Mooney. You've got to make a clean break.

– I will.

– I mean it. Stay away from Naomi.

– I will.

– Just take the money and my advice. Stay away from Suddy Joffe and his cronies, and from Naomi.

– I want to thank you.

– I'll be frank with you, I don't want to do this, but I'm doing it for Ma. So she'll stop hacking me a *chainik*. Let's order some liqueurs.

– I left the dog alone.

– It's just a dog.

– She's alone.

– It's just a dog. After fifteen minutes dogs can't remember if they've been alone one hour or ten.

– Still.

And that was a week before an unforgettable meeting took place at the casino on the west side of the city.

5

There they were, the four of them, waiting for him and it was already after ten. Nothing like it, being with this bunch, having pie and coffee, or soup and crackers. He felt manic, wanting to shout.

Mooney had always gone to the casino on Thursday nights to hang out with the boys, exactly the people his brother told him to avoid:

Oz, who was seventy-five, looking ninety, and whose second last bottom tooth had fallen out; and then there was Oz's inevitable friend Sammy, looking odd with his teeth out. The two of them as inseparable as ever, and therefore, eligible for boarding the Ark.

– Lend me a fin, Suddy said to Oz.

And then came Suddy Joffe, with his hair combed over in oily braids. Also in his seventies, Suddy was a soup mensch, and always generous with the ketchup squirter at table. Clod comfortably in his Hush Puppies, he was short but had been a great chest expander in his youth, out of necessity: he mail-ordered chest expander equipment because the bigger kids kept throwing him out the window at school on hot June days.

Suddy thought of himself as stocky some days, and just a fat fuck on others. He always looked as sad and vague, with his oily eyes, as if he had always just awoken from a nap. Yet there was lore about Suddy Joffe: he had played pinochle in the forties once with Chico Marx in LA; he was a crackerjack handicapper at the track; and most famously, his brother Duddy had once robbed a bank in East Kildonan, but was easily apprehended because he used a bicycle.

– Why did he use a bicycle? everyone asked.

– Because he didn't have a car, Suddy said innocently.

What else about Suddy?

He loved curling.

And he owned a taxi license that he exploited using two drivers, sometimes himself, even at his age.

He fiddled, as always, with his hearing aid on the table, which he never wore. The story went that he had ordered it out of the back of a racing form, and that it came from China in a large box, with a bra. The bra he gave to Sammy to give to his wife. 'The bra works better than that thing,' Sammy used to tell him.

– You should stuff the bra in your ear.

– I gave the bra to your wife.

– I know.

– Then how can I stuff it in my ear.

Sammy did not reply, but made a gesture of dismissal and frustration with his hand.

– Don't make with the hand, Suddy said.

– I should make with the finger.

Suddy was a great butt of jokes, but when you've played pinochle with Chico Marx, everyone else can go fuck themselves.

And finally there was Dennis, who now sported a buzz cut.

Dennis, in his mid-fifties, was over six feet tall, with a magnificent head. He was barrel-chested with an impressive belly: one could always find action betting on when Dennis's jeans would finally fall down, as he wore them just under his belly, while clinging miraculously to a flat ass in the back. Yet he was a nimble dancer, and looked elegant in a tuxedo, as Mooney remembered, having watched him once do the cha-cha-cha at a benefit dance for inner-city kids.

Dennis' eyes were so brown it was hard to see his pupils, so you didn't know whether he was looking at you or not. He had a radiant melancholy, but his manner was always earnest, almost vehement.

He was famous for his response to Suddy, when he had asked Dennis what it was like to be an Indian.

– Very conspicuous, said Dennis.

– Indian is not the correct locution these days, Suddy, said Oz.

Sammy and Dennis had just gotten back from playing pai gow,

where they both lost about fifteen bucks each. They were now all sitting in a leatherette booth around a table, their table, having coffee and danishes and fries, and they hadn't seen Mooney for a long time. They shoved over in friendly unison as soon as he sat down.

– Dennis, you know something about stock picking, don't you? asked Mooney.

– His reputation precedes him, said Suddy.

– That's what reputations are for, said Oz.

– How come your brother Dave never invited me to the *briss*? asked Suddy.

– You'll have to ask Dave, Suddy.

– You look different, Mooney.

– It's the eyelashes.

– He's on the same medicine as me. Thickens the eyelashes, Sammy said.

– Oz, you look like crap, said Dennis.

– That's exactly what my last doctor told me, and we planted him last week.

– Dr. Schwartz?

– Him we buried years ago. No, another one, an Indian from India. No offense, Dennis.

– None taken.

– Dr. Patel?

– Hnh.

– So you know something about picking stocks, Dennis, or not?

Yes, Dennis knew something about stocks; he was something of a hotshot day-trading stock picker. In fact, Oz called him the Equities Rabbi.

Mooney looked at Dennis, his face expectant.

– Two words, Mooney, first word: big, second word: short, Dennis said. That's all I need to say.

– Oh, yeah.

– Short the bastards, Dennis said. Get ready for it.

– But I hear we're in a bull market. My brother Dave said —

– That's why you have to short the bastards. But, just a second, we were in the middle of something.

Before Mooney arrived they had been discussing the Israeli

bombing of a house in Gaza. Sammy, whom Dennis lately took to calling Eisenteeth sometimes, had said this in justification:

– Just two words in defence of Israel: the Holocaust.

– Were you in the Nazi holocaust, Eisenteeth? asked Dennis.

– No.

– Were you in the Nazi holocaust? Dennis asked again.

– I said no.

Dennis took out a photograph of a building that looked like a cold storage warehouse built out of brown concrete and laid it out on the table.

– Do you know what this is?

– No.

– Do any of you know what this is?

He got some dumb looks.

– Did you go to an Indian residential school? asked Dennis.

– No. And no again, because I know you're going to ask me again.

– Were you in an Indian residential school?

– This is three times I'm saying no.

– I was taken from my mother at four years old and put here, into this Indian residential school. The Assiniboine River Residential School, they called it. I never saw my mother again, Dennis said. Do know what it was like going to an Indian residential school, Eisenteeth?

– No, said Sammy.

– Do you know what it's like never to see your mother again, to be wrenched out of her arms at four years old?

The photo of the Indian residential school was Dennis's trump card, Mooney thought. It could even trump the *shoah* when Dennis talked about it.

– The way I see it, said Dennis, the Palestinians are the Indians and the Israelis are the Europeans who came to take their land.

– We were given that land, said Sammy, by the British. It's the Palestinians who tried to take it away from us.

– That's what I'm saying, said Dennis. Like you people here, you were given the land by the British. Our land. It's exactly same thing.

– It's not the same thing, Dennis, said Sammy. We're the Indians.

– Exactly the same thing. The Palestinians are the Indians.

– We're the Indians.

– No, we are, said Dennis.

Dennis was fearless and relentless in argument, but Sammy could be stubborn and didn't like taking shit from anybody.

– You have no idea what the Holocaust-capital-*H* was, Dennis, Sammy said.

– Were you in the Nazi holocaust?

– Why do you keep calling it the Nazi holocaust? It was the Holocaust, capital *H*.

– It was the Nazi holocaust, small *H*, because there were other holocausts.

– There was only one Holocaust.

– Capital *H*.

– Thank you, Oz.

– You should check your history, Sammy, said Dennis.

– There was only one Holocaust.

– Not true. There were the British and Spanish holocausts against the native peoples of North and South America. One hundred million dead. The Belgian holocaust in the Congo. Ten million perished there. The American holocaust, against the native peoples again and the slaves. Then the Canadian holocaust against the Indians and Métis of Manitoba and the plains. Yours was the Nazi holocaust.

– Nobody calls it the Nazi holocaust, said Sammy. The Holocaust is the Holocaust.

– Were you in the Nazi holocaust, Eisenteeth?

– No. But I could introduce you to someone who was in the Holocaust. A survivor.

– You're lucky. I can't introduce you to anyone who was in that Indian residential school with me.

He pointed to the photograph.

– There were no survivors. Except me. The Red Army saved a few of your people, but all my friends in the Indian Residential School in my grade, they're all dead. And the hundred million Indians killed by the Spanish and British and Portuguese and Americans and Canadians, that was worse than the Nazi holocaust.

– That's obvious, said Oz, just the math alone.

Dennis always invited collusion, especially from Oz, but Dennis liked to win his own arguments.

– It's not obvious, Oz. I just explained it properly.

– Nothing was worse than the Holocaust, said Sammy. It can't even be explained. And look at you, Dennis, said Sammy. You're a survivor.

– They killed me years ago.

– I never know when to take you seriously.

– Really, I'm a zombie.

– The walking dead, said Oz.

– I know what a zombie is, Oz, said Sammy.

– You're so maudlin, Dennis, said Sammy.

– Really, they killed me years ago.

– That's why he's a stock speculator, said Suddy.

– You've really got to be dead on the inside for that, said Oz.

– You weren't always a speculator, said Suddy. You got a degree.

– You used to work at Indian Affairs, said Sammy.

– Honest job, said Suddy.

– Believe me, stock speculation is morally superior to working for Indian Affairs, went Dennis.

– You're actually a short-term investor, said Oz.

– Can I interrupt? asked Mooney. Are you finished with all the holocaust shit?

Mooney asked Dennis again about the market, what he would do with let's say fifty thousand dollars.

– Get ready to short the bastards.

The money Dave gave him was burning a hole in his pocket. He wanted to start buying stocks. The market was hot, reaching for its apogee, Dave said, and every day he was missing out.

– I want to get into the market. I want to know what to buy.

– Don't buy anything. Get ready to short.

Mooney didn't know what getting ready to short meant, but felt too stupid to ask. But Dennis hadn't finished with Sammy.

– Sorry, Mooney, but we were discussing something here. You still haven't answered my question, Sammy.

– What question?

– Were any of you in an Indian residential school?

Suddy, Oz, Sammy and Mooney all shook their heads.

– We're not Indians, said Suddy.

– Take a look at this picture. Take it, look at it closely.

Suddy had his coffee cup in one hand, a fry in the other, and for some reason a bottle of beer between his legs, so he was having trouble figuring out how to take the photo from Dennis. He put down his coffee cup and squirted more ketchup on his fries. Some of it splashed onto Sammy's face. Everybody laughed except Sammy. Mooney said:

– This is like Bugs Bunny.

Sammy was pissed off.

– You're sitting too close to me, Suddy.

– Sorry. There's no room.

– Move over.

– I can't.

– You're so close you can fart in my coffee. Why have you got that bottle of beer between your legs anyway?

– No room on the table.

– You've got plenty of room.

– Now, as I was saying, Dennis went, have you ever been in an Indian residential school, Chief? Dennis asked Suddy.

Suddy was deciding what to do with the bottle of beer between his legs, decided to ignore it and do something with his fry and the ketchup squirter instead.

– Watch where you point that, said Sammy.

Since Suddy failed to answer Dennis's question, Oz moved in.

– Never heard of them till you started talking about them, Oz offered.

– The only one who talks about residential schools is you, said Suddy, dipping another fry into a puddle of ketchup on his plate.

– Do you want a fry with your ketchup, Suddy, asked Oz.

– I don't think there were any Indian residential schools, said Sammy.

– You sound like an Indian residential school denier, said Dennis.

– They did exist, Sammy, said Oz. But they're an 'inconvenient truth'.

– It's just as bad as holocaust denial, Dennis said.

– You mean Nazi holocaust denial, went Sammy, with a touché.

– Maybe worse, Sammy, said Oz. Because although there are Nazi holocaust deniers, they need a holocaust to deny. But who knows about the Indian residential schools?

– Nobody, said Suddy.

– Stop agreeing with him, said Sammy.

– Why have you got that beer between your legs?   ·

– I don't know where to put it.

– Put it on the fucking table.

– No room. I told you.

Dennis pointed to the black-and-white photograph of the Indian residential school. Such ugly schools. Ugly uniforms. Ugly priests and nuns. Ugly deeds.

– Terrible things went on in here, he said, stabbing the photograph with his finger. Yet who knows about the residential schools? asked Dennis. Are there any movies about the residential schools? Any miniseries? Did you know you couldn't even speak your own language in the residential schools? Which meant we couldn't speak at all at the beginning, because we couldn't speak English. Aphasia is the cruellest disease. There we were at four years old, suffering from enforced aphasia. You couldn't speak your own language and we didn't know any English. And this was in 1960. And you couldn't see your mother again. The kids would cry at night. We were going mad with loneliness, in a cruel, painful way. Years later, when we were nine, the suicide thing started.

– What suicide thing? asked Sammy.

– Once you start thinking about suicide at that age, you can never stop. Do you know what the first thing is I think about when I wake up, Sammy?

– No, said Sammy.

– When Eisenteeth comes to visit and your wife is putting your teeth in and giving you your eyedrops and making you toast and coffee, do you know what I'm thinking about?

– What?

– Do you know what I'm thinking about?

– No, I don't.

– Whether to hang myself or shoot myself.

– You're too young to have those thoughts, said Oz.

– Do you have a gun? asked Suddy.

– I have six fucking rifles. And it started at the Indian residential school. When we were just nine. We would have started committing suicide at four but we didn't know it was an option. At nine we began to have 'suicidal thoughts'. Have you ever had a suicidal thought, Sammy?

– No.

– To contemplate and plan your own extinction?

– No.

– Have you ever had a suicidal thought?

– No, said Suddy.

– I suppose you haven't either, Oz?

– You're right, said Oz.

– And you, Mooney.

– He just got out of Selkirk, Dennis.

– Sorry, Mooney. So you know what I'm talking about?

– I think I do.

– To not have to live any longer. To end the thought that you'll never see your family again and that your life consists only of the priest, his man-bag, and his Indian residential school?

– We didn't go to residential schools, said Suddy.

– It was a rhetorical question, Suddy, said Oz.

– When you're old enough, Dennis went on, to realize there is such a thing as suicide and that it is an option, it's actually a relief. The first kid to hang himself was my friend George, came from my own rez. He hanged himself with his leather suspenders.

– Aw Christ, said Sammy.

– Nine years old.

– Bummer.

– And that was all it took, said Dennis. Just someone to point the way. He was a pioneer. You know all about the pioneers. Well, George was our pioneer. Hanged himself from a sash window hook with his leather suspenders in the laundry room.

– Couldn't he reach the floor?

– George was really short. Climbed up on the sill and jumped off.

– What did the government do?

– The priests changed our suspenders, from leather to elastic. Then came William. Not from my rez. The priests had locked William in the laundry room where George had hanged himself, and when the punishment was over, William was found gagging. He had tried to hang himself, too, but the new suspenders the government issued were elastic, so when he jumped off the sill, he just kept bouncing up and down.

Mooney and Oz and Sammy broke up, but Suddy just gazed at Dennis, ruthfully.

– You think that's funny?

They stifled their laughter.

– William wasn't able to kill himself like George. The priests didn't understand William's motive. Our suicides were all about resistance to our extinction, paradoxically, by means of extinction. If we killed ourselves, our spirit could be free. At nine we talked about spirit.

– Pretty philosophical.

– That's just how fucked we were. The priests had no idea about the motive because, also paradoxically, they were men of the cloth and yet couldn't understand spirit. Then other kids tried it, but then we were getting too tall for the sash window hooks.

Mooney and Oz screamed with laughter again. Suddy kept gazing at Dennis. A fry between his fingers.

– From then on there were no more suspenders, leather or elastic. They banned the suspenders and gave us belts, but Leonard tried it with his belt, not from the sash window hook but from a valve in the boiler room.

– Did it work?

– And how.

– And?

– And so they took our belts away. Ever seen me wearing a belt?

– Never, said Suddy.

– Soon you couldn't even find a rope or a cord in the entire school. The priests had them all removed. But the real problem, which the priests didn't see, was at night, when we were alone in bed in the dorms, and weren't getting buggered by the priests, all we talked about was George, the pioneer, and our own extinction, to free the spirit. In bed you're alone with your thoughts, suicidal thoughts. George had led the way. You could get out of the residential school, like George, through the laundry room. In bed you could meditate, cogitate with your suicidal thoughts. But there were no more suspenders or belts or rope, and we all wanted to commit suicide, free our spirit. That's all we talked about. We needed to find ways.

– What did you do? asked Suddy.

Mooney burst out laughing, so did Oz.

– We had to find other ways. And that's all we talked about: other ways of committing suicide. We all had suicidal thoughts. I can't remember one kid who didn't have suicidal thoughts. Suicide Residential School is what we called it. I can't even look at the name of any school and not think Suicide Residential School. Then other kids found ways, after George. We had discussed it enough, all the ways to do it. One kid even threw himself out the window. Just two storeys, but it worked.

– Must've jumped head first, said Suddy.

– Those who had a home to return to, and a gun there, they just shot themselves. Those were the lucky ones. Bye-bye Indian residential school. The conditions were ripe, as Lenin would say. The last ones left, we made a suicide pact. We'd be photographed in our white shirts and ties after glee club and then we'd have our milk and cookies and then we'd discuss our suicide pact.

– So that's why you're always so serious, said Suddy.

Mooney barked out a laugh. Dennis gave him a look, not wanting to hurt Suddy.

– And you all were living in your split-level houses as though nothing was wrong. And we had to put up with the priest, and his man-bag.

– What's a man-bag? asked Sammy.

– Must be a scrotum, said Suddy.

That slayed Mooney and Dennis.

– It's a purse for men.

– Never seen one.

– We were despondent, said Dennis, and you were all listening to the Beatles, as if nothing was wrong.

– I'm not from the Beatle generation, said Oz.

– Me neither, said Suddy.

– We lived through the depression, said Sammy. And the quota system.

– You have no idea of the concept of cultural genocide, said Dennis.

– We only know about genocide genocide, said Sammy. We know the Indians suffered. We don't deny that.

– They're not called Indians anymore, said Oz. The word is pejorative. The current term is 'First Peoples'.

Dennis put his photograph of the Indian residential school back in his jacket pocket. The waitress came by with refills. Oz was looking really sentimental.

Dennis recounted his attempt at suicide, with the waitress listening in. He had run away from the school and lay down on the train tracks in the yards behind Jarvis Avenue.

– What happened?

– The train was coming, its whistle blowing, but it suddenly stopped because someone else had jumped in front of it two hundred yards up the track.

Mooney and Oz belted out a laugh.

– I never know when to take you seriously, said Oz.

– I'm always serious, said Dennis.

After that Dennis never had time to fulfil his suicide pact. He was adopted out to a white family in Ottawa, went on to university to study economics and then got a job with the federal government in Indian Affairs.

– Honey, could you make me some soup? Suddy asked the waitress.

– That's quaint, she said. Refills?

She refilled the coffee cups and left.

– You're shitting us, said Suddy.

– I shit you not, said Dennis, stabbing at the photograph of the Indian residential school again.

– Anyway, said Suddy, trying to end the argument. It's all mute now.

– You mean 'moot'.

The waitress came back to serve Suddy his soup and clear away his plate of fries.

– Give her the beer bottle.

– I'm not finished.

– Put it on the table.

The waitress made room.

– Okay.

– Do you have soup with every meal?

– He's a soup mensch.

– He has it instead of dessert.

Oz and Sammy adjusted the bottle and bowl and cutlery in front of Mooney. Putting things in order made the conversation flow again.

– Now just what did you mean by getting ready to short? Mooney asked Dennis. Have you made much money picking stocks?

– Can't complain. But I'll tell you this, right now, now is not the time to pick stocks to buy. It's time to go short. You know, I'm not exactly sure where the top of the curve is, but I know it's just around the corner. I can feel it. So it's time to be thinking about a short.

– What exactly is a short? asked Mooney, finally.

– It's when you sell a stock before you buy it, said Dennis.

– How can you sell it if you haven't bought it yet? asked Mooney.

– You borrow it first. Then sell it. Then when the price drops, you buy it.

– What do you do after you buy it? Do you own it?

– No.

– Why not?

– Because you've already sold it right after you borrowed it.

– But you just bought it.

– But you sold it before that?

– And that's called short-selling? asked Oz.

– Or going short, said Dennis. Or being short this or that. Right now I'm short Citibank.

– My brother Dave's broker told Dave and me to buy Citibank. Dave told me he bought it.

– That means he's long Citibank.

– I thought long and short meant long-term and short-term, said Oz.

– Well, it doesn't.

– Explain the part again about selling the stock you don't own, said Mooney. How can you sell something you don't own?

– I told you, you borrow it first.

– Who lends it to you?

– Someone who owns it.

– Why would they do that?

– Well, while they loan it to you, they're charging interest on the loan of their stock. There are lots of people out there who have to hang on to stocks for a long time anyway, like pension funds and institutional players, and it doesn't matter if they go up or down; they're in it for the long term and to collect dividends for their unit holders, so they might as well make some extra money on them in the form of interest.

– So they loan me the stock and I sell it.

– That's right. Let's say you sell it at fifty dollars a share. In one week let's say it drops to forty-five dollars a share. Then you buy it at forty-five. So, you've bought it at forty-five dollars a share and sold it at fifty dollars a share. So you've made five dollars a share in one week, or ten percent on your money, which is five hundred and twenty percent a year, minus the interest, tax and brokerage fees, which are immaterial.

– But how do you sell something you don't own? asked Sammy.

– I said you borrow it first, said Dennis.

– What I don't get, said Oz, is what happens after you buy it at forty-five. Then what do you do with it?

– Nothing.

– But you have just bought it at forty-five.

– True, but you've already sold it at fifty, as I said.

– A week earlier?

– That's right. Right after you buy it at forty-five, said Dennis, you have completed the transaction.

– It makes no sense, said Suddy.

– Are you going to finish that last cracker? Oz asked Suddy.

– Go ahead, said Suddy. My soup's cold anyway.

– Ask her to warm it up.

– She's busy.

– So, said Oz, cracker in hand, to recap: you sell at fifty and then buy at forty-five, and you own it after you've sold it, but don't own it after you buy it.

– You're right, said Dennis, moving his index finger in the Oz finger-of-truth mode.

They sat silently in awe of Dennis for a moment.
- I don't get it, said Suddy.
- Have you been listening to anything I've said, Suddy?
- Everything.
- Listening but not understanding.
- What's Suddy short for anyway?
- Nobody knows.
- Suddy must know.
- Sheldon. It's short for Sheldon.
- But why Suddy?
- I didn't like Sheldon.
- His brother's name was Duddy.
- Short for what?
- David.
- What's wrong with David?
- It doesn't rhyme with Suddy.
- Who gives you these crazy names?
- It's a generation thing, said Oz.
- Sitting Bull wasn't called Dennis.
- It's a generation thing, repeated Suddy.

The waitress came by and cleared Suddy's soup bowl.
- It wasn't hot.
- Do you want some more?
- If it's going to be hot.

She left and they cogitated on short-selling.
- It sounds like speculation to me, said Oz.
- That's because it is speculation.
- It's immoral.
- What would Richie Pearl say?
- Nothing. He's dead.
- Richie Pearl's dead? asked Suddy.
- He died this winter.
- I knew him, said Suddy. I knew him before he died.
- Certainly! said Dennis.

That slayed Mooney and Oz.
- He'd say it was immoral too, said Oz.
- Richie Pearl was an activist, said Suddy.
- He was a fucking communist, Suddy, said Sammy.
- I curled against him in Thief River Falls once. Big bonspiel.

– I didn't know Richie Pearl was a communist, said Mooney. Or a curler.

– Workmen's Circle.

– They were Trotskyites.

– Everybody knew he was a communist. But getting back to what I was saying, said Oz, speculation is immoral.

– It's no less immoral than a bank deposit, said Dennis.

– A bank deposit is immoral?

– You think loaning money to a bank is moral. Since when do those fuckers need a loan from you?

– I'm not loaning them money. It's a deposit.

– Are they paying you interest?

– Yes.

– So it's a loan. Is it moral to loan money to those guys? There are people more deserving, aren't there?

– So.

– So what are the banks going to do with the money you loan them? That you erroneously call a deposit. They're going to speculate with it. They're going to push people into mortgages they can't pay, speculate on those mortgages, collateralize them, sell them as bonds, and when they have to, call in the mortgages and evict the mortgagee. All with your money.

– You have a telling insight, said Oz. But I still think it's immoral.

– You still vote NDP, said Suddy.

– What's that got to do with anything?

– There must be a better way to make money, said Oz.

– You can only make money from money, in the world we live in today.

They cogitated again.

– So how much could we make? asked Suddy.

– If the market crashes, for every thousand we put in, we could stand to make thirty times that.

– Cash money? asked Suddy.

– Is there any other kind.

There was more cogitation.

– I have fifty thousand dollars in an account with a broker, went Mooney.

– Did your brother give you that money? asked Suddy.

– He did.

– I always heard he had become a scumbag. And he was such a shy kid, said Sammy.

– A royal scumbag, I heard.

– It's burning a hole in my pocket. What do you think I should do with it?

– We can make a syndicate, said Dennis. We all pool as much money as we can and then we start shorting the American financials, or anything that is long on mortgage bonds, especially the shitty tranches.

– Why the banks?

– The banks, or anything that is long on mortgage bonds, like mortgage companies, I'm already short on one called House Capital. I'm watching the default rate on housing mortgages in the US very carefully. It's almost four percent.

– What's he talking about? asked Suddy.

– Let me couch it for you. You see, a shitstorm is coming. A huge shitstorm. The mother of all shitstorms. The default rate is going to skyrocket, housing prices will fall, and the banks will start losing money hand over fist. We'll short the bastards till they bleed. Remember Wounded Knee and all that.

– When did you wound your knee? asked Suddy.

– How much money have you guys got? All of us together, we can get some good leverage.

– You can't be serious?

– Why not? said Mooney, feeling eager.

– We'd have to think about this, said Sammy.

– We are.

– Think about what? asked Suddy.

– Getting a syndicate together, said Dennis. We could make a killing.

Dennis sounded relentlessly serious and they felt as if he would not let them leave the booth until they committed. But then the waitress appeared again balancing her tray, and staring at Suddy she asked: 'Who ordered the hot soup?'

– The soup mensch, said Oz.

– Which one of you's the soup mensch? she asked, staring at Suddy.

– I am, said Suddy. I'm the soup mensch. Is it hot this time?

– Are you paying attention?

She served the soup and left.

– I can't eat this soup.

– Why not?

– It's too hot.

– You ordered it hot.

– I ordered it hot, not too hot.

– Eat your saltines.

Suddy broke the wrapper on the saltines, munched one, watched his soup cool while the others watched him in silence.

– How much soup did you have today, Suddy?

– He eats soup with soup.

– He's a soup mensch.

The others continued to watch Suddy and his soup.

– Are you guys in?

– In what?

– The syndicate.

– What syndicate?

– To short US financials.

– Using real money? asked Suddy.

– You guys think about it.

They sat in silence.

– So? asked Dennis. Are you in?

– We're cogitating, said Oz.

– Cogitate.

They cogitated. Suddy's soup cooled a touch and he began slurping.

– That's hot.

Mooney couldn't believe that Dennis was going to finesse them into actually putting together an investment syndicate, since from the looks on these guys' faces, they hadn't understood a word he was saying. Neither did he, actually, but he was convinced Dennis knew what he was doing. Sound leadership is as good as intelligence.

– I've got fifty thousand, like I said, went Mooney.

– That money's burning a hole in your pocket, said Suddy.

– I can throw in five hundred, said Suddy. That's all I've got.

– What about you, Eisenteeth?

– I have a few thousand, Sammy said.

– What about your casino *bindl*?

– I share that with Anna.

– How much is in it?

– About twenty grand. But she's the winner. Most of it's hers.

– Tell her this is a sure thing.

– Yeah, right. She'll never put my teeth back in again.

– Learn to put them in yourself. What about you Oz?

– What?

– Oz? Are you in?

Like an actor who had forgotten his lines, Oz hesitated.

– How much have you got, Oz?

– I'll have to check.

– Check what?

– My bank account.

– You don't know how much money you have?

– I can't remember exactly.

– More or less.

– I think a bit over a million.

They all sat there looking at each other, as if they had suddenly discovered large sacks of gold in Oz's basements.

– He still votes NDP, said Suddy.

– A lot of millionaires vote NDP. They're going to be the new Liberals.

– A lot of workers vote NDP, said Oz.

– Where did you get so much money, Oz?

– He hasn't gone to a movie in forty years, said Sammy.

– But what about the casino? You're always here.

– Ever see him gamble?

– What do you come here for?

– I like to watch.

– The ultimate kibitzer, said Dennis.

– How much Jewish do you know? Sammy asked.

– I know more Jewish than you know Indian.

– I know an Indian word, said Oz.

– What word?

– *Manitoba*.

– I know that word, said Suddy.

– That's because you live here.

– But do you know what it means? asked Dennis.

– It's the name of a province, said Suddy.
– I do, said Oz. 'Lake of prairie'. It's Siouan.
– Are you in, Oz? Fortune favours the bold.
– It's speculation.
– Those guys are going down, Oz. They're pitiful.
– They're pitiless.

Wherever did Oz unearth so much innocence? thought Mooney. With or without him, they could make a syndicate. Because there was trust. He had never known any of the guys to break a promise. The only one who was hard to read was Dennis. It was not about dishonesty, because Dennis was the epitome of honesty, sometimes to the point of cruelty. But you never knew with him if people were all equally important or equally unimportant. And sometimes it was hard to deal with Dennis. He was always right. You always felt like giving in to him, but you didn't know why.

– I have a couple of properties I could sell, said Suddy. We'll stick it to Management.
– I thought you said you only had five hundred dollars.
– Cash money.
– How much could you get for them?
– I'd say a hundred thousand a door.
– Those shitholes off Main Street? said Dennis. You'd never get a hundred thousand a door.
– Where off Main?
– Near the park.
– Seventy-five a door tops, said Dennis. So that would put you in for one-fifty.
– I've got my taxi license, too. And the cab.
– Still?
– Do you still drive cab, Suddy?
– Once in a while. But I've got this kid and his brother who drive it mostly.
– How much could you get for the license?
– I don't know. I don't think I'd sell it.
– So you're in for one-fifty.
– I think I could get more.
– How much did you say was in your *bindl*, Sammy?
– Twenty thousand.

– What about you, Dennis? How much is your *bindl*?

– My stocks *bindl* is up to half a mil. And I've got another hundred thousand in my poker *bindl*. Let's do the math.

– We can't put all our money into this thing, said Sammy.

– I recommend eighty percent of your equity, max, said Dennis. It would still be an awesome war chest.

– I don't want to sell my properties, said Suddy. They're going up.

– We're betting that they're going to go down, Suddy. We're making our short on the assumption that that US property will tank, and that equities will follow, especially the US banks.

– But how can we make money if things go down?

– Because we're going short.

– What do you mean?

– Damn it Suddy, catch up. We make money if the market crashes.

– You see that's what I can't bend my mind around. How can we make money if the stock we buy goes down? How will we stick it to Management?

– It would be easier to open a bottle of beer with your penis than get Suddy to understand this, said Sammy.

– Because we sell it first, said Dennis, then buy it after it goes down. Oddly, Dennis's patience was still intact.

Suddy looked at him, his face bathed in confusion.

– But how can we sell it first if we don't own it?

– He's going full retard, said Sammy.

– We borrow it, sell it, then buy it when it crashes, said Dennis.

– So you're saying I can make money if the stocks go down.

– That's right. That's our bet.

– I understand fuck-all. You don't understand it either, Sammy, said Suddy.

– Let me couch it: it's like craps, you can bet with the roller or against him, said Dennis.

– Oh, why didn't you say so?

– I really don't know.

– You should have couched it before.

– He didn't have to couch it, said Sammy.

– But what if they don't go down. What if they go up?

– Then we lose.

– So, it's not a sure thing.

– I'm betting it is.

– Are you sure? asked Suddy.

– I'm money-sure. Because the shitstorm is coming; this is going to be a slam dunk. Look at this article.

Dennis took out a newspaper article from the same jacket pocket where he kept his photograph of the Indian residential school, and spread it out on the table.

– This article's about a Nicaraguan gardener in LA, an undocumented worker, who was given a mortgage to buy a house worth half a million. And the man might end up being deported!

– He looks like you, Dennis.

– Sha, Suddy.

– These mortgage companies are giving teaser-rates for two years at low interest, then they bugger you later.

– Why would they do this? asked Mooney. Why would they take the risk?

– Because they think housing prices are going to go up forever.

– Maybe they will.

– They can't go up forever. Credit can't expand indefinitely. Let me couch this too.

– Couch it.

– In ancient Babylon, Dennis said, every seven years all debts were forgiven. It was a way of stopping the growth of a mountain of debt. Even your ancient Jews had a Levitical year every seven years and all debts were forgiven. That's why Jesus was in front of the temple, overturning the tables of the moneylenders. It was the Levitical year and the debts hadn't been cancelled. It was a debt protest!

– So Jesus would have been short, said Mooney, metaphorically speaking.

– In any case, the debt mountain will collapse. Mark my words. We're heading for the mother of all shitstorms.

– So people will lose their houses? asked Oz.

– *Caveat* tempter, said Suddy.

– You mean *caveat emptor*?

– No, *caveat tempter*.

– *Emptor.*

– By the millions, said Dennis. They'll lose their homes by the millions. And their jobs.

– In that order.

– Or not.

– Surely there will be revolution. And Richie Pearl will have missed it.

– Nah, in America it's easy to convince people that they are being laid off for their own good.

– I don't think I can bet on that, said Oz. Wouldn't be right.

– They're human people, said Suddy.

– Of course it's not fair, said Dennis.

– It's not fair, said Oz. To be making money when others are suffering.

– He still votes NDP, said Suddy.

– What's that got to do with anything, Suddy?

– They're going to lose their jobs anyway whether you bet on it or not, said Dennis. Betting on it is not what's going to make it happen.

– I don't know, said Oz.

– Let's go back for a second to the mortgage companies giving mortgages to the gardener who might get deported, said Mooney. Why would they do it if they know he'll probably default?

– Because they don't keep the mortgage. They sell it to the banks. Once they do that they don't give a shit if the gardener pays his mortgage or not. They made their money already on the commissions.

– Well why would the banks buy this crappy mortgage?

– Because the banks take thousands of these mortgages and make them into a *bindl* and sell the whole *bindl* as a bond to other banks or investors. They make a commission on this again, in the millions, with huge personal bonuses to boot. Without the shitty mortgages, they can't make shitty bonds, sell them and make the commission.

– So why would other banks buy these shitty bonds that will go bad once the gardener stops paying his mortgage and gets evicted?

– Because the credit agencies are telling them that the bonds are triple-A. Wake up and smell the coffee: they also get a big commission from the banks to say this.

– And all this is legal?

– The Fed is encouraging it. They're all doing it. It's a bit more complex than all this, but basically, that's half the picture.

– What's the other half?

– The other half is where the real money is. Now the banks know that these mortgages are crappy shit. So they're taking out insurance on them. If these mortgage bonds tank, they'll get paid off by the insurers. This insurance is called a 'credit default swap', although it's not a swap, just an insurance policy.

– So who would insure this crap?

– Ultimately?

– Ultimately.

– Stupid people who believe the mortgage bond ratings are accurate.

– It's diabolical, said Oz. Truly diabolical.

– It's going to be a shitstorm.

– It's the maw of the market, said Suddy.

– But somebody's going to lose their house, said Oz. I don't like that.

– Not somebody, said Dennis. Millions are going to lose their houses. Especially in California, Nevada, the sand states. And others their life savings. Their pensions, their nest eggs. And others their jobs.

– It'll be a shit-blizzard, said Suddy.

– I like that, said Dennis. Do you know what a shit-blizzard is, Oz?

– Yes.

– Do you know what a shit-blizzard is?

– I grew up in the Depression. We ate beets every day for five years in a row. Our shit was red.

– Well, it's going to be like that. A shit-blizzard of Shakespearian proportions.

– I can't hack Shakespeare, said Suddy.

– Stop with the *non sequiturs*, Suddy.

– Everybody likes Shakespeare, said Mooney.

– I went to this town near Toronto with my nephew to see Shakespeare one summer. He took me. Couldn't hack it.

– Why not?

– Too many quotes.

Mooney and Oz broke up.

– Anyway, said Dennis, a shit-blizzard is coming.

– And if it does, then I'm going to make money? asked Oz.

– Tons of it. Emolument galore.

– I can't do that.

– Oz, it's going to happen anyway.

– He still votes NDP.

– You can either make money from it, or lose money.

– Rich or poor, it's a good to have money, said Suddy.

– What does that mean, Suddy?

– It means what it means.

– Look, Oz, said Dennis, you're not going to cause the shit-blizzard. The people who are cooking up the shit-blizzard are in New York and London and Frankfurt. They're bored of their fifth yacht, and now they want a yacht big enough to hold a small yacht and a helicopter. I've seen them.

– Where?

– In France. In Cap Ferrat. In France.

– When were you in France?

– What does it matter, Suddy?

– They want ice-breakers, Dennis continued. This is the New World Order.

– A diamond as big as the Ritz, said Oz.

– That's right.

– I don't know if I could live with myself if people lost their homes, said Oz.

– Oz, you don't know if you're going to live till tomorrow.

– Still.

– I say we meet tomorrow again to discuss this, said Mooney.

– Can't, said Oz, I'm getting my teeth cleaned.

– Oz, you've only got seven teeth.

– Still.

– Okay, we'll meet on Monday. We can meet at my house, said Dennis.

There was a stiff silence.

– Oh, you guys are afraid to come to my house. You think I have a rezzy house.

Silence again. After such a long time sitting in the leatherette booth, Suddy shifted on a soggy bottom.

– Who's afraid to come to my house? You, Mooney? You think I live on Jarvis, by the tracks.

– It's not that, Dennis, said Mooney.

– You think I live on Jarvis? In a really rezzy house?

– If Dennis says his house, it's his house, says Oz. *Ehr fiert die redl.*

– So now you're in?

– Out of brotherhood.

– *Ehr fierht die redl,* said Sammy.

– Tomorrow's a bad night, said Suddy. There's curling on TV. The eights.

– I have a TV, Chief, said Dennis to Suddy.

– Manitoba's down to the eights.

Just then Sammy got an importunate signal from his wife, Anna, who was bearing down on the booth with his eyedrops in her hand. Sammy could tell immediately that she was down for the night.

– Eisenteeth, your wife's coming.

– Time for my drops.

– Does she carry your teeth, too?

– I've got them in.

– Couldn't tell.

– She's down, Sammy.

Anna was already at the booth.

– Are you down? Sammy asked her.

– Here goes Dr. Doom, she said.

– Are you down?

– None of your business.

It was tiresome, but Anna came around the back of the booth behind Sammy. Sammy leaned his head back and opened his eyes, shuddering, as if she was going to slit his throat. Anna squeezed the applicator.

– I don't see why you can't put them in yourself, said Dennis.

– I put mine in, said Mooney.

– Why can't we just meet here?

– We can't watch the curling here.

– Doesn't matter where we meet, said Dennis. The important thing is that we know how much money each one will put in the pot.

– What money? Anna asked Sammy.

– That way we'll know how much money we can gear it up to.

– What money? asked Anna.

– What do you mean 'gear up'?

– Leverage. We're going to triple or quintuple our investment cash. Margin calls.

– What cash? asked Anna.

– Stop *intershtipping*.

– I'm not *intershtipping*. I'm just asking. What money?

– We're going to make a little investment.

– We don't need the aggravation.

– It's money-sure, Anna.

– You're not touching the *bindl*.

– Stop *mintering* me.

– I'm not *mintering* you. I'm just saying.

Anna and Sammy argued and Mooney slipped into his own thoughts. Oh, that Dave and his big and little treacheries. How the idea of making a mint on Dennis's big short appealed to Mooney, especially if Dave was long. The numb feelings and numb moments seemed erased by all this purpose. During these final moments of the discussion he felt the power return to his muscles, the juices flow through his brain. It was a miracle.

– Alright, we'll meet here on Tuesday.

– There's a hockey game on Tuesday.

– There's a hockey game every day, Sammy.

– We have to act fast.

– That money's burning a hole in your pocket.

– Let's meet Saturday then.

– Saturday's *shabbis*.

– Who's *shomar shabbis*?

– It's bad luck to discuss money on *shabbis*.

– Who says?

– It's in the Torah.

– It's not in the Torah, Suddy. Look, this is important, said Mooney. I've got to latch on to something in my life.

– Then Sunday, my house. And I want to see you guys come up with some real cash.

– Suddy, you're going to have to dump your property off Main Street.

– At seventy-five a door?

– Where are you going?

– I can't sit here anymore.

– I'm telling you you're going to have to sell, at seventy-five a door.

– It's not that.

– Where are you going?

– I have to get up, my ass has fallen asleep.

– So get up.

Suddy got out of the booth, walked a few paces in his Hush Puppies, rotated his neck and came back to the table.

– Suddy, how much would it total, if we all go in?

Suddy from his bookkeeping days could tally a list of three-digit numbers faster than an adding machine. He came up with the exact number in a jiffy, and then he said:

– I don't know why I should get into this. I might die next month. I have a lump on my neck the size of a ping pong ball.

– Suddy, you've always got lumps.

– This lump is different.

– Let's see it, said Anna.

– See.

– I've had bigger lumps, she said.

– It's cancer.

– It's not cancer.

– Listen, you guys, said Suddy, if there's anything of mine you want after I'm gone . . .

– I don't want the lump, said Dennis.

6

A few weeks into the short, the syndicate was already down, as stocks continued to rise, as Dave had predicted.

Mooney met his brother Dave in a Chinese restaurant run by a Vietnamese family in the old garment district. He had just moved into his mother's house, with the dog, which his mother was forced to accept.

Over a bowl of won-ton soup as big as a basketball Dave laid into him.

– You're an idiot.
– I'm not an idiot.
– How much are you down?
– A lot, said Mooney. But they're not realized losses, Dennis says.
– You're an idiot. And who's Dennis?
– Dennis, this guy we know at the casino.
– Not the guy from Selkirk I hope?
– No, Dennis, from the casino.
– I told you not to hang out with those guys.
– They're my friends.
– And I told you to buy stocks, what do you know from short-selling?
– It's when you borrow a stock, then sell it, then buy it.
– I know what short-selling is, you idiot.
– You always have to undermine my confidence.
– What confidence? You're getting taken for a ride.
– In your opinion, in your un-asked-for opinion.
– Yes, in my opinion.
– Dennis says it's money-sure. The banks are going to crash. In fact, this is the 'slowest car crash happening'.

– Who says this? Dennis? Who is this Dennis.

– He's this Indian guy, a friend of mine. Known him for years. Hangs out with me and Suddy and Oz and Sammy.

– I told you not to hang out with those guys. They're almost twice your age.

– Dennis is my age. A bit older actually. And he's a great stock-picker. He says the subprime mortgage bonds are going to crash and the banks that are holding them and the insurance on them will crash too. So we are short the financials. It's a plan with enormous possibilities.

– Enormous *im*possibilities.

– Dennis is money-sure.

– Dennis and Suddy Joffe and your stock market nutdom.

– There's nothing criminal in this.

– No, it's worse than criminal, it's stupid. And just when's this all supposed to happen?

– Well, Dennis says the two-year teaser rates on the 2005 sub-prime mortgages have expired and the interest is floating up to 12 percent so the defaults should start rolling in, and then the bonds backed by them will start to go, then the insurance on the bonds will have to be paid and the banks will crash and then the market will crash. It's going to be a shit-blizzard, Dennis says, of Shakespearean proportions.

– And you think Ben Bernanke, Hank Paulson, the boys at Morgan Stanley and Goldman Sachs and Lehman Brothers are going to be caught holding all this crappy paper? Do you think the Federal Reserve is going to let the entire US banking system crash?

– Dennis says so. He says they're either fools or crooks to have let things get this out of hand.

– You think Washington is in on this?

– Dennis says the capital of the US is now in Langley.

– I'd like to meet this Dennis.

– You should. He's a genius.

– I'd like to find out if God has blown genius into his asshole.

– He has, he has. He's a genius.

– Who hangs out with stupid people.

– He's a genius.

– You tell him for me to dump your shorts on the next dip and then buy these banks. It's 2008, not 1929. There isn't going to be a run on the banks. I have fifteen million invested in these stocks; these are blue chips, with no risk! Companies that are a hundred years old or more.

– They're going down, Dennis says.

– You're going down. Dennis is going down.

– Look, if people stop paying their mortgages, the mortgage bonds will go belly-up.

– No, they'll just borrow more on their homes, because home prices are still going up, and credit is flowing. The world is awash in cash. A one-room apartment in New York costs half a million dollars, up twenty percent from last year. Even if they just stabilize at a three percent increase in value per annum, people are still safe and making huge amounts on their homes. Mortgages are cheap because the world is floating in a swimming pool full of cash. Trillions in yen and dollars just floating around out there, looking for a safe bet. House prices will never fall, Mooney, and that's money-sure.

– Dennis says they will.

– My broker, who has a degree from McGill, and another from Harvard, says they won't. It doesn't make sense, Mooney. Look, why would these banks be buying mortgages and issuing bonds on them? They would know if they were bad. And besides, the rating agencies say these bonds are double- or triple-A.

– Dennis says you can't trust the rating agencies.

– But they're supervised! And regulated! By the Fed, and the SEC and a thousand other agencies. And let's not forget the auditors.

– Dennis says you can't trust the regulators. He says there's no oversight. The Fed is colluding, he says.

– So what you're saying, or Dennis, actually, is that there is a conspiracy involving Wall Street, the Federal Reserve, Hank Paulson and S&P and Moody's and Fitch to destroy the American banking and credit system and destroy capitalism?

– Dennis never said that.

– What does he say?

– Well, Dennis says the banks just buy the mortgages, roll them up into bonds and then sell them to suckers in Germany or Switzerland or to other, stupider banks. He says the derivatives are so complex no one can understand them and that they make their money on the commissions anyway.

– So Deutsche Bank is also in on the conspiracy?

– It's not a conspiracy, per se.

– What is it, per se?

– A clusterfuck, Dennis says. The clusterfuck before the shitstorm.

– Shit-blizzard, you called it before.

– But if you ask me, I don't really understand it.

– Well if you don't, why did you put your money into this syndicate of yours?

– Your money.

– Don't be cute.

– Don't be so negative.

– You're not getting any more from me, so I'd advise you to get out now.

– Dennis says things should start turning by the summer. He says the banks are hiding their losses. The balance sheets are opaque.

– So now the auditing companies are in on the conspiracy, too. You're saying the Deloitte and Pricewaterhouse and KPMG and Moody's, S&P and Fitch, Wall Street and the Federal Reserve are conspiring to destroy the banking and credit system? That they're the new Bolsheviks? That Alan Greenspan is Lenin and Ben Bernanke is his only son, Trotsky?

– It's not a conspiracy. Dennis doesn't believe in conspiracy theories. He says conspiracy theorists are theory-short or something. It's just gotten out of hand, because the American economy has been financialized.

– Speak English. You've probably lost twenty percent on your money so far.

– Unrealized losses. All we need is stick-to-it-iveness, says Dennis, and we'll be raking it in.

– How much are you down exactly of the fifty thousand I gave you? Twenty percent?

– More.

– How much more?

– You didn't 'give' it to me.

– How much?

– About eighty percent.

– You can't be that big an idiot! And those stocks haven't risen eighty percent.

– Unrealized losses.

– Stop with the unrealized losses. Look, if you shorted these stocks and they've gone up ten percent off the dips, and you haven't realized the loss, then how can you have lost almost all of it?

– Unrealizedly.

– Stop already.

– We're geared up. Dennis has leveraged the bet five times. Maybe more.

– You're geared up into this? All of this on margin?

– Five times. The maximum allowed, given our stake. I know, it sounds scary, and Suddy had to sell his two apartments off North Main at seventy-five a door.

– He got seventy-five a door for that crap?

– That's on his say-so. And believe me, Suddy and Sammy are pretty bummed out. Sammy's wife is ballistic. Oz is the only one not bummed out; he says he deserves it for speculating against people's homes and jobs.

'Bummed out' was euphemistic. Sammy's wife was refusing to put his teeth in, and Suddy had to be hospitalized when he learnt his bet was going south.

■ ■ ■

Suddy's hospital room looked out over the river into the early spring twilight. Mooney had gone with Dennis to visit him. Oz was there already. Suddy was sitting up in bed when they arrived, one finger in an electrode sling, his heart being monitored. He gingerly fingered his oily braids lying on his scalp with his free hand as if trilling a piano across his head.

Just the previous day he had run into Oz at Mellers'. Suddy was having asparagus soup, because he 'liked the way it perfumed his urine for the day.' Oz ordered a corned beef on pumpernickel.

– Hello, Mr. Soup Mensch.

– Sit.

– I've got something to tell you, Oz said, but I don't know how.

– Sit.

– I don't know how to tell you this.

– It'll come out sooner or later. Sit.

It came out sooner. Oz showed Suddy the latest quotations of the stocks they were shorting, how they had rebounded stiffly on a small dip. At first Suddy thought that that was good news, but then Oz reminded him that they were trying to 'short' the big US financials and had to explain for the umpteenth time what 'short' meant. Suddy began to get the jitters. So we're losing money? Suddy asked in a quest for simple information. When Oz told him how much they were down, Suddy said:

– How did I get into this predicament?

– We're all in it.

– It's *asch in porach.*

– It is looking bad.

– I could bite the table.

– Get a grip on yourself, Suddy. Suddy, don't. Suddy!

Suddy bit the table and had a panic attack right there and spilt his asparagus soup onto his cuffs. By the time the ambulance arrived Suddy had stopped hyperventilating because he had passed out cold.

When Suddy awoke in the hospital he asked Oz:

– Where am I? Weren't we having soup? This isn't Mellers'.

– It isn't Kansas either.

– Where am I?

– You're in the hospital, Suddy.

– Heart attack?

– No. Panic.

– Heart panic?

– No. Panic attack!

– What a blunder we've made!

– It'll be okay, Suddy.

– We're in the maw of the market.

When Mooney and Dennis arrived Suddy had propped himself up on his pillow and said to Dennis:

– I want to take my money out of the syndicate. We have to scrub the bet.

– Can't. It's locked in, Chief.

– Stop calling me Chief. What if I called you Chief?

– I mean it with affection.

– I wouldn't. It would be a racist remark.

– Nah.

– I'd say it because I was fucking teed off. I'd become a racist just to say it.

– It does look bad, guys, said Dennis. But we have to stick to it.

Suddy and Mooney and Oz looked at each other like the crew of a doomed submarine, while Dennis, as always, held his ground, which was built of pure self-confidence. Suddy's suffering expression was too much for Mooney. He had also been watching the quotes on TV and every time their stocks went higher by the closing bell his stomach knotted and his cheeks burned. And the thought of Dave raking it in sent an electric shock of infantile jealousy through him.

– Can't we give him any of his money? Oz asked Dennis.

– No. You can't take your money off the table once the ball has bounced onto the spinning roulette wheel. You know the rules. And it's still spinning.

– We're in the maw of the market.

– We're going to do alright, Suddy.

– All I had was those apartments, said Suddy. I'm going to lose everything.

– You're a catastrophist, Chief. When we're finished, you can buy twenty of those crappy apartments, said Dennis, at two hundred a door. The stocks we shorted are going to go down. Those buggers are going down. We're going to blow holes in them.

– But now they're going up.

– Which makes it cheaper for our new shorts. But they're going down.

– He's right, said Oz.

– Don't encourage him, Oz, said Suddy.

Oz and Dennis had remained the most resilient so far, with Mooney following suit.

– What about the losses?

– They're unrealized losses. Tacit losses. We haven't lost anything yet. If we bought them now, then we'd realize a loss.

– What do you mean yet? We have these stocks, don't we? said Suddy.

– We've just borrowed them and sold them. We're short, Suddy.

– I don't understand this. All I know is that Oz says we're down money.

– And we are. But as soon as those big fuckers start telling the truth about what their subprime mortgage bonds are worth, their stocks will drop and they'll be going down with them.

– Who?

– Wall Street.

– But that's not happening, Suddy said, blowing his nose.

– Not yet, but we're very close. By July, things will be turning our way.

– Where's the shit-blizzard you promised? You said there was going to be a shit-blizzard? Of Shakespearean proportions, you said.

– It's coming.

– So's Christmas.

– It's coming. July, maybe.

– I have to get my money out. My nephew in Toronto has been asking about my property. I haven't told him anything.

– Where's your risk appetite?

– I've lost it. I've lost my risk appetite; I've lost my appetite, period. I'm old; I made a mistake. I just want my money back. Even half of it. I'm broke.

– You have the cab, said Mooney.

– I'll tide you over, said Dennis.

– I don't want anyone to tide me over. I just want to take my money out. When my nephew finds out, he'll murder me, if his wife doesn't murder him first. I want my money, Dennis.

– You can't. It's locked in. We all agreed to that.

– Sammy's not so happy about this either, his wife is so furious, she won't put his teeth in.

– He should learn to put his own teeth in, said Dennis.

– He says it's *bakukt*.

– Nothing's *bakukt*.

– It's *asch in porach*.

– It's not *asch in porach*, whatever that means.

– His daughter Marilyn's a lawyer. And she's got a real *pisk* on her. She could sue you for the money.

– Just let me talk to Sammy, said Dennis.

– Could she? asked Mooney.

– Sammy's not going to sue us, said Dennis.

– His daughter would. She's got a *pisk* on her like you wouldn't
believe.

– I'll talk to him and his daughter.

– We both want out, said Suddy. We are the minority interest.
We have rights.

– These are desperate deliberations, said Oz. It's no way to
make a decision.

– Oz is right, said Mooney.

– We have to talk calmly about this, said Dennis. I told you the
stocks would still keep rising before they crashed.

– We're down almost ninety percent, said Suddy.

– Tacitly. We haven't realized any losses.

– I don't understand this tacit business. Am I *bakukt*, tacitly
or not?

– You're not *bakukt*, said Dennis. Nothing's *bakukt*.

– We're *bakukt*. It's all *bakukt*.

– Nothing's *bakukt*.

– It's all *asch in porach*.

Suddy turned his head to look out the hospital window. The
city glittered in the night as far as he could see. A sliver of moon
emerged from one bank of night clouds and vanished behind
another. Ice floes bigger than boulders exploded against the
bridge, making Suddy more nervous. He lightly trilled his worms
of hair.

– Why don't you eat something? Suddy.

– I need soup. I have to start with soup.

– I'll get you some soup. You're a soup mensch.

– I'm a soup mensch.

– You're a soup mensch.

Heavy-hearted they huddled by the door of his room, leaving Suddy waiting for his soup and watching a sitcom. Oz soon
received a call on his cell from Sammy's daughter.

– Sammy has succumbed to the flu, Oz said. Marilyn's on her
way right over here.

– Who? asked Dennis.

– Marilyn, Sammy's daughter. She's bringing a tort.

– That's so sweet, Mooney said.

– I like torte, shouted Suddy, who hadn't yet been put to sleep
by the TV.

– Not that kind of tort, Dennis said.

– That's right, said Oz, the finger of truth in action. Not T-O-R-T-E but T-O-R-T: a tort action. *Actus reus.* A civil wrong.

– Is this serious? asked Mooney. Can she do this?

– Just let me talk to her, said Dennis.

– Sammy's wife wants to know if you know what a *nishoma* is, Dennis.

– Tell her I don't know what a *nishoma* is. And stop with the Jewish. You guys are making me dizzy. I could go all rezzy on you, too.

Marilyn arrived, excited to be in conflict, her cheeks ablaze from the cold. Truth to tell, she knocked Dennis's eyes out. She was slender, with big knockers, and carried herself confidently, he gave her that.

Dennis took her by the elbow and led her out of the hospital. They went for a walk by the river. A crust of river ice was melting by the bank. And closer to the centre the thicker ice had cracked into huge chunks, some upending themselves and flipping over. If you saw them do that, you would dream about it that same night. These iceberglets rubbed against each other, creaked, flowed on and then detonated blindly as they smashed against the pylons of the bridge.

– We're going to sue you in open court, Marilyn said, who fancied herself a crap-cutter.

– Your father wanted in. Like the others, said Dennis, also showing he could cut the crap too.

– They had-slash-*have* no idea what they're doing.

– True, they have no idea what they're doing, but I know what I'm doing.

– This will go to court.

– So you're going to try to prove, in open court, how stupid your own father is.

Marilyn screamed with laughter, and came right back at him.

– No, I'm going to prove how slick you are.

– You're going to sue a native man for conning a retired CA, a linguist, a retired bookkeeper and cab owner and a rich retired butcher, arguing that the native man outsmarted *them* for no gain.

– You said *them* as if you meant Jews.

– I meant Europeans.

– I could've sworn you meant Jews.

– You're all Europeans to me. I don't discriminate.

– Right.

– Look, I explained everything to them. There was no arm twisting.

– But you bought them all BlackBerrys.

– It was Suddy who wanted the BlackBerrys.

Marilyn smiled.

– And I'm not slick.

– Evidently, judging from those jeans. How do you keep them up?

– It's the only proof against all the odds that there is a benevolent God.

– We are going to sue you, you know that?

– Go ahead, sue. But I've also put a ton of money into this myself. You'd have to prove what an idiot I am, too. In open court.

– I could prove your whole cousinage are idiots. It would be that simple.

He loved that word she let fly, *cousinage*. He now took a good fat look at her tits, and was surprised at himself that he hadn't copped more looks before. They crossed the bridge to the south side and stood midway looking at the ice floes below. While it was a cold night, the wind was warming up and felt spring-like. Dennis took out his picture of his Indian residential school and palmed it without showing it to her yet.

– So you're going to prove that I suckered these guys in because they're idiots.

– With wilful malice.

– How can you prove wilful? You can only infer the wilfulness of another, unless you're a mind-reader.

– That's my department.

– Or else you're going to try to show that the only native stock-picker in the province acted maliciously.

– It's not about race.

– What's it about?

– It's about being reckless with other people's money. What you did with your own is moot.

– I want to show you something.

Dennis showed her the photograph of the Indian residential school.

– Do you know what this is?

– It's an Indian residential school.

– How do you know that?

– I saw it on the Internet.

– Do you know what it's like being taken away from your mother at four years old? Being kidnapped at four years old. Never to see your mother again.

– That's all I fantasized about until I moved out of the house at twenty-one.

– I see we're not on the same page here.

Dennis put away his picture.

– Dennis, just give him back his money.

He liked the way she said his name.

– I can't. It's locked in. And besides, we're going to make a killing. They know that.

– No, they don't.

– They should.

– I don't think I like you.

– I don't need you or anyone to like me.

– Spare me.

Dennis thought Marilyn was looking at him like the school priests of years gone by when they were cross, and they were always cross. But it was just the expression she bore whenever she studied something seriously. He thought her flippant, over-bearing, overly self-confident, mischievous, a thriver on conflict. And he had heard about the lengthy exertions required if you had a Jewish wife. But she had a dynamite laugh and the most beautiful hands he had ever seen.

– Let me at least explain my strategy. Litigation might be costly.

– I'll give you ten minutes. Start talking.

She wondered if she could concentrate on his explanations, distracted by betting with herself whether or not his jeans would slip off his ass, which she thought was neither young nor old, and shocked to realize she had formed an opinion of it.

He had a fine head, she would give him that, and his expression was earnest, practically vehement, certainly not that of a con man; his was the kind of face that made you believe sincerity really existed. Perhaps that was his con. She warned herself not to get involved with someone who had been truly wretched as a child, but then the thought that her mother would flip if she dated him was just too funny.

After his explanation he walked her to her Lexus with the white leather seats.

■ ■ ■

Dave was now eating his kung pao chicken, taking in all of Mooney's story about Marilyn confronting Dennis.

– So what was the upshot of the tort?

– Marilyn's in for a hundred thou. She's mortgaged her law practice and is selling her Lexus. Here's the tort. She ripped it up herself.

– Let me see that.

Dave spread the document on the table, piecing together the parts that had been ripped in half, and examined it perfunctorily.

– So Suddy had two apartments? Dave asked. How much did he get for them? Just out of professional interest.

– I told you, about seventy-five thousand a door. Don't you listen?

– Bad sale.

– And Oz put in almost two hundred thousand.

– Oz has that much money?

– He has over a million socked away.

– You're kidding. He could fix his teeth. Anyway, I can't believe any of this, but then I can. You're such an idiot. You'll end up like Suddy. Everything's always *asch in porach* with you.

– So the tort's over with?

– Right.

– So what did you want from me?

– I want more money.

– To increase your shorts, I suppose?

– For example. Dennis says the leverage is better on the shorts while the stocks are still going up, so now's the time to increase our bet. He says it's like having the nuts right after the flop, like flopping four twos with everybody holding pocket aces or pocket kings. Slow playing them to death. You have to keep increasing your bet on the turn and river. He says the turn card has just been dealt.

– What's the turn card?

– An article he read in a little journal about mortgage default rates. The *Quarterly Mortgage Report.*

– Never heard of it.

– Look at it.

– Just keep it. I believe you.

– Read it.

– I don't have time to read it.

– He says that's the turn card. The analysis he was waiting for. And we've got to up the bet. Gear up ten times. But to do so we need to increase our deposit or something.

– Your collateral.

– Right.

– You're completely mental. And you say this guy is Indian? And he hangs out with Sammy and Oz and Suddy? How much of his own money has he put in?

– Four hundred thousand.

– Where'd he get it?

– He made it over the years picking winners.

– At the track?

– No, in the stock market. He's like this genius stock-picker.

– You know, it's odd, but you're betting against me?

– I know.

– If you guys are right, I could lose a substantial size of my equity. But that's not going to happen. There may be some minor adjustments in the market, there always are, but they will be just that, minor adjustments. You guys are going to lose every cent.

– But if we're right? This Dennis, he's a genius.

– Only because he's surrounded by stupid people.

– He says it's money-sure.

– You've always been money-sure, Mooney. Even in bankruptcy court.

– I know. But that was me. This time I have sage advice.

– Sage advice. You can't fool around in the stock market. You have to put your money in the blue chips, collect your dividends, cash out when you need to.

– But what if we're right?

– You're not right.

– Why don't you come in with us? You know Sammy's daughter Marilyn is in.

– I know. You told me that.

– She's mortgaged her law practice and sold her Lexus. She drives around in a leased Smart car.

– Who else has he suckered in?

– That's it. So will you give me another fifty grand or what?

– I have to think about it.

– Think fast. I have to get home. The dog's alone.

– Ma's there.

– But she won't talk to the dog. Won't even be in the same room with her. And she needs company.

– She said the dog had her period.

– So.

– So it made her sick.

– She just spotted a bit.

– In the living room.

– On the plastic runners.

– Can't stand those runners, said Dave.

– They fill the house with static electricity.

– You can't have a dog that has a period at home.

– I cleaned it up.

– And you can't have a dog in a Jewish house. Period, Mooney.

– That's bullshit, Dave. They told us that as kids because they didn't want a dog in the house.

– Only the *goyim* had dogs.

– The Silverbergs had a dog.

– That's because they were the Silverbergs. They had a Jamaican maid, too.

– Anyway, I have to get back. Meaghan doesn't like being alone.

– That dog's got the better of you.

– No, she doesn't.

– Does she go around picking up your shit? Does she carry it around in a plastic bag with her?

7

The month of July came and went but their short wasn't taking off. And then a hot August rolled in. Sammy had fired his daughter as his lawyer and there was talk he was going to hire a new one with Suddy.

One early August night Dennis was at the casino, sitting in their booth alone, reading stock quotations on his BlackBerry, when Suddy marched in trimly in his Hush Puppies and sat beside him.

– Just stop bothering me, Chief, Dennis said to Suddy. Your money's safe. Just have patience. You're going to make a killing.

– When?

– Soon.

– You said July.

– I made a mistake, but we're close, Suddy.

– Give me a rough idea.

– The rubber's going to meet the road, probably mid-August or September, when the big shots dock their yachts and head back from the French Riviera.

– I'm scared, Dennis. I want out.

– What you want, Suddy, is to punch below your weight all your life. Sack up.

– Dennis.

– And if we break up the syndicate, and the market crashes, I don't want you guys yelling 'Come back, Shane!'

– Come on, Dennis.

Dennis was really bummed by the harassment. And he was worried, a bit, because they also had warrant puts in the low five digits that expired at the end of September.

– We have to call a meeting of the syndicate now. And I mean now.

– Can't. I'm going away for a few weeks.

– We have to meet soon, all of us.

– Do you need some money?

– I'm okay for money. The cab is bringing in summer fare revenue. Where are you going?

– I'm going away.

Dennis had no idea where he was going. Perhaps he would go to his cottage at the Beach. He hadn't been there in July because he had rented it out, using the money to beef up the short. It actually wasn't such a bad idea: the fish fly season would be over, the nights a bit cooler.

And it was just now that the idea started rolling around in his head to get away from these guys, which meant he didn't want them to know where he was going. Without thinking he just invented a place off the top of his head where he thought he would be safe from them.

– Where are you going?

– To the Two Wolves Reservation.

– Where's that?

– In the Interlake.

– We can meet there.

– Just stop, Suddy.

– We can meet up there.

– Suddy, you're not coming up to the rez.

– Why not?

– Your money is safe, and when the market tanks you're going to make a killing. You can even get back to Vegas for a while or play at the hundred-dollar blackjack table. Or play pinochle. You're always talking about that.

– I could come up to the rez. We all could. Have lunch up there or something.

– Rez is not short for resort.

– They must have a restaurant or something.

– It's not like that, Suddy.

The next day Dennis fled to his cottage for a couple of weeks, just to get away from his partners. The fish fly season was over, too.

– Seen Dennis? Sammy asked Suddy the next evening at the casino.

– My stomach's killing me, said Suddy. I ate a pound of BC cherries this afternoon.

– A whole pound?

– I know. They were too cold.

– But have you seen Dennis?

– He's not answering his BlackBerry, said Oz.

– I can't get hold of him, said Sammy.

– He told me he was going to his aunt's reservation, said Suddy.

– Oh, so you know where he is?

– At the rez. The reservation.

– Which one?

– The Two Wolves Reservation, he told me.

– How can we find out where that is?

– Use your BlackBerry.

– He'll call, said Mooney.

– Just look it up on that thing.

– He'll call. Leave him alone for a while. You've got to have a little faith.

– Just google Two Wolves Reservation, said Oz.

– I'm bloated, said Suddy.

– Who told you to eat a pound of cherries?

– It's just that they were too cold.

Mooney thumbed on his BlackBerry and got on the Internet.

– I can't find a Two Wolves Reservation.

– That's what he said: Two Wolves Reservation.

– There is no Two Wolves Reservation.

– There must be. Google it.

– I am googling it. There's no Two Wolves Reservation.

– How did you spell Wolves? With a *v* or an *f*?

– With a *v*.

– Did you try with an *f*?

– You can't spell Wolves with an *f*.

– What about Bansche Wolf and his family. They called themselves the Wolfs, with an *f*.

– That's different, Suddy. You can't spell Two *Wolves* — the animal — Reservation with an *f*.

– Maybe they made a typo.

– They may be an oppressed people, Suddy, but they can spell.

– Just google it.

– Alright.

Mooney googled Two *Wolfs* Reservation and got no hits, just a message asking: 'Did you mean Two *Wolves* Reservation?' for which there was, of course, nothing.

– There's no such place.

– Maybe they just don't have a website yet.

– It could be under construction or something.

– There has to be. It sounds like the name of a real reservation.

– And what if he was at the 'Two Wolves Reservation', would you go visit him there?

– Why not?

– What about you?

– I don't know. I'd feel uncomfortable, said Suddy. I'd make the people there uncomfortable.

– You make everybody uncomfortable anyway.

– You don't think I know that. Look, Mooney, if I don't get my money I'm going to be hospitalized again. My blood pressure is up to one-eighty. My lump is growing.

– I'll talk to him.

– How?

– I'll google all the reservations with Two or Wolf in the name. Maybe you didn't hear him right.

– I heard him right. He said Two Wolves.

– Maybe he said Hooves, said Sammy.

– Let me work on it.

– Maybe it was Three Wolves.

– Or Four?

Mooney actually knew where Dennis was. Dennis had told him just in case an emergency came up.

He had gone to the Interlake, but not to his aunt's reservation, because he didn't have an aunt, or at least he didn't know whether he did or not, having been cut off from his family when he was abducted and placed in that Indian residential school. And, of course, he hadn't gone to the Two Wolves Reservation because there was no Two Wolves Reservation.

Dennis was quietly in hiding out at the Beach, not more than a few blocks from Sammy's cottage, in fact. But Sammy didn't go to the beach that month because he didn't have cable there and he was glued day and night to the cable stations, watching the stock market.

Sammy was being driven crazy by bull-market commentators, according to whom anyone not going long in the market was an idiot. There was one crazy guy who screamed and rang a bell. Now that was entertainment. But he desperately needed to find Dennis and get some feedback from him and either get Dennis to close the short and salvage what they could of his *bindl*, or else reassure them in some way.

Mooney told them he had found the Two Wolves Reservation and would go up there and talk to Dennis, alone. Dennis was stressed out too, you know.

Oz drove Mooney early the next morning to the bus station.

– So you found the Two Wolves Reservation?
– I did indeed.
– And you'll be okay up there?
– Dennis will be there.
– Still.
– Still.
– You're sure you want to take the bus. I could drive you there.
– I'll be safer with the bus than driving with you.
– I'm up for a review. I'd hate to lose my license.
– I was kidding.
– How do you get there?
– The bus will take me to Fisher Branch. Dennis'll pick me up there.
– And take you to the Two Wolves Reservation?
– That's right.
– So you'll be alright?
– With Dennis.
– Still.

Mooney felt a bit bad lying to Oz, but it was easier that way. He bought a return ticket and took a lonely but beautiful hour's bus ride out to the Beach.

It was a creation morning, he thought: the light was fresh and the flat fields were set between Chinese screens of trees and hedges. Although the plain to the lake was flatter than hockey ice, the effect of the screens made it seem that the tilled plots of yellow canola flowers were terraced up to the clouds. During his reverie he wondered why he needed all this aggravation. He could be living peacefully with his dog, not bothering anyone, poor, lonely; but enjoying nature. But he was driven, out of rivalry with his brother, with Larry Brickman, driven to succeed in what counted most in this world: having money. But to what end? Perhaps Oz was right, perhaps what they were doing was immoral. But Oz finally came in with them. Out of brotherhood, he said.

He stepped off the air-conditioned bus into a solid waxy block of heat. His skin tingled with pleasure.

He knew many of the people at the Beach, who nodded to him because he used to summer there many years ago in his youth. But although they nodded they kept their distance, indicating that they didn't want to stop and shoot the shit.

That was why he needed Dennis's short to work. If their ship came in — and Dennis said it would, and that the winnings would be exponential — these people would do more than nod. They would stop to talk to him, invite him over, and that was still important. If hospitalization had taught him anything, it was that you needed to be part of society, your society, and there was only one way of being accepted: having money, if only because it gave you confidence.

Money was a symbol, of course, since it was just paper. But symbols, he knew, from his university days, from his linguistics studies, were more real than the reality they symbolized.

He walked past the renovated cottages, a far cry from what they were when he was a kid, and wished he had one, not because he needed all that polished teak, but because they were symbols too, tokens that would get him accepted by his society again, or at least by himself. For whatever that was worth.

He walked the mile or so to Dennis's cottage along the lakeshore, watching the cranes dancing on the wavelets far out and then setting down on the sandbars to do bugger all. It was quiet, except for the odd distant buzz of a lawnmower, and there were fewer kids around now than when he was young, but you could still hear their screams and laughter everywhere. That sound of that sort of happiness really carried.

Dennis's cottage, solidly moderne, sat on the crumbling lake-front. The cottage used to belong to the Silverbergs and had been remodelled to Dennis's taste after he shorted some tech stocks at the end of the dot-com bubble. Years past, when Mooney summered here, he had gone to parties at this cottage, listening to ghost stories when it rained on the verandah, and playing poker with the guys. The summer after his grandfather's death he found himself in a poker game where for the first time he lost a large sum of money. He had played on impulse, forgetting everything he knew about cards, actually enjoying himself as his losses piled up and as he signed IOUs. Jeffery Nolan, who wasn't in the game, kept running in and out of the house screaming himself hoarse like a eunuch at an orgy announcing Mooney's mounting losses to the kids hanging around outside.

There was also a famous rumour that Mr. Silverberg once had an orgy at this cottage with five housewives, National Council, not Hadassah, when their kids were at camp and their respective husbands, who only drove out on Wednesdays and Fridays, were in the city working. The punch line to the rumour was this: since no one knew what to do at an orgy, nothing happened until Mr. Silverberg shouted:

– Organization!

But that was just a north-end rumour about a south-end Jew. Go know if it was true or not.

Mooney pressed his nose against the screen to peer inside the cottage while rapping lightly on the frame of the sliding door.

– Can I offer you a beer? Dennis asked.

– I'm on my meds again.

– How about some pop?

– What have you got?

– Usual crap.

– Maybe I'll have a beer.

– Do you want ice in yours? Builds up the head.

– Alright.

– Come on in, you're warping the screen.

They sat on the verandah, drank in silence looking out into the lake. They both sipped their beers with ice. After two sips Mooney was drunk on a foam thicker than a cappuccino. Things were silent and still. A hummingbird strummed a few notes. A robin twittered. It seemed they could feel the earth revolving backward on its axis.

– Why don't you unlock Suddy and Sammy's money? Mooney asked.

– It's not locked in. They can take their money out any time they want. I just don't want them to lose out. I want them to make some money. If they panic now, they'll miss out on the biggest short ride in the history of Wall Street. This is a once-in-a-lifetime thing.

– You're that sure?

– Money-sure. I put almost a half million of my own cash into this. And I've since mortgaged this place to put in more. The July mortgage default figures are in. Record defaults and evictions in California and Florida.

– Don't tell Oz that.

– I won't.

– So why hasn't anything happened?

– They're keeping the lid on things. They don't want people to panic. But my guess is the banks themselves are starting to panic. I think they're jockeying for position, figuring out which bank will be the first to hit the skids.

– You sound so sure.

– Money-sure. And tell me, is there any other kind of sure? You just tell those guys to hold on. To calm down. Not panic. If you move, you come out blurred in the picture.

– Well, give them a date.

– Alright, if things don't go my way by Yom Kippur, they can take their money out. I'll give them their money at 100 percent. I can mortgage my house. What about you?

– I'm staying in.

– Are you sure?

– Money-sure. When's Yom Kippur this year?

– How the fuck should I know? When's the World Series?

– It doesn't always work like that.

– We're going to get rich, said Dennis. An event like this only happens once every twenty or thirty years.

– What are you going to do with your money?

– Build a Canadian Holocaust Museum to inform people of

the holocaust against the first peoples of Canada. And I want you to help.

– I will, if we make the killing you say we will.

– We will, said Dennis.

– You're sure?

– Money-sure.

– Is there any other kind of sure?

They sipped their beer, the foam still holding. Dennis even knew the best way to drink beer.

– The lake is really beautiful today, said Mooney.

– I don't appreciate it as much as you.

– I have the nostalgia thing going.

– When you summered here I was in that Indian residential school. Do you want to see the picture? Dennis said, with his eyes smiling.

– Do you want to staple it to my head?

Mooney heard someone at the back of the cottage walk from the master bedroom to the kitchen. He could swear it was the footsteps of a woman.

– We have to keep the syndicate together, said Dennis.

– Suddy calls it the Eisenteeth Syndicate.

– Good name. We have to keep it together. Keep them on board.

– I'll try.

– I'd like to see those guys make money off this.

– Why do you care?

– I just care. I like to see people make money.

Then he heard the footsteps again. A woman's footsteps. Barefoot. Moving from the kitchen back to the bedroom. He did not turn around to see who it was.

They sat in silence again and watched pelicans land 500 yards out on a sandbar.

Then the footsteps again. This time he turned around and looked.

It was Marilyn, slender with that magnificent bust and that graceful way of moving, wearing a black one-piece suit, with a wrap knotted at her waist and floating around her naked ankles. Mooney thought he would choke.

– Do you know what Sammy would say if he knew?

– What?

– He'd say you don't shit where you eat.

– So?

– So you don't care?

– Why should I?

– The whole city will find out sooner or later.

– So?

– You don't care, do you?

– That's your problem. You care too much what people think. They've got you by the balls.

Mooney thought that over for a while. It was a bit brutal.

– I guess I'd better get going.

– You just got here. Stay for lunch.

– No, I think I should leave you two alone.

– It is a bit delicate. Maybe you're right.

– I won't say anything, Dennis.

– I wouldn't want anybody in my community finding out, Dennis blurted out with a roar of laughter. They already call me apple.

– Which means?

– Red on the outside and white on the inside.

Cranes landed on the sandbar, away from the pelicans.

– You know, I never know when you're serious or not.

– I'm always serious, said Dennis.

– Right.

– Tell the guys not to worry. By Yom Kippur their money will have grown exponentially. I'm looking out for their best interest.

– By *shtoopping* Sammy's daughter.

– It's not about the *shtooping*.

– What's it about, Dennis?

– It's different. Nothing to do with the *shtooping*.

– But there is some *shtooping* involved?

– There's always *shtooping* involved. But it's not about that.

– Knowing you, I give it a month.

– It's been two months already.

Mooney let himself out. After Dennis heard the screen door close he went into the bedroom.

– I'm doing my eyes, Marilyn said.

– I'll just watch.

They woke up at around eight in the evening, just as the sky was starting to redden and cool. They had slept deeply during the most beautiful part of the afternoon. Even though they kept bumping against each other Dennis found it hard to remember such a delicious sleep. The word slumber came to mind and seemed to fill his mouth.

– Are you awake?

– It must be late.

– I had a bad dream, Marilyn said.

– You're having second thoughts?

– Not yet.

– You want to end it?

– We just got started.

– Are you going to tell your family?

– No.

– I can just hear the conversation at your house. So you're dating someone. But you deny this. So who is it? They ask. You're dating a *shagitz*? Aren't you? They ask. Now you're pissed off, but instead of denying it, you can't resist what will come out of your mouth and you say: a *shagitz*!? And then you collapse with laughter.

– Well at least you're not a *shagitz*. And how do you know what a *shagitz* is?

– You have no secrets from us.

They danced on the verandah to a Mexican singer, Marilyn's favourite, Julieta Venegas, with Dennis moving nimbly, holding her in his arms, admiring the grain of her skin. Then Dennis put on the Beatles. *Revolver.*

– What's with the Beatles all the time?

– Do you want to listen to your music? Talking Heads?

– Don't butter me up.

– I can change the record if you want.

– Just wanted to know why you like the Beatles?

– Sincerity. They were about sincerity. Not like the music of your generation. Everyone just too wise already at sixteen.

– You mean cool.

– Wise, cool, what's the difference. The Beatles were about sincerity.

– Sincerity is the mark of bad poetry.

– Oh, Oscar.

– Don't get cute. And I thought you said you didn't grow up with the Beatles.

– I grew up at the same time as the Beatles, but not with the Beatles. They didn't have them at the school.

– Did you really go to an Indian residential school?

– Didn't you see me have Coke for breakfast?

– So?

– Do you want to see the photograph?

– I've seen the photograph.

– Do you want to see it again?

– I made my own copy. So what happened to you there?

– Just use your imagination.

– Don't stop dancing. You punctuate your sentences with your body.

– Do I?

– It's irritating.

– Alright.

– You've never been married?

– I've always diversified my portfolio.

– Kristeva says Don Juans are really just out to punish their mothers.

– Symbolically, of course.

– Of course, Dennis.

– I was separated from my mother at four. I can't really remember her. So there's no one to punish.

– You can't remember anything at all?

– There's a feeling there, a presence that's supposed to be there. But it's something I can't grab a hold of. I want to, but as soon as I want to, I can't.

– So how long will you hold on to me? Marilyn asked.

He had a feeling that was coming, and would have to punctuate to think of what to say. He stopped dancing again:

– That's the kind of question I would have expected from a lesser woman.

– Won't be the first.

– Do you want to keep this a secret?

– If nothing comes of it, no point in making it public and hurting anyone, Marilyn said. Mind you, the whole city will probably know soon enough.

– Why do you think nothing will come from it? Dennis stopped dancing again.

– You're punctuating again.

– Answer my question.

– Nothing comes from nothing.

– *Ex nihilo nihil fit*, said Parmenides.

– I didn't know Parmenides spoke Latin.

– What's that smell?

– Somebody's septic tank needs a pump out.

– Or a skunk.

– I'll close the windows.

– I love this place.

– Don't stop dancing.

The last cranes took flight from the sandbar. The lake was like glass, with only the slightest ripple on the shore, and the pelicans were long gone.

The next day, reading financial blurbs on the Internet, Dennis's eyes lit up.

– What are you so happy about?

– Haven't you ever seen a man this happy?

– Fuck you.

– It's the sign from God.

– You're scaring me.

– Look at this.

He swivelled the laptop out of the glare so she could read the screen. More banks, it was reported, could not valuate US mortgage assets in their special purpose vehicles.

– What does it mean? she asked.

– It means that their liability holders, who thought they could get out at any time, are frozen. It's a *corralito*. This has been happening for about a year now. Started last August in Paris.

– I have no idea what you're talking about.

– They're going down.

– When?

– I'd say by Yom Kippur the rubber will meet the road. The Day of Atonement. Last day for many.

– We used to call it Cheeseburger Day.
– You have to believe in something, Dennis said.
– I'll choose what I have to believe in.

8

Several days before Lehman Brothers collapsed, the Eisenteeth Syndicate, plus one (Marilyn, the new 'stryker', Dennis called her, which was rez talk, he explained, for gang member), sat at their booth in the casino having breakfast.

It was a hot September day, perhaps the last of the year. Enormous black clouds rolled in from the plain, a thick black membrane that was taking its time, carrying with it all that thunder and lightning. The rumblings were barely audible at first, but you could feel them below the belt. Mooney figured it would be a couple of hours before the city would be swallowed by it. And still the heat was unbearable. His shirt clung to his back.

Inside the casino, the air conditioning was up full blast but Oz was shivering.

– What's the matter, Oz?

– I'm freezing here.

– You're wearing a sweater. And wool pants.

– When you get older, you get colder, said Oz.

Lehman stock slid 40 percent that day. Dennis was watching the whole thing on his BlackBerry. When they ordered their coffee and Danish Lehman stock was over $5 a share, by the time the Danish was gone and they were on their second refill, it was at $4. They spent the rest of the day in the booth. By the time Suddy ordered the beef and barley soup for supper when the markets closed, it was at $3.03. All the financials had begun to slip.

– Ouch the financials, said Suddy.

This broke everybody up. Marilyn even screamed.

– Where did you learn that expression?

– On TV. There's this crazy bald guy who screams and bangs a bell with a hammer.

– Ouch the financials, said Mooney.

– We're going to be rich guys, said Dennis.

Suddy's eyes moistened with oily tears. He gazed at Dennis with love. Sammy looked at Dennis and cocked his head and nodded in admiration. By the time the waitress put down the check they had not only made back their unrealized losses, but were up hundreds of thousands. Dennis gave her a hundred dollar tip.

– So how much are we up, asked Sammy?

– A zillion.

– Let's sell and get out, said Suddy.

– We can't sell, Suddy, we're short. We have to buy.

– So let's buy and get out.

– We should double down now, said Sammy.

– When there's a pullback, we'll double down, said Dennis.

– Maybe we should take some profit out, said Suddy.

– Suddy, they're going down. And here's the scene-stealer: when Citibank hits two dollars a share, then we'll get out. We're going to get rich, I mean really rich.

– Lottery rich?

– Something like that.

Suddy straightened his back up in the booth, as if he had been given a massive male hormone shot. His eyes glowed. Almost everyone at the table was jubilant.

The only one loathe to celebrate was Oz. Every time Lehman Brothers dropped another buck it was like someone had cracked Oz on the back of the head with a baseball bat.

– No good will come of this, Oz said finally.

– Oz, our ship's come in.

– No good will come of this.

– They're going down, Oz. And this is just the beginning. I figure the Dow could drop as low as six thousand. Six thousand more points.

Oz felt a quaking pain all through his body.

– People are going to lose their homes and jobs.

– Not our fault, Oz, said Sammy.

– How do you know that?

– Why are asking me? I don't know how the microwave works, said Sammy.

– I have to get up for a while, said Oz.

– Where's he going?

– He's got to drop a few friends off at the pool, said Suddy. Always takes a crap at the same time.

Oz squeezed out of the booth and loped unsteadily to the bathroom. Mooney got up to follow him. Oz made it to the bathroom but slipped on a tile and ended up grabbing a urinal cake when he tried to hold on to something. Mooney ran over to keep him from falling but went crashing down with him, luckily breaking his fall. The urinal cake slid across the tiles like a hockey puck. Oz lay on top of him, heaving, frightened by the scare. All he needed was a broken hip.

– Nothing good will come of this, Mooney.

– Oz, this was all going to happen anyway. All this was decided by players a million billion times richer than us. We just made money betting it would happen.

– We're parasites, Mooney.

– But rich ones.

– I had money. You know, I had more than a million. But money's not important.

– Maybe so, but now you have more and you can do whatever you want with it. You can even give it away.

– I can set up soup kitchens for the people we put out of work.

– We didn't put them out of work. The system did.

– But we profited from it. It's evil.

– Maybe so. But being poor is also evil.

– What kind of nonsense is that?

– There is no virtue in poverty. It makes you mean and envious. Believe me, I know.

– Not everybody.

– If I have to choose between the lesser of two evils, of being poor and being rich, I choose rich.

– Fine with me, but just remember you are still choosing evil.

Oz looked more stricken than ever. Even the last tooth in his bottom jaw seemed to tremble.

– Oz, do you think you could get off me?

– I don't know.

Oz, still lying on Mooney, tried to sit up but fell back, panting from the effort.

– Why did you go in in the first place?

– I didn't think we were going to win. Or win so big. Frankly, I thought we were going to make a bit or lose a bit, the way you guys always do. I had no idea that the entire American banking system would collapse.

– It's what Dennis has been saying all along.

– I had no idea Dennis knew what he was talking about.

– Why not?

– If he did, why was he hanging out with us all these years? I thought it was all bullshit.

– He was on the level.

– I see that now.

– So that's why you weren't worried like Suddy and Sammy this summer?

– I really didn't care about losing. It's making the money like this that shames me.

– It's nothing to be ashamed of.

– It's immoral. The pensioners. The workers. The more they lose the more we make.

9

– A fine Yom Kippur this is, said Dave to Mooney.

– I told you Dennis knew what he was doing.

– Did you bring me here to gloat? I'm down millions.

Evidently, there were many on the opposite side of Dennis's bet. Lehman Brothers filed for Chapter 11 bankruptcy protection on September 15, 2008. Had there been a larger bankruptcy filing in US history? Dennis asked rhetorically. No. Lehman had geared itself to the hilt and lost everything. Dennis's syndicate had hiked up their short bets against Lehman Brothers, Citi, and threw in a British bank, the venerable Royal Bank of Scotland, in August, just when everyone else was at their cottages, thinking their stock portfolios were safe in blue chip financials.

– A fine Yom Kippur this is, Dave repeated to Mooney.

– The way you say it, sounds a bit anti-Semitic.

– Not coming from me it does. I have three fucking forests in Israel.

– I don't want to hear about your forests.

– So don't call me an anti-Semite. Not on the Day of Atonement.

– Are you atoning? For not listening?

– Are you enjoying your superiority? Fuck, an idiot like you, and Suddy Joffe. Suddy Joffe with piles of money. Go know.

– Dennis knew. You should have listened to me.

– The only time in my life I regret not having listened to your bullshit, Mooney.

– A compliment that's been a long-time coming.

– I've had a lot of time to think about it.

– Decades.

– But you know, Dave said, maybe this thing will sort itself out.

– You hope.

– I pray.

Just after the Lehman brothers collapse, Dennis read an article in one of his specialized journals that the US Federal Reserve Bank, instead of pumping liquidity into the system, which it had been doing even before Lehman, was syphoning billions from the system to fuck over interbank lending. Those fuckers, Paulson and Bernanke, he told the syndicate, were doing this to force a bailout from Congress. Motherfuckers, he said. They're putting out the fire with gasoline. It's a shakedown, he said, to pass the TARP. That vote should be fun to watch.

Dennis convened the Eisenteeth Syndicate on September 29, 2008 at Mellers', told them they were going to have a grand time. Mooney asked Dennis if Dave could come along and Dennis didn't object, it could mean an influx of fresh capital. And Dave really wanted to meet this Dennis.

For some reason, at the last minute, Dennis couldn't make it. But he told them he'd call them on his cell, and that they were to watch the news and the Dow Jones. He would try to make it later if he could.

On that day the US Congress voted on the first TARP bank bailout bill Hank Paulson cobbled together and presented with gestures of anguish, although it gave him practically dictatorial powers. Dennis told Mooney that if the vote went south for Paulson, their winnings would accelerate.

They huddled around Mooney's tiny BlackBerry screen to watch the balloting and with every nay vote Mooney thumped the table and made the pickles wobble, then snuck a look at Dave's face.

– So a no vote is good for us? asked Suddy.

– And how.

They weren't the only ones watching this. The whole floor of the NYSE was glued to the giant screens. The nays came thick and fast. Then Mooney said:

– Motherfucker. Paulson lost!

– What a rout! said Marilyn.

The market, punctured like a tire by a spike, went into free fall. Dave was stupefied, and looked at Mooney, perhaps for the first time in his life, with something like admiration. Mooney's ears burned with pride. But soon the colour drained from Dave's cheeks.

– Five hundred ticks down, said Sammy.

– That's good, right? asked Suddy, removing his feet from his Hush Puppies under the table.

– Every hundred ticks down means five-digit winnings for us. We're well up in the seven digits already.

– Six hundred, said Sammy.

– That right there is people's pensions going to shit, said Oz.

– Only the beginning, said Mooney.

– I can't see the screen, said Suddy.

– Turn on your own BlackBerry.

– Can't.

– Why not?

– It wears the battery down.

– South by seven hundred.

– Is that a seven or a one? asked Suddy.

– It's a seven. We're millionaires.

Suddy squealed. And then his face melted into rapture and he just tittered.

– All my equity is in the toilet, said Dave. And you guys are laughing.

– I'm not, said Oz.

– He still votes NDP.

– You put it in the toilet, Dave.

– It's now flushable, said Suddy.

That Suddyism slayed Marilyn.

– Seven hundred seventy-seven. And that's the close. With high volume. Record volume.

– A shellacking, said Sammy.

– Sorry, Dave, said Oz.

– How far can it drop?

– Dennis says down to six thousand. Sixty percent of its last highs, according to Dow theory.

– You don't know what Dow theory is!

– Yes, I do, said Mooney.

– You're such a bullshitter.

– But I'm up. And the market could drop another four–five thousand ticks, said Mooney.

– Fasten your seatbelts!

– Shut up, alright, Suddy.

– You shut up, Dave.

– Sorry.

– Your father would never have talked to me like that. He was a human person.

– What do you know about my father?

– How can you say that? I spent more time with your father than your mother did.

– So?

– So, I know he would never have talked like that to someone my age. He respected his elders. He was a human person.

– You're right, said Oz, the finger of truth coming down. Your father was a gentleman, Dave.

– I said I was sorry, said Dave.

– And you were such a nice kid, said Mooney.

Dave left the Mellers' stymied, his shirt drenched. When he ran into Richie Michaels, the Jew with the Yale Jaw, as he called him, his face was bleached. He didn't know how he would tell Candy about this. And Mooney's triumph now irked him to no end.

– Richie, I can hardly talk.

– What's wrong, Dave?

– I can't talk.

– What is it?

– A fine Yom Kippur.

– What's wrong, Dave?

– I'm flummoxed. The Dow just dropped seven hundred and seventy-seven points.

– When?

– When?! Today!

– In just one day?

– I'm bleeding. Blood has been shed. This is no joke.

– We've been hemorrhaging since Lehman's.

– I'm gushing blood. This is no joke, Michaels.

– I'm not saying it is.

– The whole financial system could collapse. A run on the banks and all that. A depression.

– Be patient, my broker says. It's a blip. There'll be a rebound. There always is in October.

– What if there isn't? Congress just voted against the Paulson bailout.

– Maybe we should sell and get out now?

– I'd lose almost twenty percent of my equity. By next week it could be twenty-five percent. And after that, who knows? It's seriously *bakukt*.

– You could lose more.

– So could you.

– What should we do?

– Do? For the first time in my life, I don't know what to do. When it comes to money, I have never hesitated. But this. This is sick and *bakukt*.

Dave explained to Richie Michaels about his brother's good fortune in all this. He talked about Dennis, the so-called Indian stock-picker. 'You've got to meet this guy,' my brother tells me. 'He looks right through you', my brother says.

– An Indian stock-picker.

– Yeah. The guy knows a shit load. He had them watching the vote in Congress on the TARP at Mellers'. The guy knows a shit load.

– What kind of Indian?

– I don't know. An Indian from India, I suppose.

– A Pakistani?

– No, Mooney said he was Indian.

– Have you met him?

– I was going to meet him today, but he couldn't make it.

Dave was impressed by Mooney's moves, well Dennis's moves, actually. Still, Mooney had shown gumption and good instinct. And since Dave and his friends had taken big hits on their equity he had arranged a meeting with some people — 'Just a friendly dinner', at the Michaels', he told Mooney — with some people who were desperate to do something, whose brokers had told them to be patient, but couldn't because they had *shpilkes*.

– We'll invite that Dennis, Richie Michaels said.

– Then we'll have to invite my brother.

– Your brother?

– Fuck.

– And maybe Suddy Joffe.

– I can't invite Suddy Joffe. My wife would divorce me.

– I was just fucking with you.

Richie Michaels offered to give his house for the dinner party. His wife, Barbara, who was perhaps the best cook in the city, was thrilled about preparing an authentic curry since her husband had told her that the star guest would be Indian. Barbara knew all about Indian food. Putting great store in what she thought people thought of her, she always pulled out all the stops.

The Yale Jaw Michaels lived on the river side of the Crescent in a modern manse. At the back of the house they had a picture window that ran for sixty feet across the living room from which you could watch the river freeze up now that the fall was changing to winter, or the northern lights swizzle in the sky.

True to form, Barbara Michaels brought in two Tamil refugee girls to grind the spices to make the dry masala, and a cook from the Taj restaurant to do the wet masala. All these arrangements went smoothly, as always. She thought long and hard about whether to serve wine or Indian beer. Or perhaps serve pink gins before they sat down at the table, although the idea seemed to smack of colonialism. Fuck it, she said, she'd just have everything there was to drink, and people could decide for themselves.

She called her two daughters down to watch the two Tamil girls grinding the spices. Learn something, she told them.

– Sophia, Irina, come down and see this!

– Come down and see what?

– Just come down and see this.

The girls came down to the kitchen.

– This is so awesome, said Sophia.

– OMG, said Irina.

– Stop saying that.

– Oh-My-God. How pathetic. Why don't they like use the electric grinder, went Irina.

Sophia, seventeen, already at university, had something punk-ish about her, although she never strayed far from home and was entirely good-natured. Her infantile chubbiness still clung to her, a sign of how she had been pampered. She did what was expected of her and had never even so much as broken a plate in her life. She had had few boyfriends, all within her religion, who were kind and sensitive and easily embraced by parents. She was shy but not coy, intelligent but not quick; but she had a big heart.

Irina, sixteen, was much more sociable than Sophia, but inclined to sulks and hysterics. She had a short piquant body, oval face with pillowy lips, and violet eyes. Her thoughts were sharper and immediately expressed. While incapable of keeping other people's secrets, Irina was, however, very secretive herself. Even if she was going to the ballet, she'd say she was going to the movies. She was very selfish and bore it as part of her charm, which attracted boys and girls alike.

The two Tamil refugees were sitting cross-legged and barefoot on the floor in front of a large stone mortar, hammering away with a pestle at the spices they had sautéed on the stove. The kitchen had the smell of exploding peppercorns, cardamom, fennel and coriander.

– This is so cool, Sophia had said, right before Irina poohpoohed the whole operation.

Irina said to her mother point blank after looking at the two Tamils:

– Don't exert yourself, mother.

Barbara wouldn't let Irina get her goat. But Irina started up again, relentless.

– So this is it? This is what you called us down here for? I was on the phone, you know.

– I just wanted you to see how they did this.

– Ok, I get it. They grind the spices and throw them in a stew.

– Don't be sarcastic.

– Okay. I get it. I'm going to make a few calls. I'm going out for supper with Jamie and Leslie.

– No, you're not.

– Yes, I am.

– Your father's invited a new friend. Someone from India. We're having a dinner party. The Kaufmans are coming, too.

– Now for sure I'm not staying.

– You can go out after dinner. And you should watch this.

– Really, mother. I get it. They fry up the spices and then they grind them. Okay. But they could have used your thousand-dollar electric grinder. It can grind an elephant tusk.

– I'll watch, said Sophia.

– It didn't cost a thousand dollars.

– Well, something like that.

– Nothing like that.

– All you know how to do is spend Dad's money.

– It's half my money.

– Right. Like you worked for it.

– I worked.

– For like ten seconds.

– You can be so difficult, Irina.

– I'm going to get a profession.

– I hope you do.

– What if this guy doesn't like Indian food?

– He's Indian, why wouldn't he like Indian food?

– How pathetic. I'm Canadian and I don't like Canadian food.

– There's no such thing as Canadian food, said Sophia.

– That's my point, Barbara said.

– What point? I don't see a point. You just latch on to what other people say, mother.

– No, I don't.

– I don't see why you have to make this guy an Indian meal. It's going to be so embarrassing. This whole show you put on. It's going to make him barf. Like at Sophia's bat-mitzvah, you hired a reggae band and had Jamaican kosher food. That was so embarrassing. I'm going upstairs.

– You stay here.

– What for?

– Turn around. Don't talk with your back to me.

– OK, I'm turning around. What?

– What are you going to wear? her mother said.

– What am I going to wear? What are you going to wear?

– Dress nice, said Barbara.

– I hope you're not going to wear those capri pants, mother.

– Just dress nice.

– Should I wear a sari?

– I don't like your sarcasm.

– Live with it.

– I don't like it.

– You know where the door is.

– Just tell me what it is you don't like about me, and I'll try to fix it.

– Just your mere existence irritates me, mother. The phoniness. The trying-too-hard-ness. And let's not forget your big mouth. That's what everybody at the club calls you, you know? The big mouth.

– I take after you.

– You wish.

– And they don't call me that. Irina, come back here. Let's talk about this!

– I'm going to put on an unprovocative mini-skirt! I'll stay for half an hour but then I'm going out. There's really no sense arguing, mother. What? Can I go? I'm going upstairs.

Irina, her lips holding firm, headed for the stairs. Sophia continued to watch the Tamil girls grind the spices, while her mother clung to the argument with Irina, following her to the foot of the staircase. She wanted to ask her again to dress nice, but knew Irina would make a grievance out of the request. She tried to keep from doing so but it came out anyway.

– Dress nice!

– Can't hear you!

– I said dress nice! Don't dress like a you-know-what.

– Say it. Like a slut.

– Okay, don't dress like a slut.

Sophia appeared behind her and broke in:

– Mom, all sixteen-year-old girls dress like sluts.

– No, they don't. I didn't. You didn't.

– And what are you going to wear? screamed Irina from the upper banisters as she ascended. Are you going to wear those capri pants?

– What? I can't talk to your back.

– I said are you going to wear those capri pants?

– I might.

– With your calves? You're so embarrassing! And all your shoes. They call you the Imelda Marcos of the Crescent.

– Don't scream at me from up the stairs! Come down and talk like a normal person.

– Just don't embarrass us!

– What?
– Just don't embarrass us!
– I can't hear her.

Sophia and Barbara went back to watch the Tamil girls grind the spices.

– This is so cool. Why are their feet like that?
– Like what?
– They're so calloused.
– I suppose from not wearing shoes when they were kids.
– It's really gross.

■ ■ ■

Punctual, Dennis was the first one to ring the bell. Barbara opened the door, having watched his cab pull away, and she then took a good look at him. She gawked.

– I didn't have the right information, she said to herself, almost mouthing the words.

She felt foolish and sick. A tide of panic rose up through her body and tingled in the roots of her hair. 'This man is not Indian,' she said to herself, 'he's *an* Indian.' Richie said he was Indian. He said Dave said he was Indian. Fucking Dave Kaufman did this on purpose to make me look foolish, she thought. That royal scumbag. It was an awkward moment like she had not had for a long, long time. 'He's Indian, the guest, I mean,' her husband had told her, which is what Dave Kaufman had told him. Dave fucking Kaufman, the royal scumbag.

Barbara gawked. Dennis stood awkwardly at the door, suddenly not sure if this was the right address. With her intestines in a clover hitch, acting moderne, she said:

– Come in. You must be Dennis.
– You must be Barbara. How very nice to meet you.
– Thank you.
– Smells like curry. I love curry, he said, almost courtly.
– It's a Tamil curry, Barbara said ingeniously, avoiding the word *Indian*. She would rework this somehow. Her armpits were drenched.

– What an amazing house! Dennis said. You must be very proud.

Dennis had let his hair grow during the summer and it hung straight over his forehead, almost in a Beatle cut. The invitation had been come-as-you-are and Dennis wore his jeans and a suede jacket with huge pockets over an immaculately pressed paisley shirt.

– I'll get through this, she thought. I just didn't have the right information.

She fought to retain her usual buoyancy, but realized she was faced with two options. Her therapist had advised her to resolve all conflicts as soon as they cropped up, which here meant that she could come clean, explain that she lacked the right information, and simply apologize if there was an offense. On the other hand, she could ignore the obvious. Why couldn't you serve curry to a native person?

Barbara had always tried to lead a comfortable life, with plenty of lifelong friends and many pleasures, immune because of their wealth and her natural conformism to the bullying of the community. But she always felt a nagging uncertainty as to whether she was pulling it off, whether the community liked her or not. But this story would get out, she realized, and she almost started to cry.

– I'll get you a drink, she said.

– Do you have any Indian beer? he asked. And can you put it in a glass full of ice?

– Cubes or chips?

– Up to you.

She couldn't tell if he was pulling her leg so she went into kitchen to get him a Kingfisher and a glass with ice, her eyes were burning from trying not to cry.

Dave and Mooney were the next guests to arrive. Mooney had picked Dave up in his mother's Lincoln after dropping Suddy off at the casino. The night was prickly with frost.

Suddy had felt dejected that he hadn't been invited, and looked foggily through the windshield and said a very Suddy thing:

– If you hang out with the Michaels, you'll be too good for us.

– Nah.

– Does your brother Dave have something against me?

– Nah.

– As a kid it was hard to connect with him. But he was a good kid.

Then he said another Suddy thing:

– Family has to stick together to be cohesive.

– You're right.

– Your dad always wanted your family to stick together.

As soon as the car pulled up under the casino marquee Suddy's mood swung and his eyes lit up. He hopped out of the car and almost ran inside.

After parking the car in the drive, Dave and Mooney walked up to the house. The door was ajar as Barbara had been too agitated to close it.

Dave strode into the Michaels' place and immediately smelled the curry. It was so strong it almost bore a hole through his nasal wall.

Then he saw Dennis sitting on the sofa with his beer in one hand, talking to what looked like a sixteen-year-old prostitute. Putting two and two together he pivoted and turned 180 degrees and muffled a bark of laughter into the elbow of his car-coat, as if he were doing the Canadian sneeze, and strode right back out the door.

Mooney followed him out, saw tears slip from his brother's eyes as Dave stumbled back out onto the front porch and onto the frosty lawn. Luckily Dennis had been absorbed in conversation with Irina and hadn't heard Dave's yelp. Mooney went out to shut Dave up, but Dave was hysterical already, laughing and staggering across the lawn, finally blurting out:

– You said he was Indian.

– What?

– But you didn't say he was *an* Indian.

– I distinctly said he was an Indian.

– You said Indian. And I told Richie Michaels he was Indian. He must have told Barbara he was Indian.

– He is an Indian.

– I can see he's an Indian. But you said Indian without the thingamajig.

– What thingamajig?

– Without the 'an'. You didn't say *an* Indian.

– You mean the indefinite article.

– Whatever.

– That's what an 'an' is. It's not a thingamajig.

– You didn't say an Indian. You just said Indian. I assumed you meant an Indian from India.

– I said an Indian.

– You said Indian.

– Even if he was an Indian from India he would also be an Indian, with the indefinite article.

– No, you would have said Indian, which is what you said.

– I think I said 'an Indian'.

– You said Indian.

– How many Indians from India do you know called Dennis? said Mooney.

– Why couldn't an Indian from India be called Dennis? They all anglicize their names sooner or later. And what makes you assume that Dennis is the name of an Indian who's not from India. Tell me that.

– It's a generation thing.

Just then a cab came up the drive, honked, and the two Tamil girls ran out from around the back, crossed the lawn sparkling like glass, and hopped in. Dave shrieked with laughter as the cab drove away.

– Barbara went whole hog! Mind you, she always goes overboard; I heard once she breastfed her poodle.

– Christ, Dave.

– And a phoney to boot. Look! She probably hired those Indian girls to make the meal authentic. Didn't I tell you this city was more sophisticated than Toronto, didn't I?

– You're still trying to prove that point? said Mooney.

– I'm not trying to prove anything.

– Yes, you are. I'm sure she's very embarrassed.

– And it's your fault, Mooney. Fucking indefinite article.

– I didn't need the indefinite article. Admit it, you just made the wrong assumption. You should have asked for clarification.

– I didn't need clarification, Mooney. You said Indian, not an Indian.

– He is Indian, and he is an Indian.

– No, Mr. Chomsky, he's not Indian. He's an Indian.

– Gandhi was an Indian, wasn't he?

– You know what I think, I think you left out the indefinite article on purpose, Mooney.

– I didn't leave out the indefinite article on purpose. Maybe you misheard.

– Maybe you misspoke.

– How do you know I said Indian and not an Indian? Do you have total recall?

– Why didn't you say First Peoples?

– I couldn't say he was a First Person.

– What are you talking about?

– You can say First Peoples but you can't refer to a Canadian aborigine as a 'first person'. Since I didn't think you were sensitive to the issue I used the word *Indian*.

– But not an Indian. Proves my point.

– I did say 'an Indian'. Maybe you heard Indian when I said an Indian, and it was you who elided the indefinite article because in an unconscious act of racism you assumed that an Indian couldn't be shorting Citibank.

– Don't be ridiculous.

– I'm not.

– You always say such ridiculous shit. Try not to open your mouth tonight. Sooner or later I know you'll say something stupid.

– Now that I recall, I didn't say he was Indian. You asked me who Dennis was and I told you he was 'this Indian guy'. I didn't say he was Indian.

– And you didn't say 'an' Indian guy.

– That's right. I said he was 'this Indian guy'. You shouldn't have assumed he was an Indian from India.

– Just don't say anything stupid tonight. Don't embarrass me or yourself. And don't be pedantic. Don't talk about bagels and don't talk about Israel! Nobody wants to hear your opinions about the Ashkenazi Jews being originally from Mongolia.

– I never said that!

– At the *briss* you did.

– No, I didn't. It was the kid next to me. You shouldn't have sat me at the kids' table.

– I shouldn't have invited you.

– We've already had that argument, Dave.

– And Naomi and Larry Brickman are coming, so behave.

– What do you mean behave?

– Don't talk to Naomi.

– I have to say hello.

– Say hello and keep your mouth shut.

There were about twelve people there, with a few more to come, plus the Michaels girls, and a uniformed maid to serve and clean up. Mooney restrained himself, on Dave's advice, from getting into conversations.

It had been a long time since Mooney had seen private luxury in full swing. The table glittered. Mooney looked at every object and while astonished, acted blasé. And the women were so beautifully dressed that they aroused in him his easy love of them.

There was a couple there, the Bergers, running very hard after this crowd, without ever succeeding in catching up. They looked at Mooney as a dangerous newcomer and weren't very friendly. But almost everyone else was, at least with smiles, although they were too shy to approach him, and he to approach them. The news of his coup in the market had preceded him here.

There was Morty Miller, the lush, and his wife Shelly, whose primary missions was to make sure he didn't drink too much.

At first he only nodded back at the warm hellos he received. People were nice to him! Was it because now he had money?

All this goodwill made him feel like an astronaut re-entering the atmosphere but who needed brakes, so he took refuge with his drink by the block of windows to watch the river, trying to look interesting and lonely at the same time.

– Mooney?

It was a raspy, woman's voice, one that came out of time lost. He turned his head to the left, from where the voice came. He recognized her voice immediately. It was her fault he had been institutionalized.

– Naomi.

Her fingernails were varnished the same red as the lipstick smear on her cigarette filter. He had never known her to polish her nails, or wear lipstick, or smoke. But there was no doubt that it was her. Oh, how she used to snuggle him into her cashmere sweater. She was still tall, on impossible legs, no waist and flat tush, and her black black hair with that cowlick in front. God she was gorgeous. He hugged her when she opened her arms, holding her cigarette free and up in the air as he squeezed her.

– So, weren't you going to say hello? she said.

It was really her voice, really her, he thought, amid the welter of emotion.

– I didn't see you come in.

He had so much to say to her, but he just stared at his drink now.

– It's good to see you looking better.

– Oh.

– There's something different about you.

– It's the eyelashes.

– You're right.

– It's from the medication.

– I like them.

– Do you?

– And now you're turning red.

– You never came to the hospital.

– Too busy.

– I'm fully recovered. Some memory issues, but I'm good.

– I heard about your stock market operations.

– Are you here alone?

– I'm here with Larry.

She tilted her head towards that big fat fuck Larry Brickman, talking to the Bergers, his head bobbing; just one of those guys whose head is always bobbing in agreement, even when he doesn't agree.

– How could I have missed him?

– He's lost a lot of weight.

– Yeah right.

– Your resentment shows, Mooney. Try covering it up.

– I don't resent Larry.

– You used to.

– No, I didn't.

– Yes, you did. You were jealous of him.

– Me? He's such a phoney.

– You resented him because he was rich and he was doing what you wanted to be doing.

– To you. He stole you from me.

– I would have left you anyways.

– The fat fuck.

Larry Brickman really wasn't fat anymore; he was actually looking kind of trim. Naomi took charge of the conversation, as always, and kept her eyes on Mooney. He didn't dare return her look.

– How long have you been out?

– About six months.

– That's what I supposed. Where have you been?

– Everywhere and nowhere.

– Are you living alone?

– No.

– With someone?

– You might say that.

– What's her name?

– Mother.

– You always had to have a woman looking after you. Why not the real thing.

– I suppose.

– She still hates me, doesn't she?

– Nah. You shouldn't have left me.

– It was an honest breakup.

– Honest?

– I did what I had to do. Didn't mean I didn't care for you.

– Is that how you cared for me?

– Was bankruptcy how you cared for me?

– You were seeing Larry Brickman.

– I was honest about that.

– Thanks.

– You had your funny business, too. I knew you were sleeping with Natalie.

– You knew that? How did you know that?

– She told me. Women love to talk about sex. It's actually better than sex.

– She told you?

– Even about how you did it with your clothes on at her house. She said their humidifier had broken down and there was so much static electricity, that since you were fucking with your sweaters on she thought her husband would find you both electrocuted. All those infidelities to prove yourself.

His glass was empty, but he had no recollection of drinking from it. He looked up from it finally and into her eyes and said:

– So, are we going to see each other or what?

– Here we are.

– I mean privately.

– What about your mother? What are you going to tell her?

– I'll just tell her I'm going out. Meeting a friend.

– She would kill you if you saw me.

– Give me your number.

– I'm not going to give you my number.

– Come on.

But before she could, Dave came over and she left without saying a word to Dave.

– I told you not to talk to Naomi.

– I just said hello.

– You said more than hello.

– I was just being polite.

– Don't get involved with her.

– I'm not getting involved with her.

Dave pushed off and Larry Brickman floated over, drink in hand, head bobbing.

Mooney's conversation with Larry Brickman went like this.

– What's the story? Mooney.

– Hey, Larry.

– I heard you and Dave are making a killing in the market. This market!

– I am. Dave's not.

– I thought you were going halfers.

– I'm not in it with Dave.

– That's not what I heard.

– You heard wrong.

– He did stake you though?

– That he did.

– How soon after declaring bankruptcy can you start getting back into shit?

– Right away, actually.

– Great. Great for you. You fuck over your creditors, and now you're back in the bucks.

– Those are the rules.

– I don't know what you see in speculation.

– The proportion of work to money is good.

– I don't think I could get into it. By the way, where are you living now?

– With my mother.

– You know everybody else is hurting with this Lehman business, but you.

– That's because they don't understand the market, Larry.

– And you do?

– Dennis does, he said, pointing his head at Dennis.

From time to time the curry wafted in from the kitchen and everyone looked at Dennis, making them aware of Barbara's painful embarrassment.

This would get out, Mooney thought. To the whole city. And maybe it was his fault. He should have made it clear to Dave that Dennis was not an Indian from India.

Dennis was still sitting where Mooney first saw him on the sofa next to Irina, who was aggressing; she hadn't left his side, now joined by a few other guests. Dennis was looking venerable while he spoke of his reasons for shorting the US financials, and having gone on margin to do so. Barbara didn't like how close Irina was sitting to Dennis with all these people around.

– Irina, she said, why don't you give Dennis some room?

– I'm okay, he said.

– Come and help me in the kitchen. Maybe he'd prefer to talk to the adults.

– I'm an adult.

– It's okay, said Dennis. It's good to meet to young people. This way at least someone will come to your funeral.

– Irina.

Irina got off the sofa, mostly to show Dennis how responsible she was. She smoothed her mini-skirt and went with Barbara into the kitchen.

– I thought you were going out.

– Changed my mind.

– You're bothering him.

– He's cool.

– Give him some room to breathe.

– Didn't you know he was an Indian Indian?

– I got the wrong information. I thought he was from India.

– It's obvious he's not.

– I can see that now.

– You've really embarrassed yourself.

– Why do you treat me like this?

– I treat you the way you treat your mother. By the way, are you going to let her come down?

Barbara had forgotten all about her mother, who would be wearing who knows what.

– Of course. She's changing right now.

– You treat her like shit.

– No, I don't.

– We'll see.

– And I told you to dress nice. You look like a slut.

– Everybody likes what I'm wearing.

– There are other people here to talk to.

– I'm talking to Dennis.

– Let other people get a word in edgewise.

– Like Leah Berger? Why do you invite those people? They're such suckholes. They run after anybody with money.

– Where did you get that *pisk*?

Irina went back to the sofa and wedged herself between Sophia and Dennis. Sophia had recognized Mooney, and whispered to her sister:

– That's the bagel guy from the Kaufman *briss*.

– You're kidding. Go talk to him.

– Shut up.

– He's all alone.

– Shut up.

– It's fucking Dave Kaufman's brother.

– Really?

– Go talk to him.

– You go.

– You go, you're the nice one.

Sophia got up and went over to Mooney, standing now by the dip.

– Hey, I know you, you're the bagel guy, at the *briss*; you caused that bagel fight that was so funny.

– The mother of the kid who lost a tooth didn't think so.

– Yeah, things did get kind of heavy, but I learnt a lot about bagels. I laughed so hard that day. So did my sister, and she doesn't usually like *brisses*. Frankly, she doesn't like anything.

– That's your sister?

– Yeah.

– She dresses like a hooker.

– What sixteen-year-old doesn't?

– Still.

– She keeps telling my parents she wants to be an escort. Drives my mother nuts.

Sophia drifted away from Mooney. To cover up the fact that he was standing alone he walked over to the big windows again, nursing another gin and tonic, staring at the black lawn rolling down to the river, looking philosophical.

He overheard his brother say to Richie Michaels at the other end of the glass wall:

– What's with the plastic chairs in the patio? It looks like a Palestinian funeral.

Richie Michaels dropped his Yale jaw. Dave had a way of insulting you that you didn't know if it was out of affection or malice.

– We haven't got around to changing them.

– They look like shit.

– We'll change them in the spring.

– Look, Morty's already drunk.

Understatement city. Morty Miller had already begun to spill liquor. Morty's stock portfolio had taken a big hit, overweight with financials as it was, and he could have killed himself for taking his broker's advice and not dumping his stock in the summer when it was up. Now it was down sixty percent and falling fast, and he didn't know if he should weather the storm or cut his losses and run. He was in a panic. He had almost all his equity in stocks after selling the business and the thought of going broke was keeping him awake nights.

Mooney had been friends as a kid with Morty's youngest brother. He used this as a conversation wafer when Morty came up to him.

– Do I know you?

– Hi, I'm Mooney Kaufman. I knew your brother Lyle.

– I don't have a brother.

He had forgotten that Morty had not spoken to his brother for years, when they had a falling out over the business. He had forgotten who had cheated who.

– I think I know you from the Beach, Morty said.

– You used to dunk me in the lake. Hold my head under the water.

– Nothing personal. I did it to all Lyle's pisher friends.

Morty loped off, really gassed, switched his liquor to rye and kept drinking. Drinking for Morty Miller was always a sloshing of the broadloom, upholstery and his pants. At one point he knocked the maid over when she bent down to clean up a puddle of rye on the carpet.

– Where's the food? I need to eat!

He went up to a coffee table on which there was a tray of poppadums and he hurled one like a frisbee across the room at Mooney.

– Catch!

Mooney watched the poppadum career towards him. He ducked but it dipped like a knuckle ball and hit him on the forehead before falling to the ground in bits and crumbs.

– You were always such a spaz, yelled Morty to Mooney from his poppadum mound.

Morty's voice was hoarse and loud. It was hard for Irina to hear Dennis's explanation of short-selling. And things got worse when Morty approached them from behind.

– Why don't you drink? Morty said to Dennis, leaning over the back of the sofa.

– I am drinking.

– Those are just courtesy sips. You're not drinking.

– I am drinking.

– You've got ice in your beer.

– I know.

– People shouldn't come to parties unless they come to drink. Who do I have to let blow me to get a refill?

– Who'd want to blow you? asked Irina.

– You?

– Not me, said Dennis.

– Who then?

– I don't think you have to let anyone blow you to get a refill, said Dennis. I think you just have to ask politely.

– Where's Imelda Marcos? She'll give me a drink. Barbara!

Dennis's deportment at affairs like this was always extremely aristocratic, of unshakeable confidence; but it was hard to handle Morty.

– Please don't get into an argument now, darling, said Morty's wife, coming to the rescue.

– Shut your cunt, he said.

– They're separating, Barbara whispered to a friend.

– Please don't get into fight with this gentleman, his wife said.

– He can't even drink, said Morty.

– Come on, darling. Let's go lie down.

– Mind your own business, for fuck's sake.

To Dennis, he said:

– You call that a drink? What's in your hand?

– I have a drink in my hand, said Dennis. I am drinking.

– Let me see that drink.

– Here.

– Let me see that drink.

– You're looking at it.

– So you're the stock-picker. The Indian stock-picker? I thought you were an Indian from India. So did our hostess with the mostest.

Morty began to laugh, almost losing his balance.

– Why aren't you drinking?

– I am.

– Show me your drink!

Morty, still behind the sofa, lunged for Dennis's drink, lost his balance, warped backwards and tipped over the cocktail cart. The crash brought out the Indian chef from the kitchen.

– Fucking cocktail carts! Morty shouted, sitting in a pool of gin and rye and blood from where he cut his knuckles on an unfiled screw head.

He pounded his temples viciously with his fists.

– Fucking cocktail carts! With all their money they can't put in a fucking bar. What are they saving it for? I know where their money came from.

People would have scattered if they had eaten, but they were too hungry to be ousted by Morty's conduct. And he was already, suddenly wan, sitting there on the floor in that puddle of liquor, and soon he would vomit and then his batteries would run out, but they had to act quickly.

– Come lie down, his wife whispered, kneeling by his side.

– I'm like the Energizer bunny. I am the Energizer bunny. I can drink all night.

– You have drunk all night.

– Nothing will be the same, he shouted. There's going to be a depression. You'll all be broke by the end of the year. All of you. There'll be soup kitchens on Portage Avenue. And then there'll be a world war with Iran. A nuclear war. Because of the stock-yards, this city will be a prime target. Nothing will be the same! You'll all be evicted from your fancy homes. The bailiffs are doing the paperwork as we speak! Oh, look, it's Dave scumbag Kaufman. I didn't see you, Dave.

– If we're going to get nuked by Iran, it's pretty moot what the bailiffs are doing, said Dave.

– It's a moot point, eh Sir Dave, Royal Scumbag?

– Pretty moot, Morty.

Morty was about to join the people of Lost Money, like I did once, Mooney thought. The people of Lost Money were sort of like refugees, always nostalgic for the homeland of when they had money. Morty's self-pity was more tangible than his own, though. And so much on the public stage.

Morty's wife and Barbara led him out of the living room into the dark adjacent den in a complete and total rout, where they jostled him onto a sofa to sleep it off. When Barbara came back she stood in the centre of the room.

– Supper's ready, she said, smoothing down her long blouse over her capri pants. It's ready.

And it was a real feast.

Barbara's mother, Mrs. Goldenberg, had come down from the granny suite, dressed in one of her hideous silk foulard blouses that made Barbara cringe. Normally she was not allowed to mix with the guests in the evening, but tonight was special. She was allowed to have dinner with everyone, but at the appointed hour Barbara would say: 'Say goodnight to everybody, Mother,' and the old lady would make a charming exit, after everyone had been impressed by Barbara's kindness to a mother that her other friends would have put in a home years ago.

– Ma, Barbara Michaels shouted, Ma, come and say hello. I want to introduce you to someone. Ma? Look who's here. It's Duddy Kaufman's grandson, the little one, Mooney. You remember Duddy Kaufman?

The old lady squinted at her, then at Mooney.

– Duddy Kaufman's *einekle*?

– That's right.

– I knew your *zaida*. He put my husband out of business.

Mrs. Goldenberg was supposed to sit next to Dennis, but Irina pushed her into the adjacent chair and sat beside him, filling up his wine glass.

Truth to tell, Barbara's mother was a bit loopy. Right before the steamy samosas were served in a cold yoghurt and chickpea sauce, she leaned across Irina, grabbed Dennis's hand and said:

– The cleaning lady is stealing from us. Last week she stole a shoe from me.

– Why would she steal just one shoe? Dennis asked, leaning across Irina's chest.

– Next time she comes, she'll steal the other shoe.

– Did you know my mother has five hundred pairs of shoes? Irina said to Dennis.

– No, I didn't.

– They call her the Imelda Marcos of the Crescent.

Dennis and his short-strategy was the centre of the dinner conversation. For the rest of the evening Barbara's mother behaved well and only made one interruption.

– We didn't talk about money at our dinner table, she said, to Dennis.

– That's because you didn't have any money, Mr. Michaels said, making Barbara blush, ashamed as she was about her life before getting rich.

– She's out of it, he said to Dennis.

Everyone's broker at the table had advised them to hold tight, not to panic, as the market crashed faster and faster.

- My broker told me things would stabilize with the Dow at around eleven thousand.

- Pure treaty talk, said Dennis.

- But that's what he told me.

- I know your guy.

- He's honest at least.

- Nice guy, Fitz, said Dennis. Honest but stupid. So stupid even the other brokers noticed.

- 'Panic is the enemy,' that's what they're saying.

- Nonsense, said Dennis. Don't truckle to your brokers. The Dow will have to shed about six thousand more points. It has to lose about sixty percent of what it went up since the Iraq war rally.

- Who says?

- Dow theory. Elliot waves. Symmetry. That's how these things go. It's like love: first two years it goes up and up and up, and then it comes down.

- About sixty percent?

- Thereabouts. So my advice is to sell your financials, write off your loss, take all your available cash, and short those same stocks before it's too late.

- That's not what my broker says.

- It's not his money.

- But he depends on me.

- To keep your money long with him. Anyway, it's up to you. I'm just here as a favour to Mooney. You can take my advice or not.

Mooney felt a rush of pride.

- But let's say, went Richie Michaels, for argument's sake, that we sell our financials at a loss now. And then we short them. What if they go up again? We'll have missed the rebound and lost another twenty percent.

- But there isn't going to be a rebound. Not yet. The market is going to tank. The US banks are insolvent.

- All of them?

- All of them.

- They don't say that on TV.

- Since when have you heard a truthful word on TV? The day before Lehman Brothers collapsed they were recommending it as a buy on TV. What you people don't understand is that we're in a shitstorm. No, a shit-blizzard.

– Of Shakespearian proportions, added Mooney.

I knew he would say something stupid sooner or later, Dave muttered to himself.

– The banks are sitting on tons of crappy paper, Dennis said. Trillions, not billions, of bonds and CDOs and CDSs on CDOs that are worthless.

– The US government will backstop them.

– There isn't enough money in the known universe to backstop them. It'll take them years to de-leverage. They won't loan money to anyone, not even to each other because they don't know who's next to file Chapter 7. The financial system is hanging by a thread.

– It's a shit-blizzard, Mooney said.

– The Dow is headed for 2003 levels, said Dennis. It'll end up down sixty percent off the highs.

– And so? said Mr. Michaels.

– And so what? asked Dennis.

– So what's your advice?

– I already gave it, said Dennis. If you don't close your long positions, you'll lose at least another fifty, sixty percent of your equity, for sure, and possibly eighty percent if things go really badly. And it could take year to recover. Years.

The room hushed. Dave had said very little all evening, listening to Dennis's every word, trying to think why Dennis was right and why he had not seen this coming. 'What have we learned from this,' he kept saying to himself. 'What have we learned from this?' His idiot of a brother had turned his $50,000 stake into real money, maybe into well over a million dollars with the leverage, and it would grow if the market continued to collapse while he had already lost about $4 million, maybe more, by last Friday. His fucking brother, falling into shit and coming up smelling like roses. It wasn't fair. He couldn't believe how envious he was feeling.

– Mother, say good night to the people.

– That's my cue, Mrs. Goldenberg said. Good night people.

Barbara's mother put on a brave front and rose from the table, walked out to the hall and took the stairs one at a time.

After dinner everyone sat on the sofas around the coffee table. The maid served coffee, milk tea and Indian pastries and sweets. Irina sat beside Dennis again, on his right, her sister Sophia on his left.

It's an avuncular attraction, thought Barbara.

The others sank back into the lavish upholstery with their cups, waiting for the conversation to rekindle. Even Morty had been woken up and fed in the kitchen, and now sat contrite next to his wife, his eyes red with drink, sipping his coffee. Mooney sat next to Morty, feeling sorry for him.

– How much have you guys made so far? asked Mr. Michaels.

– Well, we started with about a million, which was geared up five times, and then we raised our bet with another two hundred thousand, which was geared up ten times. With the hit the financials have taken so far, I'd say we're up about five million.

– Not bad, said Dave, four hundred percent in a month.

– It's just the beginning. And if we ride this thing all the way down, we'll make about three thousand percent. When he said 'we' he nodded at Mooney.

Another wave of pride swept over Mooney. He didn't know why he had been so reserved all night. He looked at Naomi, but she was watching Dennis, her hand in the hand of Larry Brickman. The painful memory of the day she left him welled up. He was furious with her. He had been hospitalized because of her. Sure, he had gone bankrupt and they were suddenly of the Lost Money tribe, but that was no reason to leave him. As kids they used to believe that money wasn't important. When had they begun to give it value? Who started it?

– What are you going to do with your winnings? Barbara asked Dennis.

– I'm going to use the money to build a Holocaust museum.

– I know just who you should talk to, said Barbara. Sharon Goldman, she knows everyone.

Irina laughed at her own coming remark:

– You mean, she knows everything about everyone.

– Irina.

– You said it yourself about Sharon Goldman.

The company laughed at Sharon Goldman's and Barbara's expense. Two birds and all that.

– She's the one to talk to, said Barbara, driving right over her daughter's remark with a straight face.

– How pathetic, said Irina.

– Mrs. Michaels ploughed on. Sharon Goldman. If you want something done, it's Sharon Goldman. She even helped build the Holocaust Museum in Washington.

– You're always chasing after Sharon Goldman, Irina said.

Barbara blushed. 'I could buy and sell Sharon Goldman five times over,' she thought, 'and she's the one who chases me.' But she kept her mouth shut.

– I wasn't referring to the Nazi holocaust, Mrs. Michaels, said Dennis. I was referring to the Canadian holocaust, against the first nations. Let me show you something.

Dennis took the neatly folded photograph out of his pocket, unfolded it and spread it on the coffee table, smoothing out the crimps. Mooney noticed it was the same picture Dennis had shown them at the casino. Everyone, even Dave, bent over to look as he rotated it slowly for them.

– What do you think that is? he said straight to Irina, although everyone hung on his question.

– I don't know.

– What do you think it is?

– It looks like a penitentiary, said Sophia.

– This is an Indian residential school, said Dennis. My Indian residential school.

He pointed at the photograph.

– That's where we slept. And that down there is the room where George hanged himself from a coat hook with his suspenders, and where we caught the suicide bug. Every one of the kids I shared my dorm with is dead now. Now take a look at this picture.

He took out another picture, of a group of Indian kids in pyjamas.

– That's me. All the others are dead. You see that kid smiling, the only one, that was George. This was taken the night before he killed himself.

– We had no idea that was going on, said Barbara.

Irina howled. Dave sniggered. Barbara fired off her Dave-the-Royal-Scumbag-Kaufman look at him and turned her head back to the photograph again.

– Maybe I shouldn't have brought these, but I do wonder if you people knew about the Indian residential schools. I was kidnapped by the Canadian government at four years old. I never saw my mother again.

– Kidnapped is a bit strong, don't you think, said Dave.

– He was a kid and they nabbed him, said Mooney.

– I'm convinced we knew nothing about any of that, said Barbara.

– You were listening to the Beatles and giving each other wedgies while I was institutionalised.

– But to compare it to the Holocaust, Morty said, irked.

– It was genocide, said Dennis.

– Cultural genocide, there's a difference, said Morty.

Then Dennis pulled out another photograph. It was reproduction of the great Sioux hanging of Minnesota. In the picture there were Dakota men and boys hanging from an enormous square gibbet. The caption under the picture, dated December 26, 1862, Mankato Minnesota, read: '38 Dakota hanging from a square gibbet.'

Everyone stared at the bodies dangling from the thirty-eight stretches of rope.

– One of these men is my great-great-great grandfather, who had been exiled in Canada during the Indian Wars. Captured, drugged and returned by the Canadians to Abe Lincoln. Then hanged there.

– Oh, said Irina.

– Just a few of the hundred million native Americans that were killed by the Europeans.

Morty was pissed off and anxious to get a word in:

– You just can't make a Canadian Holocaust museum; and you can't use the word *holocaust*. You'll dilute it. If you use the holocaust word for other tragedies then it belittles the Holocaust, capital *H*. Morty was fuming, his hands shaking. What happened to the Indians was a tragedy.

– We're not talking about a tragedy. Hamlet is a tragedy.

– I can get pictures too, you know, said Morty, of Auschwitz, Bergen-Belsen.

– Are you in them?

– No.

– Are you in them?

– Just what are you saying then?

– If exterminating six million people is a holocaust, then what do you call exterminating one hundred million people? Either the six million was not a holocaust and the hundred million is a holocaust, or they are both holocausts of different proportions.

– You have to talk to this Sharon Goldman, said Barbara, trying to defuse the conflict.

Mr. Michaels rolled his eyes. Irina snorted.

– So do you really think this Sharon Goldman can help him? asked Mooney, colluding with Barbara to guide the conversation onto a milder path.

Now it was Dave's turn to roll his eyes. He always said Mooney was such a suck. But sucking up to Barbara Michaels was so unnecessary because she could be so easily intimidated anyway.

– I don't know if this guy is serious or not, said Morty, aggressively.

– I'm always serious, said Dennis.

– It's insane. A Canadian Holocaust Museum. I'm no hater, but it's ludicrous.

– Look, I'm not taking pledges, said Dennis.

– What did you mean by that?

– We're just having a conversation.

– What did you mean by 'pledges'.

– I mean I'm not raising money.

– We can't have this conversation, said Morty, trembling. This is an insult to the Holocaust victim.

– Morty, said his wife. Stop it.

– And I don't like that word you used, said Morty to Dennis.

– What word?

– You know what word.

Some spittle collected at the edges of Morty's mouth and the veins in his temples throbbed. Everyone had thought that Morty had settled down. But now he was getting into a conniption.

– What word? said Dennis.

– You know what word.

– No, I don't.

– Pledges. I feel the hate.

– I wasn't being derogatory.

– So appalled. I'm so appalled. And ashamed you people aren't saying anything. Nothing. Nothing at all in defense of the Holocaust victim.

Morty thought that if this do had been at his house, he would be screaming 'Out of my house, all of you!' Why wasn't Michaels saying anything? Money, it's always about money with the Michaels, with their moderne house and season's tickets to the ballet, always about money. 'Get out!' he would have screamed.

– Do you know how much the average Holocaust survivor gets from all the retribution paid for Nazi war crimes? Mooney asked Morty.

– Tell your brother to shut up, Morty said to Dave.

Dave shook his head subtly at Mooney, willing his brother into an early grave. 'Don't go there, Mooney,' he said to himself.

Luckily, no one had paid attention to Mooney's question except Morty. Dennis began folding up his pictures and placing them back in the inside pocket of his jacket.

– We didn't come here to talk about holocausts, said Dave. There'll always be holocausts. It's human nature.

– It's all politics, said Mrs. Michaels, welcoming Dave's attempt at détente.

– He can do what he wants with his money, said Morty. I don't care. I didn't even want to have this conversation. He was indignant, but cowed by Dave, who held his eye.

– Let's talk candidly, said Dave. We came here to talk about how to stop the hemorrhaging.

– We're dying here, said Morty. I'm dying. If this goes on, I'll be broke. When I sold the business I sank everything into equities, into US financials. It's what my broker told me to do. He's such an idiot.

– You're the idiot, said Dave. We're all idiots.

– Well, I've given you my opinion, said Dennis.

– My broker says we should concentrate on the dividends.

– Now that's a sucker's bet, said Dennis. They deduct the dividends from the quotation price of your stocks, so what do you gain?

– I'd like to hear an opposing view, said Morty.

– You get the opposing view every day.

– They hit you on the head with it, said Mooney.

– What's he doing here? said Morty to Dave.

– He's part of the syndicate, said Dennis. A founding member. A fond member.

– A fondled member, said Morty.

– It's the New World Order, Dennis said. Up is down, down is up. Nothing will ever be the same. We're heading into a shit-storm. America will go bankrupt. Is bankrupt. Don't say you weren't warned.

– Why do you want our money?

– I don't want your money.

– But if you had more money to invest, what would you do with it? asked Dave.

– With more money we could gear up even more, said Dennis. The more cash the greater the margin calls and guarantees we can muster. And on the next rebound, we can short the bastards again. They're going down.

– Maybe they want us to panic. And as soon as we do, up goes the market and we're fucked again. They'll get us all in a hot-box.

– They've got you in a hot-box now. Who's going to lift the markets if the smart money is now going short? asked Dennis. The bums that inflate the markets are now riding them down. I'm talking Armageddon. Breaking the Seventh Seal.

– Hold on.

– And I stand behind what I'm saying. With my own money. I'm not a broker.

– Are you sure the market will tank?

– Money-sure.

– Say something, Dave, said Mr. Michaels.

– I think I'm in.

At the door Dennis thanked Mrs. Michaels graciously, Irina hovering.

– I would really like to have you and your family over for din-ner one evening. To reciprocate, Dennis said to her.

– That would be nice.

– I don't think I could match your Indian dinner, though. It was lavish. Very authentic. Best Indian meal I've ever had.

Barbara wasn't sure if he was serious, but she accepted the compliment, avoiding his eyes. There really was kindness from strangers.

– No, really, I'd like you both to come, bring the kids. You have two very bright kids.

– We could arrange something.

– What about next week?

– I don't know where you live. Richie? Richie, come here a minute. Go get Dad.

– Get him yourself.

– Say Saturday night? went Dennis.

– Saturday night?

– Are you busy?

– Richie? I don't know. Richie? Why don't I get back to you?

– If you're not busy.

– I'm not busy. But maybe Richie is.

– Let's just say it's a date, my house. Bring your mother, too.

– I don't know.

– If Richie is busy you can come without him.

– No, I don't think so. We go everywhere together. Shall I call you a cab?

– That would be great.

– Don't you have a car? asked Irina.

– I do.

– What kind?

– A Lexus R400.

– Why didn't you bring it?

– If I have something important to go to and I don't want to be late, I take a cab.

– How come?

– I might get stopped by the cops.

– Why would you get stopped? asked Barbara.

Irina screamed.

– Mother, you're so pathetic.

– No, why would he get stopped? Tell me, I don't know. I don't know what's always so funny with you. Why would he get stopped?

Irina howled. Mrs. Michaels smoothed her dress over her abundant hips.

– No, really, why would he get stopped?

– You're so out of it, Mother.

– No, why. Why would he get stopped? Explain it to me.

– You're pathetic, she said to her mother. I'll give you a lift, Irina said Dennis.

– This is a school night.

– So what?

– Richie?

– I'll be back soon. You don't live on a reservation or something?

– I live on a beautiful street that slopes onto the river. Like you. But east of Main.

Once the dishwasher was humming softly and the rest of the house was dark and quiet, Barbara took one long last breath, surveyed the calm, and walked slowly up the stairs to bed. The dinner party had been like a strenuous picnic for 150. But she had got through it, like everything else in her life, which brought her to the conclusion that her life, for all its privilege, was really just getting through one thing after another. It was always like keeping dates that she hadn't made with people she didn't like. Yes, that was it.

There was no real enjoyment in things, just getting through them.

As she entered the bedroom she noticed her husband was having a laughing attack by himself in the en-suite bathroom while brushing his teeth, causing tiny flecks of toothpaste to fly about pell-mell.

– What's so funny?

– I can just see your face when the Indian came to the door and smelled the curry.

– Dennis?

– Yeah, Dennis.

– You're so demeaning.

– It's just funny. I'm not trying to be demeaning. I give to inner city charities.

– I lacked the right information. Fucking Dave Kaufman could have told you he was an Indian.

– He did. But he said he was Indian, not an Indian.

– You should give him shit, just once.

– Not going to happen. He's a good client.

– You're shit-scared of him.

– No, I'm not. He's just a good client. I don't really give a shit about Dave Kaufman. But I'm no idiot. You know, he made a remark about the plastic chairs on the patio. I told you to change them.

– I'm changing them in the spring. I might have served a curry anyway.

Her husband laughed again and the toothpaste specks flew. But the laugh was a tiny bit forced this time.

– No, you wouldn't have. You wouldn't have served a curry. If you knew he was an Indian, you'd have served venison or something.

– You are so demeaning.

– And you go too far, you know that? You just go too far, Barbara. To the point of embarrassment. What does Irina say, How pathetic?

– I can see where Irina gets her lack of respect for me.

– Yeah, from your stupidity.

There was just one more thing to get through. Irina had driven off with Dennis an hour ago. She stretched out in bed next to her snoring husband, listening to every sound, waiting for the whirr of the garage doors and the sound of the engine turning off. Once Irina came home she would take another Valium and go to sleep, but first she just had to get through the wait.

10

The TARP bailout bill was pushed through Congress on October 3 despite opposition from ordinary citizens, which was ignored. Nevertheless, the markets continued to slide.

The first arctic front of the year shuckled over the city and swallowed it with a cold that made your ears and nose red and numb. Lips were chapped. Snow fell and lay, white-hot and unbearably bright at first, but then it had to be shovelled or snow-blown, and six months of this white crap lay ahead, thought Mooney. But he loved it anyway, as both as something real and as a sign.

And now they were making big money. The market was sliding inexorably into the shit. By mid-October the Dow was down to 8,500 points, and Suddy decided it was time for them to get an office downtown. He lobbied the others for it:

– Besides, Dennis is exceptional, he deserves an office. He's got a brain the size of a . . .

– A what? said Oz.

– I don't know. Something big. A pumpkin.

They had looked at several places to rent, and were wandering around the last one that was on Suddy's list. It was in a tall but squat office tower, the highest on the plain, on the 14th floor. Suddy thought it was the one with the cleanest toilets. And the faucets turned on and off automatically. He also thought there were a lot of sockets in the walls.

They had begun their short in March with the Dow at 11,800. They had suffered for several months when the Down went up into the mid-12,000's, then just up and over 13,000 in early May, which is when Suddy had been hospitalized, and Marilyn wanted to bring her tort action. But then it went down, all summer, to Dennis's relief, with a few one-off upswings plunging them deep enough into the red again to cause another panic. But after Lehman Brothers crashed they were in the black for good, and earning the big bucks. By the end of September the Dow was at 10,000, then dropped sharply in the first week of October to 8,000 or so, then made a short comeback to 9,000 by Halloween, only to hit the skids again in November. Their initial million, leveraged by an average of seven times now, had made them millionaires. On some of their bets they made 70 or 80 percent profit which, multiplied by their leveraging, hit four-digit percentages. If they cashed out now they'd have realized millions, Dennis and Oz taking the biggest slices, followed by Marilyn, Suddy, Sammy and Mooney, in that order. Suddy, elated, thought it was time to rent an office.

– We don't need an office, said Dennis. All we need is a computer and a modem and an ADSL pipe. Which I have at home.

– I don't want to go to your house, said Suddy.

– What's wrong with my house?

– It's too far away.

– This place is even farther from your house, Suddy.

– But the bus route is faster.

– Besides, Mooney drives you everywhere, anyway.

– Mooney's good that way.

– Why don't you take your cab?

– I've got two guys working the license.

– You hardly come over anyway, said Dennis.

– I want an office. We need an office in this financial frenzy.

– What do you need an office for, Suddy?

– I just want one. Makes it more professional. More dignified.

– Dignity costs money.

– We have the money.

– Let him have an office, said Oz.

– We don't need an office.

– What do you think, Sammy?

– I could care less. I'm not going into no office in the morning. I've been retired for twenty years now.

– And I didn't like the fact I wasn't invited to the Michaels, said Suddy. He wouldn't stoop to call me.

– Suddy, come off it.

– And I knew his wife's mother when she was a Goldenberg.

– Didn't they change their name to Golden? said Sammy.

– But she married a Goldenberg, so it went from Golden back to Goldenberg.

– I hear now they're thinking of changing it back to Golden.

– Yeah, Suddy said, there are so many Goldenbergs in this town. Still, I should have been invited.

– Forget about it.

– No, I didn't like it. I have a *nishoma*, too.

– None of us were invited except Dennis.

– Mooney was.

– Because Dave organized it. His mother probably made him invite Mooney.

– I wasn't invited either, said Sammy.

– You don't like the Michaels.

– My wife doesn't like the Michaels. That little shit Barbara Michaels snubbed her once at *shlikes*, the little shit.

– They could have asked all of us, said Suddy.

– Don't worry, they didn't have soup.

– Was it a wine and cheese party?

– Those went out in the sixties, Suddy, said Mooney.

– What did they serve?

– Indian food, said Dennis.

This broke them up.

– Was it authentic, Dennis?

– Very.

– You wouldn't have eaten what they served, Suddy.

– You would have made a face.

– Dave says we should get an office, says Suddy.

– When did Dave tell you this? asked Mooney.

– I saw him at Mellers'.

– Dave? He doesn't go to Mellers'. They don't serve *bunyiet*.

– I know your brother, Mooney. I knew you kids when you were *pisherlach*. Always a sullen kid, that brother of yours, but a nice kid. But he was going to go places, that kid. Your dad said so. But he never had your charm, never wanted to give me a kiss when I came over to see your father, *alevasholem*. Now your

father knew how to play pinochle. He had such elegant melds.
And a great skip, too. I can't understand why he voted to dissolve
the curling club. They all did.

– What's the curling club got to do with anything, Suddy?

– It's the way this world is going. Anyways, Dave said we
should get an office. Otherwise we'd look like hicks.

Mooney shuddered. For a moment he had forgotten that Dave
was in now, spending more time with Dennis than he was, as
they were arranging the influx of more capital from Dave and his
friends, even from Larry Brickman, who looked down his nose
at stock speculators, fucking hypocrite. Their plan was to open a
new short as soon as the Dow rebounded up from 8,500 into the
9,000s. The fluctuations were getting wilder every day.

■ ■ ■

– Why do you have to *intershtip* yourself in my thing, Mooney
asked Dave one day.

– I'm trying to save my fucking equity. And it's not your
thing.

– Make your own investments.

– I am.

– Just do it with your friends.

– We need Dennis. We don't know how to do it ourselves.
Anyway, what's it your — business?

– It's just . . .

– Just what?

– I don't know.

– All I know is you haven't paid me back the money I lent
you.

– I'm good for it, wouldn't you say.

– No.

The Eisenteethers, who still had their shorts going, wouldn't be
able to join Dennis and Dave's new initiative, unless they cashed
out and re-shorted, or brought in fresh capital, which none of
them had or were willing to do, as Dennis insisted that the Dow,
in spite of the volatility, no, because of it, was going south, deep
south, to Miami, no to Guatemala, and by 6,000 more ticks.

Mooney was tempted to cash out his short and wait for the

dead-cat bounce that would bring the Dow up to 9,000 or so and then short it again. Come in as a partner with his fucking brother Dave and fucking Larry Brickman and fucking Richie Michaels. But he didn't, out of fear, he thought: he lacked the balls, he told himself, and kept his short.

But it wasn't a question of balls, or rather, not that set of balls, but a different set of balls. Truth to tell, Mooney was distracted by love. If he couldn't make a decision it was because he had become obsessed with Naomi after seeing her at the Michaels' do.

The night after the Michaels party he couldn't sleep for thinking about Naomi, her raspy voice, the way she held her cigarette, the way she flirted with him. In the hour of dawn he realized he had to find her, talk to her. Instead of concentrating on the market, making a decision, he obsessed on Naomi.

He found out where Naomi worked and waited one day for her to come out of her building. He walked behind her for half a block as if he were a detective. If she saw him he would pretend he was just there on an errand or something and that they had bumped into each other by accident. All of a sudden she turned around. He was in some sort of trance between sleep and consciousness, with a cast of two, Naomi and him, rolling in and out of a delicious embrace on a large bed.

– Are you stalking me? she said.
– No. I was doing some errands around here.
– I think you were stalking me.
– I wasn't.
– What errands?
– This and that.
– You were stalking me.
– I was waiting for you.
– I knew it.
– So, are you going to see me or what?
– It's complicated.
– Just once. Come on.
– I don't know, Mooney. I don't know what I ever saw in you. I gave up other men for you.
– I don't know what you saw in me either.
– Then why are you stalking me?

    – I was just waiting for you.

    – You were stalking me.

    – Alright, I was stalking you.

    – I knew it.

    – So, are you going to see me or what? I still adore you.

    – I don't know.

    – Is it Larry?

    – I'm free to do as I please.

    – You keep getting tougher and tougher.

    – That's what you saw in me.

    – And what did you see in me?

    – I told you, I don't know. But you always get under my skin.

    – So?

    – So what?

    – Are you going to see me, or what?

After that he saw her once for coffee, twice for lunch and, finally, they arranged to meet at a hotel downtown, but not for lunch. Since they made the date he had been restless, feeling guilty about Larry Brickman!, nervous about how he would perform. Naomi was hard to make cum, and he was no expert on the bedsprings.

The days before their date he spent just filling in time. The office hunt was useful in that direction. And so was spending the money from the small cash-out Dennis had made about a week earlier by closing a highly leveraged warrant put on the Dow at 8,500 and realizing a profit in the low six digits, which they divided up in proportion to their stakes. Suddy was the only one to complain.

    – I thought it was locked in, said Suddy.

    – I lied, said Dennis.

    – You mean we could have cashed out in the summer?

    – And lost.

    – Well? Could we have?

    – Yes, you could have.

    – So you made that up about it being locked in.

    – I did, said Dennis.

    – For your own good, said Oz.

    – How can we trust you? asked Suddy.

    – He did it for your own good, said Oz. That's how.

    – I can't trust you now, Dennis.

– Suddy, if you had taken your money out in the summer, you would have lost a bundle, said Mooney.

– Dennis was protecting us, said Sammy.

– He should have told us.

– No, he shouldn't have.

– My *nishoma* is not a *roszenker*.

– Your brain is, said Sammy. Your brain is a *roszenker*.

– I'm a human person, said Suddy. A human person.

Suddy forgave Dennis finally and took his money and signed up for a pinochle tournament in Vegas for the end of November, and went to the casino with a thousand bucks with the intention of sitting at the $100 blackjack table.

When he strode into the casino that night he moved so smoothly for his age that it was if he was walking on his own travelator. He bust each of his ten hands and lost the thousand dollars without feeling the pain.

Sammy used some of his money to recapitalize the *bindl*, and used the other portion to buy a double plot at the Rosh Pina Cemetery. When he told Suddy that his wife Anna had got herself an iPad, Suddy's reaction was Suddyish.

– What's wrong with her eye?

Oz gave most of his money to his kids, some to the NDP candidate for Inkster, some to the food bank and some to Dennis's foundation for his Canadian Holocaust Museum. He could hardly wait for the syndicate to stop making so much money and cash out completely. The news about foreclosures and evictions, mass unemployment in the US and the general misery that was spreading across the world made him feel sick and guilty. He was glad for Suddy, Sammy, Dennis and especially Mooney, but it all made him sick, and if he looked like shit more than ever, it was because he felt like a shit.

Dennis set up his foundation to promote his Canadian Holocaust Museum project and reminded Mooney of his pledge to help him. Mooney said he would get round to helping out, but that he had a few things to do first.

Dennis also took Marilyn to Ireland, secretly, for a week's holiday.

The day Mooney stared at his new bank balance he felt it was nothing short of a miracle.

He was crawling out of his skin and went in Suddy's cab, him driving, with Suddy for chips on Main Street. A big fucking order of fries they gave him too. Bigger than usual. Money goes to money, he thought. Suddy drenched his in ketchup. Mooney was generous with the vinegar bottle, so much so he almost choked on the vinegar fumes on the first chips he stuffed in his mouth. He was so hungry he gobbled too fast and burnt his tongue. They ate their chips walking in the snow to the car. It was perhaps the best order of fries he had ever had in his life, he told Suddy, thinking about what he would do with his money.

He used his first profit-taking to pay back Dave, and then move out of his mother's house with Meaghan. As luck would have it, the first place he looked at, a sublet of a swanky new apartment on the Crescent overlooking the river, with white leather furniture and a good parking spot, was available immediately. Another miracle.

Mrs. Kaufman was dead set against his renting the flat.

– Renting is like flushing money down the toilet.

– It's okay for now. We'll see how things go.

– Down the toilet.

– It's not down the toilet.

– And what about the dog?

– What about the dog?

– Are you taking the dog?

– Of course, I'm taking the dog.

– What for?

– It's my dog.

– What you need is a car.

– What?

– What you need is a car.

A car dealer offered him a humongous Audi SUV at a discount with certain heft if he took it right away. An Audi as big as a fucking tank, with just a thousand kilometres on it. Another miracle. And while Dennis poked some fun at it, calling it the Rez Rocket, he didn't mind, because the miracles were coming thick and fast, as they can only do when you've been a loser for so many years. The Rez Rocket was complete with beige leather seats and a television in the ceiling, which he could never figure out how to work.

It was great having money in the bank and your pocket. Like

his father, he made a thick wad of fins, tens, twenties, fifties and hundreds. In his wallet he placed more hundreds between the silk folds. He had no credit cards because he had no credit, having been blacklisted since his last bankruptcy. Life was never better when you could reach into your pocket and come up with a wad of cash, almost like pulling a drowning kid by his hair from the lake in front a big crowd.

He was even pleased to receive a letter from the tax authorities, in a white envelope, his name clearly visible in the cellophane window.

He had had his hair cut properly, making a changeover to a more rugged look. And he had joined a gym with the idea of turning his abdomen from a soft dome into something that would look like the squares of a chocolate bar. He spruced up his wardrobe and notified the welfare people that he wouldn't be needing their cheques anymore. Now he made out his own cheques. He joined Greenpeace and decided to send them a cheque each month. Making money from financial speculation required giving to good causes.

Suddy took him to get a couple of new suits made, which turned out rather dumpy. When his brother asked him where he got his suits he told him.

– Suddy took me to a tailor.

– No, he took you to someone who thinks he's a tailor.

So he went to Dave's tailor and gave the Suddy suits to the Salvation Army. Looking good, he went to the hotel to meet Naomi and fuck her, and fuck over that Larry Brickman while he was at it.

Naomi was already waiting in the lobby of the hotel. And that was another miracle. She had not changed her mind. They held hands all the way up the stairs to the room, which steadied him, as his ankles felt like styrofoam. It was all a bit raw. In the hall outside the room a painter was placing strips of tape around the frame of the door of the room next to theirs. The painter was dressed in white coveralls that had been spotted over many times with many dots and squiggles of colour, and he was humming 'Blackbird' by the Beatles.

Mooney and Naomi entered the room. It was just about noon. Mooney took out two condoms from his wallet and placed them on the night table side by side. He was still holding her hand. She laughed when she saw the condoms. He undid some buttons of her dress, thinking to undress her all the way, as if she were a baby, but then they thought they were too old for that and they undressed themselves.

She slipped off her dress over her head.

Under her clothes she wore a cotton bodice, like a bathing suit, actually. She rolled it down her chest, the breasts popping up, continuing to roll, down over the hips, down her thighs and down to the ankles. He thought it would stop his heart.

Suddenly, she was shockingly naked. He peeled back the bedcovers. As they got into bed they could hear the painter on the other side of the door still singing 'Blackbird'. Mooney didn't have an erection and he thought it was because he had left the door unlocked. He got up to check, but it was locked.

When he got back into bed he had an erection, his first in four years: the miracles were still happening. She made a happy grunt as he penetrated her, slowly, as if he were sitting down in a scalding bath. Yet, few things had been so familiar to him. At the moment of penetration, odd as it was, they were holding hands again, fingers interlocked on the pillow. She was crying.

He freed his hand and stroked her hair, which crackled. He looked at the expression in her tearstained eyes. For the first time he kissed her lips and it felt as if her very life flowed right into him. But he also thought: fuck that Larry Brickman to shit.

From above the bed he saw himself making love to Naomi, and he saw that he had forgotten to use the dubes on the night table just as his sperm flowed into her. His shoulder collapsed on her collarbones. He had that specific feeling of being a man again. And then they fell asleep for two hours.

He woke up first, worrying that his dog was alone. But the anxiety was more than worries about Meaghan. Naomi had changed, especially with her face full of sleep. She had aged. He hadn't seen it before. She was paler, her lipstick was smeared, and she was breathing with difficulty, as women who have aged do.

And he didn't know what to do with her now. What next? Just the way it was with someone you hardly knew and who you had just met by accident. He thought that they could go to a movie after, which is what people do when they don't know what to do.

Naomi awoke and saw him staring at her, or judging her, which made her shy. She drew him into her arms.

– Maybe someone saw us come in? she said.

– Someone did.

– Who?

– The painter.

– I've never done this before, she said.

– Not with me, you mean?

– Not with anyone.

– Where did you do it with Larry Brickman?

– Not in a hotel!

– You know, I still remember seeing your breasts for the first time.

– Hnnn?

– I was afraid then.

– Of what?

– Of being disgusted by them.

– Were you disgusted?

– No. Not at all. I had seen breasts before, in *Playboy*, and they were quite dirty.

– Now they're disgusting, she said.

– They're different. But they're still not disgusting.

They were silent for a while. After all, things were pretty raw, being with her after all these years, and with the anger he sometimes had felt towards her. But the sex had made him feel he was quite above anger and revenge, almost having transported him above his fears, into the sky, and into immortality. He even felt bad for Larry Brickman.

They still had lots of time to be together. The afternoon stretched out before them and sometimes it was impossible for him to find his bearings. He felt again like he didn't know what to do with her. Maybe another go. Maybe a movie. He held her hand, but he could feel his own indifference, and yet he was obsessed with getting her back, or at least building his new life around her, or the idea of her. That made him feel sad and mean and trapped, and he only squeezed her hand harder to make himself feel something else.

He stood up violently and started dressing.

– What's the rush?

  – I have to get back to Meaghan.
  – Meaghan, your bitch?
  – Meaghan, my bitch.
  – Right now?
  – Right now.

Naomi jumped out of bed and made two fists, so small when
balled up, and banged him on the chest violently. He grabbed her
wrists because she was hurting him.

  – You know, I have to get home, too. I told Larry I was just
going to the . . .
  – How's life with Larry?
  – You're so mean. You were always mean.
  – No, I wasn't.
  – Your father was such a sweet man, too.
  – He didn't think that much of you.
  – See what I'm saying. You're mean.
  – I wasn't mean.
  – You were to me.
  – You're the reason I had my breakdown.
  – No, you were.
  – You know, I couldn't remember my last name.
  – Get over it. That was in the past. Stay with me a while
longer.

He never understood why she had ever loved him. Even though
she had explained it to him — that when she was with him she
did not feel lonely — he still could not understand why that
made her love him, because he had not been able to understand
her loneliness, had not believed it possible.

■ ■ ■

The Eisenteethers took the office in the clouds with the cleanest
toilets and automatic faucets. Phones were installed and office
supplies purchased. Suddy and Mooney went in every day, Oz
never, Sammy and Marilyn from time to time, and Dave and
his pals looked in when it suited them. Suddy brought a folding
card table, but they sent him home with it the same day in a cab.
Real office furniture arrived that Marilyn ordered. There wasn't
much to do at the office, however, except watch the stock quota-

tions, keep an eye on the VIX, Google and print out reports that no one but Dennis understood, or just stare out the windows and watch the snowflakes, like little parachutists, float down from the sky.

Suddy put up a small poster in the office, one about the stop-loss: Safety is job one! it said. And he enjoyed watching the stock bulletins.

- Bank of America is unched.
- What? said Dennis.
- It's unched.
- What's unched?
- Bank of America.
- No, what does unched mean?
- Look, it says here 'unch'.
- Unchanged?

Dennis spent a lot of time at his foundation for his Holocaust Museum, always reminding Mooney of his pledge to help out. But Mooney found himself busier than ever, juggling his trysts with Naomi, walking Meaghan in the park, and driving Suddy around in his Audi SUV to the casino and Mellers'.

Suddy learned how to turn the printer on and off and how to load it with paper. And also how to order in, clean up the mess and get the office in order for the next day. It was a grand time for Suddy especially. He was enjoying his winnings like never before.

Mooney found it easy to spend the day with Suddy, who always spoke nicely about his father, and because Suddy was a terrific napper. He would fall asleep in the Barcelona chair that Marilyn bought, his head falling to one side so heavily that it looked as if his neck had been wrung. It was the typical Suddy nap position.

Whenever Dave came over and saw Suddy asleep like that he would say:

- You'll end up like Suddy one day, Mooney.
- Good!
- No, really.
- What's wrong with Suddy?
- He's a simpleton.
Bizarre word choice, thought Mooney.
- He has a big heart, Dave. You should have a heart that big.

– He's a simpleton.

Mooney didn't care. With Suddy awake he could discuss hockey and baseball and curling, the times when there was a Jewish club in the north end, where you could order milkshakes and nips at the counter. About the space-age bun-warmer. Those were grand times, before the rich Jews moved south and sold the club.

The office had a little conference room they would sit in when Dennis came, where they would discuss the evolution of the markets and then eat Chinese food.

It was all fucking A, thought Mooney. The office, the money being made in the zillions, seeing — no, *fucking* Naomi.

It was Suddy's brainwave to have a cash float for petty expenses, like the Chinese food. An army marches on its stomach, Suddy, who was a veteran, would say.

Suddy had a lot of ideas. So many that he sometimes gave Dennis a headache.

– Give it a rest, Suddy.

Sometimes they were all there, even Marilyn. By Christmas, by the time the big cold was there to stay, they were already up millions, and it was sheer pleasure sometimes to get together and watch the Dow slide a hundred points on a big screen, with Suddy cranking out the exact sum of their winnings on his old key-punch adding machine, with a handle as big as one on a meat grinder. Suddy's adding machine really was a number cruncher, and Suddy from his bookkeeping days could do multiplication with crackerjack accuracy on it by adding up sums many times in a row, cranking the handle over and over again.

But other days were slow, and if Dennis didn't come in, there was nothing to do. The doldrums, Suddy called them, when the highlight of the day was leaving at lunch and going for chips and vinegar or just ordering in.

No one except Mooney had caught on to the relationship between Dennis and Marilyn, and all three kept their secret as professionally as spies. Their public indifference to each other was absolutely brilliant, Mooney thought. But then again, he was also in a secret relationship with Naomi. He loved that part of it, but worried it was perhaps too big a part of what it was.

Yet, that was his ultimate plan, to win Naomi back from Larry Brickman.

But sometimes things got hot when you least expected. Like when a warrant was about to expire. Dennis would bark out orders and Mooney would close a position here or open another one there. Mooney got good at keying in passwords and orders on the computer. Dennis always came over to check before he hit the enter key though. All this action geared Suddy up, which Dennis humoured.

– There's no paper in the printer! he shouted.
– Load the printer, said Dennis.
– There's no paper.
– Go downstairs and buy some.
– I don't have any money on me.
– Take it out of petty cash.
– There is no petty cash.
– Go to the bank and get enough for a new float.
– How big a float?
– The same as last time.
– How much was that?
– A few hundred.
– I'm on it.

Things were really hopping some days. Outside the snow came down thick and fast, and sometimes the air chilled to 30 below.

One winter's night the Eisenteethers organized a big dinner at the Steak Palace to celebrate, on Suddy's insistence. And they were to order the prime rib, Suddy said, glowing as happily as a baby in a Chinese poster. You can't go wrong with the prime rib, he said. 'And you get a cut like this thick.'

Mooney thought to invite his mother, but she refused to go.

– You always say you're so alone.
– Like a stone.
– So come with us.
– I won't know anyone there?
– Sammy and Anna will be there.
– I don't like Anna.
– What's wrong with Anna?
– She has a big mouth.

– That's what she says about you.

– But she has the big mouth. A real *pisk*. She's the one.

– You know Suddy.

– I can't stand Suddy Joffe.

– Dad liked him.

– Dad like everybody. And everybody liked him. He was the one people liked. I did the dirty work, but everybody liked him. Of course I never tooted my own horn. I'm not like that, but he was the one everybody liked.

– Suddy likes you. He always speaks highly of you.

– Suddy's an idiot.

– Dad liked him.

– Who didn't he like? Your father liked everyone. More than his own family. He'd give money to people he didn't even know. Money that could have gone on my back.

– You have tons of clothes.

– Still. He was generous. A fin here, a twenty there. I had to stop him sometimes from giving away the furniture. Once he wanted to give Mrs. Stein my Persian lamb coat. Mrs. Stein! With their stinking millions.

– You hated that coat.

He was invited to people's houses. Twice to the Bergers, the couple that was running after the Michaels. They had a very modern house built out of polished timber and glass and filled with white furniture.

Mooney took Suddy with him to make up for not taking him to the Michaels. Suddy said it was like walking through a lumber-yard full of snow.

The Bergers were a bit shocked to see Suddy at the door. They looked at the way he dressed and his oily braids of hair combed over, and thought 'shlepper', but they were otherwise very polite. Right away Suddy knew there would be nothing he could eat there and that there would not even be soup. He eventually had to ask for bread and butter, which he ate in great chunks, smear-ing the balls of butter with pleasure.

Naomi and Larry Brickman were also at the Bergers, which was awkward as fuck, Mooney thought.

It was awkward for Larry Brickman, too, but not for the rea-son Mooney thought.

The last time Larry Brickman went to the Bergers was for a party, to which only five couples came. For some reason the Bergers were being snubbed, and he didn't know why. Maybe there was no reason, except that they were pegged as people who were chasing after people richer than themselves, or maybe it was all just a misunderstanding, as the Bergers seemed rather easy-going, and were flummoxed by their precarious standing in the community.

Now, instead of throwing large parties and risking a shutout like the last time, the Bergers were reduced to organizing small dinner parties, where they could get confirmation of attendance. What was being done to the Bergers was something of a shunning, and he had accepted the invitation against his better judgement, only on Naomi's insistence, because she felt bad for them. He personally had no need for the Bergers, for shit's sake, and why Naomi felt sorry for them was beyond him.

The time dragged on at the dinner, and with the wine Mooney was getting drowsier and drowsier. Each course seemed to take longer to get through than the last. Mooney found the conversation excruciatingly boring. They didn't even ask him about the markets. He remembered the hot arguments with the young people at Dave's grandson's *briss* and thought he got along better with people under twenty, or over seventy.

When he saw Naomi get up to go to the bathroom he followed her inside, locking the door behind him.

– How can you hang out with these people? he asked.

– I have to pee.

– Just answer my question.

– They're friends.

– But they're so boring.

– No more than me.

– That's a lie.

– You always exaggerated how smart I was. How interesting I was. But it was just to make you think you were smart and interesting.

– You were smart and interesting.

– No more than these people thought they were. So why did you come?

– They invited me.

– You could have blown them off. Everybody does.

– I had nothing better to do. I already walked the dog three times today. In the snow. My mother bought him boots.

– I thought she hated dogs.

– She's in love with that dog.

– And so are you.

– I should've stayed home with Meaghan.

– Maybe you should have.

– I thought there was going to be more stimulating conversation.

– What made you think that?

– I don't know.

– Can I pee now?

– Don't. There's no toilet paper in the dispenser.

– See if there's some in the cabinet under the sink.

– I can't go into other people's cabinets.

– Just look, for fuck's sake. I really have to pee.

Mooney was seeing Naomi pretty regularly for sex, usually at his new apartment. Of course, she wouldn't let the dog in the room while they were doing it. Meaghan mewled with jealousy outside the room, and scratched the paint off the door with two paws in her despair. Lately Mooney had begun dropping the dog off with his mother before getting together with Naomi. Just the day before the dinner at the Bergers' they spent the afternoon in bed, eating Chinese food out of cartons.

She had rolled his ball sac gingerly between her fingertips.

– Nice move, he said. But you can stop now.

– I've been practicing.

– I said you can stop right now. Practice on someone else.

– I do.

– My mother was right; you're such a slut.

– Is that what she thinks of me now?

– She always thought you were a slut, with no rear end. And who didn't want kids. I don't know what she complained about more.

– You didn't want kids either.

– You were supposed to have saved me, in her mind.

– No one could have filled her job description.

– No one else wanted to.

– Can you blame them?

– Still.

– I won't tell you what my mother thought about you, or your mother.

– She couldn't stand me. Or my mother.

– When I left you, she gave me a hundred grand.

– Cash money?

– Cash money.

– She could have given you that money when we were broke.

– She would only give it to me if I got rid of you.

Sometime it came over him to tell her he loved her. But he never did. He would just mouth the words when she wasn't looking. The feeling of wanting to tell her he loved her would burst open, and he would mouth the words. But he was still too angry for her having left him for Larry Brickman, so he held back from giving them sound. If only he could say them out loud, he would be reborn, he thought, but he couldn't forgive her.

– Can you nap yourself to death? asked Suddy.

– I don't think so, said Oz.

– Never heard it happen, added Sammy.

It was mid-February, into a new year of arctic cold, and the whole Eisenteeth Syndicate had been convened for lunch at Mellers' to talk about whether they should make another cash-out, but for now they were listening to Suddy talk about his Vegas trip. Suddy was wearing a floral patterned shirt, and beneath his chair there was a puddle on the floor from the snow that had melted from his half-rubbers.

– I think I almost died in Vegas, said Suddy, from napping.

Suddy looked like he did when he had a hunger pang.

– You probably had another panic attack.

– No, I was in bed. Very relaxed.

– You can have a panic attack in bed.

– It was my second nap. My pyjama and bedpan nap, Suddy said. I was exhausted, I guess. Vegas kills me.

– That's 'cause you gamble at night.

– You lose track of time there. You don't know when it's day or night.

– You entered the pinochle tournament, didn't you?

– They put us up in a crummy hotel.

– So?

– So I thought it would be a bit more luxurious. And I didn't like the pricing. The charge for the first night was double the charge for the fourth and fifth nights. Cockamamie.

– You're a whiner.

– They were giving you a discount, Suddy.

– It just wasn't fair. Not in my books.

– How did you do in the tournament?

– They play Vegas pinochle rules there. I don't like the way they meld. And there's no bad language allowed.

– I've never heard you swear, Suddy.

– I do when I play pinochle. And the cards have to be shuffled five times there. The first day they filed a Sportsmanship Violation against me. Me! Suddy, who played pinochle with Chico Marx.

– You talk too much when you play cards, Suddy.

– You open your hand and always go 'beautiful'.

– That's irritating.

– It dekes out the other players, said Suddy.

Go take the orders from the *goris*, the Indian from India told his son. The kid came over shyly to the Eisenteeth table. They ordered their usuals and he wrote them down on a restaurant pad.

– What happened to the Mellers?

– They sold the place.

– To Indians.

– East Asians.

– From India?

– Where else?

– They could be from Uganda.

– Or the Caribbean.

– Now they're here. Fucked just like everybody else.

– You don't mind the cold? Suddy asked the kid waiting on them.

– You get used to it, the kid said.

– Nobody gets used to it.

The kid left.

– I don't think we should keep the office, said Suddy.

– It was you who insisted on having it, Suddy.

– It's too hard to get there in the winter. Too much snow.

– Take a cab. Take your own cab.

– I'm not taking cabs. And Oz can't pick me up anymore.

– They took my license away.

– Oz never came in anyway. Mooney's always driving you around.

– In the Rez Rocket.

– Just take a cab, Suddy. You can afford it now.

– Mooney, is that the biggest SUV there is?

– I don't know.

The kid came over balancing an enormous tray.

– Who ordered the soup?

– Suddy!

– What?

– Didn't you order the soup?

– I did.

– Where's your head?

Suddy's head was occupied with his trip to Vegas.

– What are we doing here anyway, asked Suddy?

– We're closing the shorts, Suddy, said Dennis. We're closing the syndicate.

– What about the office?

The Dow had fallen by mid-February 2009 to around 7,300 points. Dennis was suggesting they get out now: it could fall even further, true, but why chance it. These were pretty good lows. Four thousand ticks, with their leverage, was a pretty good run. Five thousand ticks would be fabulous, but things could turn at any minute now. They had already multiplied their initial bet thirty times.

– I thought you said it would go south to 6,000, said Mooney. As far as Florida, you said.

– It could get to Guatemala or Antarctica, said Suddy.

– I did. I did say that. But somebody out there is going to start bargain hunting. The big boys are planning to blow a bubble back into the market as we speak. And they're a sly bunch of pricks. Let's not be too greedy.

– We are greedy, said Oz.

– But not too greedy. Maybe we should just close all the shorts.

– Dissolve the syndicate?

– We've done pretty well.

– Mooney, you're sulking.

– I'm not sulking. I just don't think we should close yet.

– We've ridden this thing down pretty far, now it's time to cash out.

– How much have we made?

– Millions. Thirty times what each of you bet, less a ridiculous tax, some commissions, and some interest on the margin calls.

– Thirty times?

– Thirty times. Three thousand percent.

– Cash money?

– Cash money.

Dennis cashed them out in the millions after their meeting and they dissolved the syndicate. He still kept things going with Dave and his friends and kept the office, cashing out but preparing to go long, waiting for the formation of the Triple Cross of Death of the 200-, 50- and 18-day moving averages.

Oz came by the office the next day and picked up his cheque, in the high seven digits. He said his cash-out was enough to make up what all his four kids lost on their pension plans.

– Oz, you look like shit.

Oz was looking drabber and frailer. No one had ever seen him looking so bad.

– I'm not feeling so great, but I am relieved it's over.

– You should see a doctor.

– I've just been to the doctor. He wants to run some tests.

– What tests?

– Tests. Blood work. The usual. But he won't find anything new.

– No?

– There's no cure for being a shit, Dennis.

– You're not a shit, Oz.

– You're not, because you don't think you did anything wrong. But I did.

– Look, if you hadn't come in with us, your kids would be out more than half their pensions. You just hedged things for them. Other people's kids won't be so lucky.

– Other people's kids are our kids, too.

– You're right. But all this wasn't your fault. Or theirs.

– Maybe, maybe not. But I'm a shit.

Mooney's final cash-out came to about $1.5 mil on a $50,000 stake. It was another miracle. Dennis cut him the cheque and he deposited it in an account at his branch of the Royal Bank. The manager called him into his office and offered to help him invest it. Mooney said he knew how to invest the money himself, thank you, his chin tilted up, a swagger when he walked out of the prick's office. That afternoon he phoned Naomi and told her to come over.

After sex Naomi fell asleep and he stayed up, back against the headboard, hands behind his head. Outside the snowflakes fell on the white river and the evergreens. Big mothers. He both wanted to keep this a secret from Larry Brickman and have Larry Brickman know all about it. But that made him feel like a prick, like Larry Prickman, and he didn't want to end up like Larry Prickman; he wanted to be *morally* superior to Larry Prickman, though sleeping with Naomi didn't make him *morally* superior to Larry Prickman. The conundrum got him down and he woke Naomi up with a gentle nudge.

– Marry me.

– What?

– I want to live with you. See you every day. Marry me.

– Again?

– Marry me.

– I didn't sleep last night, let me sleep, Mooney.

– Marry me, please. It's the only thing that will solve my life.

– Why buy the cow when you get the milk for free? she said, followed by a fake laugh, followed by a real laugh.

– Let me pay you the ultimate compliment.

– That I'm not a cow?

– I'm paying you that compliment, yes. Now marry me. Don't you see, it's *bashert*. We were made for each other. Just forget about Larry Brickman. He's a prick. He really is. He's as bad as my brother.

– Your brother's a scumbag. Which is worse, by the way, a prick or a scumbag?

– A prick. A prick is worse than a scumbag.

– I know he's a prick. But he's nice to me.

– Hitler was nice to Eva Braun.

– Right. He got her to commit suicide.

– Bad example. Please, just marry me. Don't go home tonight. Stay here with me. Don't get out of bed. Go back to sleep. We'll order in more Chinese food and eat it in bed.

– What'll I tell Larry?

– I'll call him.

– You'd love that.

– I'd rather eviscerate him, but I'd settle for that phone call.

– I like this arrangement. We can see each other twice a week.

– Fucking afternoons.

– What's the difference?

– I want to see you at night. I don't sleep well.

– Why do you let your insecurities spoil everything?

– What else do insecurities do?

– Well, I can't give up the security I have. I won't lose everything for love. Not a second time.

– But I have money now.

– For now.

– These are tough terms.

– But you're the one who made them, if really you think about it.

Mooney accepted Naomi's terms. But they unsettled him. There was no way he could be morally superior to Larry Brickman if he was sleeping with Naomi behind his back, even if Larry Brickman had slept with her behind his back. The fuck he knew why he needed the high ground; he had just speculated massively against the US banking system.

■ ■ ■

Not long afterwards, Dennis called Mooney and told him to meet him at the casino in the afternoon. They sat in their booth and ordered coffee and muffins. They ate in silence.

– Are you going to finish that? asked Mooney.

– You can have it. Can't stand raisins in muffins.

– Why didn't you order it plain?

– Forgot.

– Why did you want to see me?

– Couple of things.

– Like?

– Like why you've never come to the foundation to help out with the museum. You promised.

– I did.

– You reneged.

– I'll get around to it as soon as I get settled.

– You are settled.

– Not really.

– Where's your mind at?

– I'm involved with this woman.

– Naomi Brickman? Your ex-wife.

– How did you know?

– Half the city knows.

– I never know when you're serious, Dennis.

– You're trying to woo her.

– I haven't heard that word for a long time.

– My advice: don't get involved with an ex. Dating your ex is like dating the dead. You're looking at her with beer glasses on.

– I can't seem to focus on other things, Dennis.

– You should be helping out. Come down to the foundation. It'll give you focus.

– I know. I promised. I'll set aside next month. The whole month.

– You promise.

– Yeah, I promise. What else did you want to talk about?

– I'm going to go long soon, said Dennis.

– The Triple Cross of Death?

– Yeah, the Triple Cross of Death. It'll soon be time. Just thought I'd tell you, in case you wanted to come in.

– With Dave and his friends?

– Yeah.

– Dave and Richie Michaels?

– And Larry Brickman.

– Fuck.

– It's business, Mooney.

– I thought you wanted to short the buggers till they bled.

– We did. They bled.

– But now you're going long.

– The Fed is pumping trillions into the system. They want to reflate the market. The guys we bled, they're getting a transfusion, thanks to Mr. US Taxpayer, the stupid fuck. So, it's time to go long.

– I think things are still going south, Dennis.

– The financial lava will start to flow, Mooney.

– They're going down, you said so.

– They might, for a bit longer. But then they'll turn. And when they do, it will be swift and brutal. *V*-shaped. Fuckers that they are, they'll pull things down first, to suck people in, then give it to them like a native fisherman, push it up thousands of ticks. And I'm talking Cape Canaveral. A real space shot.

– Above the ski tips?

– Cannonballs.

– I'm opening up another short, Dennis.

– Don't do it, Mooney. We'll be on the opposite side of the bet.

– You said yourself the market was going down to six thousand.

– Could do. But markets don't move up and down. There are these immensely rich fuckers who move them up and down. And they might just keep moving them down for a while — but just to fuck with you. Besides, the risk is too high for the reward of another five hundred to a thousand ticks, max. There are no pot odds anymore.

– Dave is really in on this with you?

– He listens.

– I'm sure.

– If you go it alone, Mooney, you'll be left looking at the stars.

– I'm opening another short.

– If you do, just make a small bet. Don't max out and don't gear up.

But Mooney bet it all, about a million five from his cash-out, and bought highly leveraged warrant puts on the Dow. At first, when the Dow tanked at 6,626 on March 6, 2009, he made a few hundred thousand, more than enough to make his head swim because he had done it on his own.

By March 16, a week later, the Dow had bounced back up to 7,223, which flushed his gains down the toilet along with about a hundred thou of his initial stake.

The feeling in his gut at the final bell was horrible. He had cramps so tight he thought he would shit himself. It was panic, and in spite of a brewing snowstorm he saw from his floor-to-ceiling windows he called Dennis the next morning and invited himself over. He fed Meaghan and chased her and her squeaky bagel around the house, made sure she had water and went down to the garage to get the car.

The snowstorm had gathered howling on the plain and was about to push into the city.

The Rez Rocket crept up the dark ramp and out into the dim raw morning. The car had been dented here and there now, and scratched to shit. It seemed like every time he parked it outside, some kid vandalized it.

Visibility was poor, but the Rez Rocket ploughed through the starter drifts with ease. The snow at first came down in white bars, but when storm rose and slouched off the plain, the wind began to gust.

– Motherfucker.

The radio said the wind speed was gusting up to 60kmh in some spots of the city, which meant it was a blizzard. Of course the DJ started spinning records about snow, which wasn't funny, given how people were caught out there in the freezing cold and wind. But in the car it was warm as toast, and the enormous wheels ground through the drifts, pushing ahead into a wall of flurries, pursued from behind by billions more, whipped up into a frenzy.

– The fucking flurries chasing Orestes.

The snow that had already fallen was being blown up into the air, mixing with the new snow and forming *pisher* tornadoes. Confirmation: it was a ground blizzard now, the DJ hooted. The Rez Rocket was being attacked from above, behind and in front, but still it pushed ahead on its massive tires.

He could still see about a quarter of a mile ahead, which he thought made the drive still safe, and began his creep across the bridge east to Dennis's, going through a drift about two feet high that had formed at the head, coming out the other side onto a smooth patch of pavement that seemed to have been swept clean and then polished by a Zamboni. He skidded, doing a 360-degree spin, and continued on his way. Outside the wind howled and thumped. This is fucking amazing, thought Mooney. The river below was white, the bridge had been packed white, the sky above was white. The world had turned white, and Mooney felt he was trapped inside an immense chest freezer.

He called Naomi on his cell that was hooked up to the dash.

– You'll never guess where I am.

She gave him good shit for going out in a blizzard; she didn't think it was romantic at all.

– You're an idiot.

– It's all completely white.

– You're still an idiot. And you're scaring me.

– It's our day today.

– Are you nuts? I'm not going out in this.

– You said twice a week.

– I'm hanging up, Mooney.

He kept creeping across the bridge, churning the snow under his monster Pirellis. The Great Iran Blizzard of 1972 killed four thousand people, he remembered. The Great Schoolhouse Blizzard of 1888 trapped kids on the US plains in one-room school houses for days. The Winnipeg Blizzard of March 1966 paralyzed the city for two days. Thinking about blizzards was not helping any.

Another asshole, Mooney said, when he saw a black figure trudging along the bridge through snow drifts up to his knees, followed by one up to his crotch. He would have to pick the bugger up, he thought, and he did. The guy was shaking, his teeth chattering.

– What are you doing out in this? he asked, as the guy got in the car, his coat blasted with snow. He had snow down his boots, snow in his eyelashes and snow clinging to his balaclava.

– What are *you* doing out?

– I asked you first.

– I went to work.

– Are you nuts?

– I just got the job. They sent me home anyway; they could've let me weather the storm at work, you'd think.

– What's your name?

– Paul Schroeder.

– Mennonite?

– Yeah.

When they got to Dennis's, a drift had formed waist-high up to the front door. They pounded on the door. Dennis came to the door and told them there was a shovel in the back. They went around the back but there were drifts up to the windows and the shovel must have been buried. They came back around the front and dug with their fists around the first door, which they managed to pry open a bit into the drift and squeeze through. By the time they stood all frosted in Dennis's front hall, Mooney's nose was numb and his fingers and toes tingled with a touch of frostbite.

Dennis smelled a snow drift in the room.

– Who's this?

– I picked him up walking across the bridge. He's Mennonite.

– How can you tell?

– He told me.

Since their trousers and socks were sodden Dennis gave them each a pair of jeans and clean socks to change into. He put their boots to dry on the radiator in the laundry room. The Mennonite was still shaking, his teeth chattering. Dennis fixed him hot chocolate and tossed in some little marshmallows. They left him alone in the kitchen shaking, trying to calm himself down and went to Dennis's study.

– You brought the Rez Rocket.

– Smooth ride. In a blizzard.

– I thought it was a snowstorm.

– They upgraded it to a blizzard.

– Nobody is going out today.

– We did.

– You're mental.

– I'm panicky, Dennis. It's a hairy situation.

– I told you they were just trying to sucker you in.

– What should I do?

– You're even?

– More or less. Down a hundred thou.

– Then get out now. We're going long. And really geared up.

– It's just a bear rally, Dennis.

– No, it's the real thing, Mooney. There's trillions of dollars being pumped into the system at interest rates that are actually negative. This thing is going to the top of the charts. This is 'I Want to Hold Your Hand'.

– But the economy is for the shits. There are mass evictions, factories closing right and left. There are soup kitchens!

– So?

– So if it happened to me I'd want to go out there and bite the ankles of the banksters.

– You'd have to wait in line. What the fuck do they care anyway. This is the Bizarro world, Mooney. They're going to take the Dow back up to at least sixty percent of the drop it just had, just on this first round of easy money alone.

– Are you sure?

– Money-sure. Just get out, Mooney.

– I'm going to see what happens tomorrow.

– Don't. Close the position now. I'll do it for you. What's your password?

– meaghan36.

– What's the '36' for?

– Twice *chai*.

Dennis worked the keyboard, brought up Mooney's bets on the screen and keyed in the order to close his positions. All Mooney had to do was press enter.

– Press enter, Mooney.

– I don't know. Tomorrow it might tank again.

– Press enter, Mooney.

– Let's see what happens tomorrow.

– Mooney.

– It might go down tomorrow. I could break even.

– Have it your way. But you like that car out there?

– You mean the Rez Rocket? Yeah, sure.

– Press enter or get ready to kiss that motherfucker goodbye.

– I'll give it another day.

– You're gambling now, Mooney.

– Just another day.

– We said no gambling.

That night Mooney and the Mennonite had to crash at Dennis's.

He couldn't sleep thinking about Meaghan alone. She'd probably be crying. He woke in a sweat and saw a crack of light under his down, relieved that it was morning and that he could get home to Meaghan, on snowshoes if necessary. Dennis had to have snowshoes. But when he got up he found out the crack of light was because the Mennonite had left the bathroom light on and it was actually just 3 AM. He was despondent.

The next day the sun shone and the city was out cleaning the streets. Mooney went home, and found Meaghan in his bed, in a foul mood, having shat and peed on the parquet floor in the living room. He begged her forgiveness but she was sullen for the rest of the day. He checked the market report, and since the market was flat, he kept his short. He had a moral obligation to be hopeful.

The day after that it actually fell a bit and Mooney's panic ebbed. He called Naomi and she came over and they had sex.

Something about her that day gave her a glow that bewitched him like never before and he bathed in it. He had never been more attracted to her, her smell, her skin, her feet, her fingertips, her voice.

   – Why don't you leave Larry?

   – Can't. And we can't keep having this conversation.

   – Marry me. I'm crazy about you?

   – Can't.

There was no use in arguing with the way she said 'can't'. The matter-of-factness of it precluded any discussion. She brought the word down an octave from her normal voice and dragged it out: it was as nasty as love could get. But he persisted.

   – Can't or won't?

   – Can't and won't.

   – Why not?

   – Just not going to happen.

   – Should I beg?

   – If you have to ask that.

   – So I'm losing you, again.

   – You haven't lost me. I'm just not leaving Larry. You're too unreliable.

   – I'm earning good money now.

   – You'll blow it.

   – I won't blow it.

   – It's not the money, now.

   – It was then.

   – But it's not the issue now. You know, I didn't want to be rich, Mooney; I just wanted a normal life. I didn't want to live like the Michaels or their friends. I just didn't want to clean my own toilets.

■ ■ ■

By March 27, 2009, the Dow had gone up to 7,776 points and Mooney was down more than just a hundred thousand.

Then, stupidly, like a cow staring at a barn door, as the Ukrainians say, he watched all his warrants get gobbled up as the Dow rose first to 8,000 then to 9,000 points, his strike price. A new bubble had been blown up the ass of equities, and about $1.1 mil of his not-hard-earned money had evaporated. Just like that. In under three months. But Dave and Dennis had tripled or quadrupled theirs. Larry Brickman, too.

He stopped going out for those three months, stopped calling Naomi — losing money like that was a libido-buster — didn't even take her calls, and hardly saw Suddy or Oz or Sammy or Dennis. He was stuck, just looking at the stars, as Dennis warned. He didn't see anybody, because people just seemed trivial.

When Dennis reminded him of his promise to help out at the foundation for the Canadian Holocaust Museum, Mooney had to tell him that he was feeling the shits, and wasn't in the mood for much of anything. Dennis insisted, almost nagged, Mooney thought. Accused him of breaking his promise. He did manage to promise him again that if the market turned around for him, he would do some work there. But now he was just useless, to himself and to everyone.

One day Suddy called him up and asked him to pick him up and take him to the casino, you know, get out of the house. When Mooney said no, Suddy suggested that they go out for chips and vinegar. Mooney said it was not a question of venue.

– A man has to get out of the house, Suddy said.

– I'm down, Suddy, really down.

– How much?

– About $1.2 mil. Just three hundred thousand left. I can't go out. I can't see anybody. I'm sick.

– So, that's greed for you, Mooney.

– I wasn't greedy.

– What was it then?

– I was driven. It was the miracles.

– I don't know what you're talking about. But you need to get out of the house.

– I can't.

– You're whining. Your father was never a whiner.

– Just let me sulk, Suddy. I can't be around people

– He never gave up. Will and resistance till the end.

– I know.

– A jewel of a human being. A real jewel. I just have to think about your father and I get a good feeling about people.

– My luck has changed, Suddy.

– You need to turn it around.

– I can't.

– Why don't you go see Mitzi Dervitch, the psychic. Your Dad and I used to see her. She could pick the winners. We'd see her before going to the track and always pick up an Exacta or a Daily Double. She's psychic.

– Nobody's psychic, Suddy.

– Believe me, she's psychic. You know, I consulted her before giving Dennis and you my money. Before I sold my properties.

– I don't believe in psychics, Suddy.

– Mitzi's a clairvoyant, too.

– Christ, Suddy. I don't believe in it.

– But you believe in miracles?

– I had proof.

– What proof.

– The miracles. They were coming thick and fast.

– And now?

– They've stopped. Maybe they have to do with not helping Dennis. I told him I'd help him with his museum shit.

– Go see Mitzi. What have you got to lose? And stop with the miracles business. They'll lock you up again.

– I don't know where she lives.

– Pick me up tomorrow; I have a doctor's appointment, and I'll show you where she lives.

– How would that help?

– You get a feeling about a person from their house.

– Why do you have to see the doctor?

– My stomach. I ate a pound of unshelled peas this morning.

– And now you want to go for chips?

– I used to be able to eat two pounds of peas no sweat. And I'm listless. Sometimes the room spins. I should go to Rochester.

The next day was a lovely June day, a day of assurance that summer was coming. The leaves on the trees were still small and rubbery. He picked Suddy up and drove to the clinic. There was a lot of road work and the drive took forever. Suddy fell asleep, his head falling to one side, as always, as if his neck had been wrung. Suddy could fall asleep anywhere, anytime, even, it was rumoured, standing up.

Mooney waited for him at the doctor's office. When he came out he asked him:

– What'd he say?

– He says I have garbage symptoms.

– Is he going to do any tests?

– No. He says at my age intervention is worse than a cure. Big Doctor Pincus.

– Pincus?

– Pink Ass. You know what he can do with his garbage symptoms.

Then they cruised by the front of Mitzi Dervitch's house. He took a good look and decided it was safe.

– It's a nice house from the outside, said Suddy.

– She seems to be houseproud.

– I told you.

– Seems safe.

– What'd I say?

He made an appointment with Mitzi Dervitch to see if the miracles were coming back. Upon further research, Mooney found out she had a very good reputation as a card reader and for being discreet.

Years ago Mitzi had been a south-end housewife who had a knack for making predictions that came true. Feelings bubbled up inside her that gave her premonitions about the sex of fetuses, or about the names of horses at the track, about people's careers and affairs and the coming of blizzards and electrical storms. After years of being told that she was psychic by her family and friends she began to believe she really was, and decided to set up shop and sell what she had been giving away.

She held her sessions in her living room, which was not unlike his mother's. It also had a plastic runner from the chesterfield to the TV, because she didn't know how to replace the batteries in the remote.

– Why a Jewish psychic? Sammy said. She'll talk. The whole

city will know everything. I know a Ukrainian who's a lot cheaper than Mitzi Dervitch. Cheaper than all the Dervitches.

– It's the candour. You can be candid with her, said Suddy.

– How embarrassing to have a family member who's a psychic, Sammy said. But I see how it could be useful.

– I've heard of her, said Oz. She can pick winners.

– She always picked winners for me, said Suddy.

– She's a bit of a show-off, said Sammy.

– But she can pick winners.

– How does she pick winners?

– If I knew, I'd be the psychic. She just picks winners.

– She's a show-off. And if she could pick winners, she wouldn't have to work as a psychic.

– Maybe she likes her work.

– Nobody likes their work, said Suddy.

– You don't like to work, Suddy.

– I worked.

– You worked, right.

Mitzi was anything but a show-off. After seventy-five years on earth she was an excellent judge of whether people or horses had character and determination or not.

– Sit. I knew your father, she said to Mooney.

Mooney sat on the opposite side of the card table beside the TV. He tried to adjust his chair, but kept pushing the legs up against the plastic runner.

– Everybody knew my father.

– The nicest guy, Mitzi said.

– I know.

– We all loved him.

– Everybody loved him.

– Are you here about money or love?

He hadn't thought about asking her about Naomi.

– Money.

She heaped the cards in a pile and shuffled them on the table. She made a neat deck and Mooney cut the cards. She laid out her first of her fortune melds.

– This is about money? Mooney asked.

– Material wealth and fortune.

– What do they say?

– Oh, the miracle card!

– I have had miracles lately. But they've stopped suddenly.

– That's obvious from the cards, she said.

– Why have they stopped? I was having an incredible run.

– Why does anything stop? A cycle ends.

She melded another card. The Nine of Pentacles. Surrounded by grapevines a poised, confident woman stood with a falcon on her forearm. In the background a plantation boiled with riches.

– You have been working hard.

– Sort of.

– You have been enjoying your rewards for hard work.

– I wouldn't call it hard work.

– But there were risks.

– There were.

– Oh, sorry.

– What? What's the matter?

– I put down the card upside down.

– Does that change the meaning?

– It can mean deception. Bad faith.

– How do you know it's upside down?

– Because it's not upright.

– Depends on how you look at it.

– And it's not upright.

– What else does it mean?

– Roguery.

– So what would you advise? Regarding financial matters.

– Prudence. Security.

– Well, let's say I haven't been prudent. That I've taken a risk.

– In business?

– You might call it business.

– With your brother Dave?

– How do you know that?

– The whole city knows.

– Well, it's not with my brother Dave. The city is wrong.

Mitzi put down another card. The Knight of Swords. Mooney tried to push his chair in to get a better look, but the leg caught against the runner, so he stood up, picked up the chair, and tucked it forward, right under the card table.

– What's that?

– The Knight of Swords.
– Is it upright?
– Yes.
– So?

The card showed a knight charging on his horse, his sword above his head. It gave Mooney vertigo watching the horse swoop across the clouds and sky. You could feel the wind blowing behind the horse's ass and bending whole trees.

– This knight, Mitzi said.
– What about him?
– He's impulsive.
– Rash?
– Rash. And foolish. But it is only appearance.
– What do you mean?
– His decisions are actually swift, the result of experience.

Mooney thought that his short was impulsive, but he did have experience; he had learned things from Dennis. He was just being audacious.

– Does it pay off?
– Sometimes you have to act quickly.
– So it's a positive card.
– Upright.
– And it's upright, right?
– Yes. Only one problem, though. It can signify something horrible.
– How horrible?
– Death.
– When it's upright?
– Right.
– And it is upright?
– I said it was upright.
– Death for who?
– For you. You cut the deck.
– I don't think I did the last time.
– I saw you. But don't worry. It needs to be in the proximity of other cards of fatality.

The phone rang and she answered it. She listened to the other person on the line for what seemed to be a long time. Mooney could hear sobbing. He checked his wristwatch and wondered if this interjection would be deducted from his time. Mitzi continued listening and then spoke into the receiver:

– Don't do anything today. Stay at home and stay away from gambling.

She hung up the phone and melded another card. The session was almost up and her next appointment was already knocking at the door.

– Just a second.

She got up and went to the door, leading a woman into her den to wait for him to finish. He couldn't get a look at her, as she wore huge sunglasses and a hat. They spent a while together in the den. Again he wondered if that time was being deducted from his session.

The last card was The Wheel of Chance. She smiled.

– What's so funny?

– Nothing. This is a good card.

– It's reversed.

– Thank God.

– Why?

– If it had come out upright, it means that destiny is waiting for you and it is beyond your control.

The telephone rang again. She held the receiver and listened patiently.

– I told you no casino today.

She hung up and looked at the cards on the table, getting back into her role.

– Where was I?

– Destiny is waiting for me.

– That's right.

– But the card is reversed, right?

– So it is. Which means your luck is about to change. It means abundance. I see great abundance for you.

– I have my answer.

– What?

– Nothing.

He had his answer, which is what he had come for. He sat at the card table staring benumbed at the Wheel of Chance. He sensed that Mitzi was growing impatient, drumming her fingers on the edge of the card table, so he extricated his legs from under it and stood up.

– I think it's been very useful for me, he said.

– I hope it has.

He moved towards the front door.

– Aren't you forgetting something? she said.

– No, that's all I wanted to know.

He took another step towards the door, first trying to get a peek at the woman waiting in the den, but was unable to see her face, as she was tucked into a corner by the window.

– Aren't you forgetting something?

– Oh, thanks, he said. Thanks a lot.

– You forgot to pay me.

– Oh, sorry, sorry.

He fumbled for bills in his wallet and laid them out on top of the cards, which apparently was a no-no.

– Don't put money on the cards.

– Sorry.

She snatched up the bills, opened her purse on the floor and placed them inside.

– Can I ask you must one more question?

– I have another visitor.

– It won't take long.

– Go ahead.

– Do you communicate with the dead?

– Sometimes.

– Can I ask you a favour?

– What?

– If you see my father, don't tell him you saw me.

He left Mitzi's feeling reassured about what had been worrying him before he went in. He would keep his short. The market would have to plunge again. Economists were talking about a double-dip recession. And his luck was about to change.

The markets slumped the next day. All of a sudden he was only down about $900,000 and it looked as if Mitzi was right. There was another neat little crunch the day after that and he was only down $800,000 by closing bell. He phoned Mitzi to thank her and decided he'd call Dennis and offer to come down to the foundation to work. But Meaghan was sick so he took her to the vet instead. On the third day the market fell again, and he was back up to a million.

He closed his position, having recouped about two-thirds of his losses. Then he decided he would make one final bet. He geared up on another short near the close of the market on a Friday.

The following week was the shits, beginning with the rebound later on Monday, which was impressive: 150 ticks. Tuesday was worse and by Wednesday he was down to the $300,000 he had when he went to Mitzi's. He cancelled yet another arrangement to see Dennis at his foundation and stayed closed to the TV for the next ten days. Only once did he drive Suddy to the casino.

He watched the final massacre at home on TV that July, a tremendous rally that wiped him out completely.

When it was over he stood up, his guts roiling, and shut off the TV. As the juice to the TV wound down with a whine, he felt as if he was going to fall over. His brain raced to find a thought to latch onto and his hand felt out for something to clutch. He grabbed a fistful of air. The miracles were over.

The world tottered. He had to get out of the apartment. He hooked up Meaghan to her leash and went out for a walk to get chips, a walk that lasted an hour and a half, right across the city to the north end. It was a hot, dry day and the sun flamed straight down. He thought he would get sunstroke and die before he got there. Meaghan's tongue was hanging out and she was breathing rapidly to cool herself.

They gave him the chips and he thought he could almost count each one, so miserly had they been with the order. Fuck this, he said, and ordered another and had them double bag it. One of the chip-makers looked at his workmate, lifted his chin, tapped himself on the temple to indicate that Mooney was mental. Mooney felt rage boil up from his gut, but he kept his cool.

After dousing the chips with vinegar he thought he should have ordered gravy instead.

He felt miserable, and when he paid for the chips he thought that the money in his wallet was all he had left in the world. His fingers moist with vinegar and oil, he pinched the bills, as if by magic he could make them double or triple their worth. But in

the end he just handed them over to the cashier. He had no idea
how he would pay his rent at the end of the month, until he realized he could sell the Rez Rocket, but it was so scratched and
dented from vandals that he didn't know how much he would get
for it. And besides, how would he be able to pick up Suddy?

He left the restaurant with his double-bagged fries and dog
and walked on the hot evening payment towards the south end,
first past the shithole hotels, one of which his father had owned,
then into the downtown, seeking the shady side of the streets.
The chips tasted like crap because they had mixed the cold ones
from the first order with the hot ones from the second order. He
walked for several hours, dizzy with heat and fatigue and ended
up at his mother's house, almost collapsing on her stoop.

– Don't bring the dog into the house if she's having her
period.

– She's not having her period. I think she's menopausal.

– I went through that. Twice. Dr. Bernstein said it was pure
affliction.

– I think it's different in dogs.

– She looks terrible.

– She's thirsty.

– Poor dog. That's the way I felt. Worse.

– I'm going to stay over for a few days.

There was no way he could go back to his apartment. It had
been contaminated with financial news.

That night he couldn't sleep and wondered whether he would
ever sleep again. The anxiety was not unlike the beginning of
his nervous breakdown after Naomi left him, which also began
with insomnia. First came the tossing and turning phase, and
just as he settled into one spot on the sheets, he reminded himself that he wouldn't be able to fall asleep like that and changed
position. He then recognized the phase when you don't know if
you are asleep or awake, when all thoughts coagulate into a hard
ball that bounces off your forehead a thousand times before they
form an actual word, which is not a word with any meaning,
but more like a rocket you board to travel round and round in a
frantic loop.

In the loop he could recognize computer screens, tallies, cash-
money flushed down toilets, Naomi being stern. In the loop he

promised Dennis he would help with the Museum. And how he didn't help. He was always arriving just when Dennis was out and his foundation closed. Round and round in the loop.

His teeth were chattering when he woke up, and he was drenched in sweat, especially under the chin. He tried to calm himself, but the panic just pressed on his sternum.

He got out of bed and went to the kitchen, a haven in essence, having actually wanted to wake up his mother, ask her something, like why she didn't stab him in his crib when he was a baby. He boiled water, not knowing if it would be for tea or to use to scald himself back to reality. The hiss of the kettle was numbing, at last.

The dog and his mother both woke up and wandered into the unlit kitchen, both knowing something was wrong with him. The dog rested her snout in solidarity on his thigh and let all the air out of her lungs. His mother turned off the kettle and sat down with him.

– You're sick.
– I'm not sick. Not that way.
– What are you sick with?
– I'm not sick that way.
– How can I help you? What can I do for you?
– Help me.
– How? How can I help you?
– Help me with my head.
– How can I help you?
– With my head.

She grew despondent and changed tack. Tragedy is not just failure, it is specifically failure in front of your mother. Like Oedipus: if his mother hadn't been around, it wouldn't have been tragedy.

– What can I make for you? Do you want some fried matzo.
– No.
– Can I make you a hard-boiled egg?

She drew out a pot from the cupboard and started boiling an egg. He watched her standing by the stove. Soon the lid shook and danced.

– Your father had problems, too. He faced them head on.
– But he made money, had a family. He succeeded.

– He always told me his problems. Then the solutions came.

– I lost money, Ma.

– How much?

– A million and a half dollars. In three months. Just like that. *Asch in porach.*

– I lost a lot more than that.

– A million five.

– I lost a lot more than that when your father died.

– A million five!

– It wasn't going to last forever.

– I've got to latch onto something in my life. I'm running out of time. Help me.

– How?

– With my head. With my life.

– I want to see you settled. I'm here for you. This is your house. What do you want with your egg? I'm here for you.

– *Asch in porach.*

– Nothing's *asch in porach.* When you're dead, then it's *asch in porach.*

For a moment he wondered if this is what he really wanted, to have his mother to himself. Or have her so that Dave could not have her.

Did he just think that?

And now that he had her, is that what he wanted? In any case, he would have to move back in with her.

– Don't tell Dave.

– Dave knows. I know. The whole city knows.

– Christ. How could he know?

– He's known for weeks you've been losing money.

– Christ.

– But he's grateful to you. He says since you introduced him to Dennis and saved his equity, he'll give you a job.

– Christ.

– Take it.

– He hates me.

– He doesn't hate you. Take the job.

– I can't work for Dave. He hates me.

– He doesn't hate you. Take the job, give me some peace.

He knew just where Dave could shove his job. But he had to get his life in order. He had to latch onto something, and settle things with Naomi, because that was a bad situation. He had to end that relationship. All those conflicts in the loop had to be resolved.

■ ■ ■

The next morning Naomi phoned him on his cell, which his mother answered.

– Oh, it's you, she said, her mouth frosted. I'll get him.

He went for a walk in the park with Naomi and Meaghan. Naomi was wearing sunglasses and a sundress. She asked him why he hadn't called her in months, why he had never returned her calls. He told her he had lost all his money and hadn't seen anyone, except Suddy.

– I know.

– How do you know?

– The whole city knows.

She didn't care, she said. She just wanted to help him.

– I have some money I can loan you.

– It's not money I want from you. I can't do this, anymore. I can't share you.

– I know. You told me that.

– Especially now that I have no money left.

– I don't care about your being broke.

– You did before.

– I cared that I was broke.

– I can't give you what he can.

– I don't need you too, do I?

– You don't understand. I can't compete with him.

– Why bother?

– Listen, Naomi: I have to break up with you. I am breaking up with you. This is crazy. You're never going to leave him.

– Can't.

– Don't you understand? I'm breaking up with you.

– Can't. We're not a couple. We just see each other.

This stymied him.

– You think I'm selfish, she said.

– A bit.

– It's true. I am selfish. It's crazy, I think about you when you're not around.

– So do I, but I can't do this anymore. I have to get my life in order. Latch onto something.

– Mooney, you'll never get your life in order. But you're terrific. You've got a big heart.

– I'm turning into Suddy.

– What?

– Look, Naomi, we have to break up. You're just seeing me out of guilt for leaving me. And that just confirms your worst feelings about yourself. I'm letting you go.

– Can't. It's not a unilateral thing.

– Yes, it is.

– What if I say no?

– It won't do you any good. The truth is I love somebody else. Now that was a big, fat spontaneous lie. Why the fuck did he say that? And Naomi burst out laughing. So did Mooney.

– Who?

– I can't tell you that.

– Do I know her?

– No. Look, you're wasting real affection on the wrong person. I was always wrong for you. Your mother was right. Eventually they all are.

– My mother was a snob and a bitch.

– But that didn't mean she couldn't be right.

– Stay away from me. I have to accept my limitations.

– I do.

– So why do you want to see me, I don't know why. I guess in marriage when the sex goes.

– It hasn't gone.

– I didn't need to know that.

– Now you do.

– Maybe he neglects you in other ways.

– He's always there for me. What do you care anyways? You're in love with somebody else.

– I still care for you.

– You mean you can still hurt me.

– I don't want to hurt you.

– Then you love me.

– Of course I love you. I've always loved you.

– But now you love somebody else.

– That's right. Why should I feel guilty about this? You should devote yourself to Larry Brickman, body and soul. He's a prick, but he's your prick. Your words.

– So you've had your revenge.

– It wasn't about revenge.

– Bullshit.

– Life can resemble the tackiest soap opera.

– I suppose all you need is for me to say I'm carrying your baby.

This broke him up. Then he panicked.

– Are you?

– No.

– Christ.

– Just wanted to see how you'd react.

– How could you say I was out for revenge?

– That's what this was about, wasn't it? You're following me that day.

– What?

– Why did you follow me from work that day? Why did you do this to me?

– Not for revenge. I wanted you back.

– Oh no. You liked the competition.

– No, I didn't.

– You liked the conflict. Always have, Mooney.

– That's not why I went after you.

– You men just love to have a woman to fight over. So that you can knock each other down.

– Don't make this into a feminist issue.

– Do you really love somebody else? I can tell when you're lying.

– I do.

– Who?

– It's nobody you know. I'm in love with her. She's not like you.

– In what way.

– Well, she's not thin.

– I knew it.

– And she lets me make love to her from on top. She looks at me when we make love.

– We went past that phase when we were kids.

They walked on ahead, confused. He listened to the great voice of the empty park. And to the great lie he had told Naomi.

– You know, when I had money, last year, the million five, people treated me differently.

– Because people like rich people.

– I thought people hated the rich.

– You finally made people feel comfortable around you. Poor people don't make people feel comfortable.

– But I'm poor again.

– Maybe you'll be rich again. It's a financial world now. Fortunes made and lost in an instant.

– In my case, lost.

– Why are you giving up, you were doing great.

– Not now I'm not.

– You yo-yo, Mooney, that's your problem. You were hot for me, now you're in love with somebody else.

– I don't want to yo-yo anymore. I want things settled. I wanted you, but that's out.

– You had me. You could still have. But just two days a week.

– No way.

They reached the pavilion and the promise of coffee. But there might be people they knew there, so they turned around and walked back. Naomi was starting to cry.

She took her sunglasses off to wipe her eyes and dropped them on the grass. Her eyes were moist and swollen. Mooney picked the glasses up and felt it was like holding two big tears.

– It's getting hotter, she said.

– Hnnh.

– So do you love me or what?

– I can't see you anymore, Naomi. I can't. I have to get on with my life.

■ ■ ■

Suddy, Sammy and Oz were outside his mother's house, hammering on the screen door. His mother let them in and they went downstairs to the rec room, where his father once kept his stamps and coins. They sat in big leather chairs by the Hawaiian bar, where a new miracle unfolded, a miracle that only the seriously fucked-up can appreciate.

 – We thought we should stake you, Sammy said.
 – We heard Dave wants to give you a job.
 – He's a scumbag, said Sammy.
 – He's offered me a job.
 – The money was my idea, said Suddy. I said to cut you a cheque.
 – We pooled fifty thou for you.
 – Dennis chipped in, too.
 – It was Suddy's idea, said Oz.
 – I said that, said Suddy.
 – I heard.
 – Did you go see Mitzi? asked Suddy.
 – She's good, said Mooney.
 – Dennis says hello.
 – Dennis said he was afraid to come to the house, said Suddy. Afraid of your mother.
 – So am I, said Sammy.
 – Suddy's the one who should be afraid. She can't stand Suddy.
 – That's bull. She's really a good person, your mother. And your father was a good person. A *shtik* gold, said Suddy. A human person. Does your mother have something against me?
 – Nah.
 – He was a good person, your father. A human person. We had good times in this room. After a bonspiel, he'd invite the whole team over for drinks. He let the liquor flow.
 – You don't drink liquor, Suddy.
 – I had a beer or two here.
 – I can't accept this.
 – Take it, Mooney.
 – I think I've had enough.
 – You can't give up, said Sammy.

– You're no quitter, said Oz.

– You're no quitter, said Sammy.

– I'm fucked, said Mooney. Royally fucked.

– Not true. You're unfuckable, said Suddy.

That just about murdered Oz and Sammy.

– Suddy!

– I meant it in a good way.

– How can you mean that in a good way?

– I mean Mooney can't be fucked. You made a comeback. And the syndicate was your idea.

– It was Dennis's.

– No, you thought of it. You brought the first money to the table. Dennis executed your idea.

– I'm fucked now, Suddy.

– No, you're unfuckable.

– You mean unsinkable.

– That's what I meant. Unfuckable. Unsinkable. You know what I mean. I meant it in a good way. Words aren't only for description.

– Dennis says you should come down to the foundation. See his operation. I still don't have a clue what he's doing, but he's busy. Things are going good, he says. Maybe he'll hire you.

– That'd be volunteer work. I need to latch onto something. I wanted to see Dennis's thing, but just haven't got around to it. Do you guys want anything to drink?

– I want to. Haven't got around to it. Do you guys want anything to drink?

– I'll have some Danish.

– He said 'to drink'.

■ ■ ■

The fifty thou lasted until October. Wild fluctuations and indecision vacuumed up his whole *bindl*.

The heart can clench like a fist, Mooney found out. And now he would have to go work for Dave.

12

Why didn't he tell him to shove his salary you know where? Because he was a retard, that's why. But still, it was regular money. And yet, sometimes he almost broke down and wept.

He was working for Dave and Dave's friends now, who were being advised by Dennis. It was Dave's nth successful business venture.

He regretted just opening his eyes in the morning since it meant the long dreaded day ahead at the office, where once he was making big money, eating Chinese food with Suddy and playing with the printer.

His mother was happy that he was going to work in the morning, working under Dave. Except for walking the dog in the park after work, he stayed home in the evening playing gin rummy with her. He could tell by the way she lay down her melds that she was in a better mood. A mother's disappointment in her son is a terrible thing, and it was good to see her living the fiction that he was under Dave's protection. She made him fried matzo every day, because that was really the only thing that didn't upset his stomach.

She kissed him goodbye before he went to work.

– Christ, he said, softly.

Then he was off.

Mooney dreaded going up the elevator too. But the worst part was loading the photocopier, which is what Suddy used to do. God how they ran through paper. He almost cried when there was no paper left to stock and he had to go the stationery store and buy more, then lug it back. Dave called Mooney into his private office. Of course, Dave had to have a private office. How many private offices could someone have? With the Eisenteethers no one had a private office. Dennis had called it primitive communism.

– Mooney, could you bring me copies of that report? said Dave. The one you downloaded yesterday.

– I was just about to go for lunch.

– We need it.

– I have to print it up.

– So print it up.

– I'm entitled to my lunch break.

– You can have it later. The crowds are smaller.

– I'm hungry now.

– Stop fucking around. This is important.

– I'm entitled to my lunch break. If there was a union —

– There's no union here.

– I could join one.

– Stop fucking around.

– I'm not fucking around. I'm not your gopher. I'll get it after lunch.

– Just get the fucking report printed up. We have a meeting. And you are our gopher.

– Why are you doing this?

– What?

– Why are you doing this to me?

Mooney was white with humiliation. Dave was indignant, with having always helped him and getting this backtalk as thanks. Like waiting for a sneeze to build up, they were both paralyzed, and for the longest time.

– Let's see if the fucker is out of paper.

Dave stormed out of his office and went over to the printer, Mooney following. He positioned himself in front of the printer and ripped out the paper tray. Empty. I didn't even want him around, thought Dave. It was his mother's doing, the Queen of the Intershtippers. He had to put a stop to listening to her, because even if he did, she still didn't give a shit about him. But that was only the paranoia talking. She probably did give a shit. Possibly did. He was shackled to the stupidest family on earth, in spite of how clever he was, how ruthless in business, with acumen galore.

He wanted to scream, Enough! Enough! This has gone on far

too long! Time to cut Mooney from his moorings. Cain slew Abel alright, but not with violence, but by driving him crazy. He was Abel! Mooney was Cain. He was Abel!

    – See, it's out of paper, said Mooney.

    – I can see that.

    – So, I told you.

    – So why are you putting on this act?

    – It's not an act.

    – This trade union rights shit?

    – I'm entitled to my lunch break.

    – Do you want to go back on welfare?

    – Of course not.

    – So just print up the report.

    – It's out of paper. Can't you see?

    – So load the paper.

    – There is no paper.

    – What's this?

    – You load it.

    – Alright.

    – You're not doing it right, Dave.

    – I am so. Fuck you, Mooney.

    – You're going to break the tray.

    – It's my tray.

    – Suddy could load the paper better than that.

    – Suddy's not here. Get out of my way.

    – Get a grip, Dave.

    – Don't tell me to get a grip. I'll load the paper myself. Go for lunch. Take an hour. Take two hours. Go. Get the fuck out of here.

Mooney's face burned. His throat was tight. The rage built up in him. And that was just day one.

His two afternoons a week with Naomi were gone, and now he missed them. He certainly buggered that up, but it was a stupid situation. Dennis was right about exes. They're like dating the dead. And working for Dave was undermining his confidence. The salary wasn't bad, and he could move out with the money he made, but he was just too depressed to go apartment hunting.

One evening in the fall, more than a year after the collapse of Lehman Brothers, after the leaves began to turn colour, stiffen and drift to the ground, and the temperatures began to chill, winter settling in, Dave invited Mooney to an exhibition hockey game of old-timers, as their mother insisted he get Mooney out of the house.

The aurora borealis burned red and green in the sky that night. Below, in the arena parking lot, Mooney refused to get out of the car.

– Are you getting out of the car or what?

– No, they're crappy teams, he said. Real crap. Bound to be a shitty game.

– Still, it's free for you, Dave said.

– A *shnorrer* invite.

– Better than nothing.

– Really shitty teams.

– It'll be fun.

– It's a crappy exhibition game.

– All exhibition games are crappy. So what?

– Ma asked you to take me, didn't she?

– So what if she did?

– I knew it. Does she know what a bunch of crap the teams are?

– She knows fuck-all about hockey.

– She asked you to give me the job, too?

– She didn't ask me.

– Yes, she did.

– No, she told me. She ordered me.

– I knew it.

They sat in Dave's car. Just sat there, the motor running to keep the heat on. Mooney thought about going in if only to throw himself under the Zamboni, but then decided it would be best if Dave just drove him home.

– Come on, get out of the car. The faceoff is in ten minutes.

– If the players were any good, they'd still be playing.

– When's the last time you saw a real hockey game? Not on TV?

– I can't remember. I don't even like hockey that much.

– You love hockey.

– Only when millionaires play.

– These guys were millionaires.

– But now they're so old they can't see the puck.
– No need to shout.
– Sorry.
– So what's the difference if the teams are crappy? You're so fucking sullen all the time.
– I lost a million and a half dollars just a few months ago.
– You should have got out when Dennis told you to.
– I know. I know.
– You deserve to suffer. A million five.
– I know.

Mooney slouched, his cheek against the car window, looking like someone had taken the air out of him. Dave continued to gloat.

– You could have got out after losing two hundred thousand or even half a million. You'd still have money now. A lot of money. I mean, for you.
– I know.
– You know.
– I don't need the sarcasm.
– What else works with you?
– I need you to stake me again.
– Here we go again. Just draw your salary. It's not that bad.
– It's humiliating.
– Just accept your limitations, and get on with your life.
– I paid you back, didn't I?
– Don't shout.
– Didn't I?
– Yes, you did.
– Now who's shouting?
– You.
– Get out of the car.
– No.
– Get out of the car! We're going in.
– I'm not going in.
– Get the fuck out of the car.

Dave leaned across Mooney's chest and worked the door handle.

– Get out of the car, he breathed.

Dave got out and went around the other side to open the door.

Mooney hit the door switch. Dave got out his key and activated the doors. The electronics whirred and Mooney's door was unlocked. Mooney hit the button and locked them again. Dave counteracted. Mooney hit the button again, and Dave counteracted again and quickly yanked on the door handle and pulled Mooney out by the collar, which ripped. Mooney spilled out on to the pavement and landed on his knee, before he even realized he was no longer sitting on the hot car seat. His knee began to swell instantly.

– What the fuck!

– When I say get out of the car, I mean get out of the car.

Mooney hefted himself up and took a good swing at Dave, clipping him across the ear. It was like a radio went on full blast in Dave's head.

– I'll pound you out.

Dave hadn't heard that expression since high school and screamed. But then Mooney hit him again and he went down. As he did Mooney thumped him on the back with his elbow, trying to flatten him like a big crease in a rug that keeps bulging.

– Stay down.

– I'm down. Just get a hold on yourself.

– You treat me like such a piece of shit at work.

– That's what work is.

– I'm not used to being treated like shit. I never treated my workers like that.

– And how many times did you go broke?

– Stay down.

– I'm down.

– You don't have to treat me like that.

– You should be more cooperative. Do as you're told sometimes. That's your problem. You can't take orders.

– I do my work.

– With a grudge.

– Life hasn't been easy for me.

– No, that's your problem: it's always been easy for you. You think every day is your birthday. Everybody owes you. Just cause you smile you think everybody owes you. Just get your shit together. Give us all a break. Give Ma a break.

– I'm the victim here.

– You wish.

– I'm just asking to be treated with more respect at work.

– Join a union. You like unions.

– Just fire me.

– Can't. Ma. Besides, what would you do?

– Drive cab.

– Right. Ma's going to have to tell people you're driving a cab.

– Why not?

– Not going to happen. You're not driving cab. You're going to continue coming to work. And try not to fuck things up. You're such a fuckup! I'll pay you just to stop fucking things up.

Dave finally got up because Mooney let him, but as thanks he kicked Mooney in his swollen knee. The pain shot up to his brain and out the crown of his head.

– You're such a prick, Mooney said, grabbing his knee. I could have kneed you in the face just now.

Dave just kicked him in the knee again. Mooney felt the sole of Dave's shoe scrape the knuckles on the hand that was massaging his knee.

He backhanded Dave with his other hand and knocked him down. There was an ugly crunch as Dave hit the pavement again. He would have a sore tailbone tomorrow.

What's his name, Clara Mass's grandson, the one Dave called Yahweh, saw the whole thing and went over to break up the fight. He first picked up Dave and then held Mooney back when he tried to punch him, during which time Dave got in a couple of feeble punches. Mooney flailed right and left in Yahweh's grip. They were both heaving. Their lungs burned.

– Calm down, you guys.

– Let go of me, said Mooney.

– I will. But just stay calm.

– Alright. I'm calm.

– Are you calm?

– I'm calm.

The kid released his grip a bit and Mooney went to grab him by his hockey jacket, but the material was as slippery as fish and his hand slid until it got a hold of his *tsitsis*. He yanked hard and he could feel the whole tallis start to slip out.

– Let go of my tallis!

– Let go of me.

Clara Mass's grandson pulled back but Mooney hung onto his *tsitsis* and soon he had dragged Mooney half way across the parking lot over the icy patches, and only came to a stop when Mooney had succeeded in pulling the entire tallis out through his jacket hem. It was like one of those operations in which they remove the gall bladder through the navel. The kid's mouth dropped when he saw the fringes of the other side of his tallis appear with Mooney now holding the entire prayer shawl in his hand.

The tallis coming out of the jacket just broke Dave up. At first the laughter was that of someone being strangled, but then he let rip.

– Sorry, said Mooney, looking at the bunched up tallis in his hand.

– Fuck sorry.

– I'll pay you for it.

– That's a three-hundred-dollar tallis.

– You were rooked. It's acrylic. You overpaid.

– It's not acrylic. It's pure silk. It's from Israel.

– It's not silk.

– Give it here.

The kid inspected the tallis for damage and then took off his hockey jacket and put on the tallis, saying the prayer for putting on the tallis. Dave cracked up.

– They have a prayer for everything.

– The commandment of fringes, said Mooney.

– They're going to destroy the Jewish community, these people, said Dave.

– They are the Jewish community, Dave.

– He's going to miss the faceoff.

Now Mooney started to laugh.

– Everything is a joke with you people. I was only trying to help you guys. Christ, you're sick. Both of you.

– You're a *pisher*, said Dave. Jews never went around dressed like that before.

– Yes, we did.

– In the seventeenth century.

– Let him pray.

– And you're a scumbag. I know you. Dave Kaufman, isn't it?

– Just finish the *brochah*, put your tallis on and fuck off.

– You should *leg tefillin* with me.

– Are you carrying extra *tefillin*? asked Mooney.
I have some in my car.

Dave got hysterical, until the pain tightened in his spine like a self-tapping screw, and he had to sit down on the pavement. Mooney was also in stitches.

– I'm not, we're not, *legging tefillin*, said Dave.

– When's the last time you *legt tefillin*? the kid asked him.

– We're not putting on *tefillin*.

– When was it?

– Thirteen. The day after my bar mitzvah. Once and that was it. I lost my *tefillin* bag.

– So did I, said Mooney.

– In a poker game.

– Look, why don't we *leg tefillin* together, the kid said. You'll see. Whatever's eating you guys, well, you'll get over it.

– We're not putting on *tefillin*, said Dave.

– What kind of Jew are you?

– One with three fucking forests in the Negev.

– But who won't *leg tefillin*?

– My father knew the *siddur* off by heart and never walked around with his *tsitis* hanging out.

– The eyes of God are upon you.

– How many eyes does God have?

– What?

– You said the eyes of God are upon us. How many eyes does He have?

– Two.

– How do you know that?

– It's a metaphor.

– So God is a metaphor?

– No. He's God.

– Just fuck off. They're dropping the puck.

They both got hysterical again. The kid put on his hockey jacket over his tallis and hurried off to the arena.

– Scumbag!

   – *Pisherle!*

Mooney hobbled over to Dave.

   – Can you walk? Mooney asked him.

   – I buggered up my back. No: you buggered up my back. You'll have to take me to my masseuse.

Mooney carried him piggyback to the car and stuffed him into the backseat.

   – Drive me to my masseuse.

   – I want to go home, Dave. I want to die.

   – Drop me off at my masseuse first. Then you can go home and die.

   – Where does she live?

   – Just drive. You're depressed again.

   – I'm not depressed. I'm suicidal.

   – Do you want to have sex?

   – Not with you.

   – I'm trying to help.

   – Believe me, that wouldn't help.

   – I meant I could call Charlotte, my masseuse.

   – Your dominatrix?

   – That too.

   – I'm not going to have sex with your prostitute.

   – She's my masseuse, too.

   – So?

   – So why not?

   – It's sick.

   – She won't mind. I won't mind.

   – I would. Besides, I only think I can have sex with one woman.

   – Naomi?

   – Yeah.

   – Bullshit.

   – I swear to the Jewish torah.

   – Is there any other kind of torah?

   – I'm miserable without her.

   – Have you been seeing her?

   – I'm going to vigorously deny it.

   – Don't bother.

   – For a year.

– On the sly?

– On the sly.

– The whole city knows, Mooney. I told you not to see her. What she saw in you, I don't know. Why she married you, that will never cease to mystify me.

– Hey, I gave her some good years.

– She could have had anybody. Fuck, I liked her.

– She was too beautiful.

– Except she doesn't have a rear end. Ma was right. You can't trust a woman without a rear end.

– Do you hate women, Dave?

– Frankly, I have a bit of a grudge against them; but I don't hate them. Everything is so extreme with you.

– I haven't talked to her for three months. And I broke it off.

– Why?

– Embarrassment.

– Hers or yours?

– Mine. Of how I buggered it all up.

– That's not why.

– How would you know?

– I don't believe it.

– Well, if you want to know. I did. I broke it off, because she wouldn't commit. She prefers Larry. She wanted to keep seeing me. Two days a week. Afternoons.

– So, it's over.

– It's over.

– So let me drive you to Charlotte's. I need her to fix my back anyway. She's certified.

– I have to meet this woman.

– Then let's go. Now.

– I don't think I could get an erection with your Charlotte.

– She can give any man an erection. Just like that. She knows men.

– Is she one?

– Fuck you. She grew up with three older brothers. She's studied psychology. At Purdue.

– I don't think seeing her would help.

– It's what I do when I get depressed.

They drove over to Charlotte's split-level in the south end. The

house used to belong to the Birnbaums before they lost the cater-
ing business. Dave had a key and let himself in. The house was
dark and only the cat was slinking around at the edges of the living room, lurking at the baseboards.

    – I think she's sleeping. I'll wake her up. See if she's in the
mood.

    – I thought you said she was a prostitute.

    – Even prostitutes have to be in the mood.

    – I thought that was the point. That they didn't have to be in
the mood.

    – You know nothing about prostitutes.

    – I'll take that as a compliment.

    – It wasn't.

    – Don't wake her.

    – I'll just be a minute.

    – No. No. Don't wake her up.

    – Relax.

The house was sparsely furnished, but stylishly Sixties retro,
except for the bedroom, he would find. The cat kept circling the
living room along the baseboards. It was a fat wicked cat named
Juliette, he would find out. When Dave came out of the bedroom, fear rose in Mooney's throat.

    – She's up.

    – I told you not to wake her.

    – She's up already.

    – Christ.

    – It's all arranged. But she's got a little cold. You go first, Dave
said.

    – Well, I'm not going after you.

    – She showers in between.

    – It's not that.

    – Use protection.

    – Can't.

    – Can't?

    – I'd need a three-foot condom.

    – You're such an idiot. Just get in there.

    – I can't believe I'm going to do this. I've never been with a
prostitute before.

    – It's an acquired taste.

– Like sushi?

– Or wine. Or whiskey. Nobody like how they taste.

– Some people do.

– They say they do. But they don't. Stuff tastes like shit.

– So why do they drink?

– Because getting drunk is cool.

– I may be too old to acquire this taste.

– Just go in.

– Are you going to wait here?

– I'm not waiting in the car.

Charlotte was sitting up serenely in bed, under a throw, wearing a short quilted pyjama jacket. She looked as if she were in her late twenties and had just given birth, and now was waiting for the nurse to bring in the baby for feeding. She patted the bedspread beside her, making him feel like when you were in school and called to the blackboard.

He hesitated.

– Sit.

– I'm okay.

– I won't bite.

After settling down next to her on the bed he was almost horny in an unhorny kind of way. He noticed how hot and red her cheeks were, and how she narrowed her eyes to look at him. She was a lot plumper than he had imagined. Even her bottom lip was plump, as were her upper arms, even her toes, which poked up under the throw, the nails painted bubblegum pink.

He had to make a new estimate of her age, up by five years. She then removed the quilted top, one strap of her satin nightie slipping from a sturdy shoulder, exposing a plump tit with the reddest, tiniest nipple he had ever seen folded in.

He heard Dave put on music in the living room.

– You know, he said, I don't think I'll be able to have an erection.

– Why not?

– I'm depressed.

– Why?

– I lost a million and a half dollars a few months ago. Everything I had.

– How?

– In the stock market.

– I lost money too, she said.

– Sorry.

– That money won't be coming back. But your erection will. I promise.

She shifted buttocks and made him come around the other side of the bed and sit.

– So? she said.

– Is the meter running?

– What do you care? He's paying.

– Could we try not to mention him?

– Alright. I'll apply more tact.

– Thank you.

– So.

– So, do you really think I'll get an erection.

– You will. You Jewish guys are all over-libidinized.

– Strange word choice.

– By your mother's always telling you how great you are.

– True.

– True you're great?

– True they always tell us that.

– So what do you think would get you excited?

– I think talking? Mostly talking.

– That's what most of you want to do.

– I mean talking dirty.

– Is there any other kind?

– Can you pretend to be someone and tell me how —

– Sure. I can do that.

– I haven't finished telling you.

– I know what you're going to ask. Who do you want me to be?

– A woman I know.

– Sure, as long as it's a woman. Does this woman have a name?

– Yes.

– What is it?

– I'll whisper it. Later. When we get going.

– Do you want any props?

– No. Just the pretending. Just your voice.

– You make it easy, she said.

– Aren't I supposed to say that?

– You could.

– I mean you don't make me feel like a fool. Even if I am one.

– Well you're not.

– I'm not?

– Maybe a bit of a fool. One million five hundred thousand dollars. That's a lot of money.

– In three months. I had made it in less than one year. Almost a three thousand percent profit.

– How did you make so much money?

– Shorting the financials on margin.

– Three thousand percent?

– Three thousand percent.

– And you lost it all back?

– A million five.

The moon dipped below an oak limb.

– Will Dave need one bill or two? she asked.

– I don't know.

– Oh, sorry.

– Tactless.

– Tactless.

She got up, went to her desk and printed up an invoice, slipped it under the night table ashtray filled halfway with ash and butts, and bounced herself back onto the bed and under the throw. The gesture made him revise his estimate of her age back down.

He made his way timidly under the throw. Charlotte uttered little moans as she snuggled him close to her. She must have been a child of heartbreaking warmth, before toughening up. She spread her legs.

– Watch the knee.

– Sorry.

Adjustments were made to legs and hips and elbows.

– Can you give me my lines? she breathed in his ear.

An hour later they stopped, exhausted, her voice hoarse, his knee on fire. She had said her lines with exceptional zeal, and over and over.

– Stop. Stop. I need air, she said. And a cigarette.

She got out of bed and opened the window to a blast of frost.

The bill fluttered under the ashtray. She sneezed seven times in a row. Mooney snuggled deeper under the covers.

– I thought you had a cold.

– I like colds.

– Could you close the window?

This done, she got back under the covers.

– That was nothing short of miraculous, Mooney said. I didn't expect that.

– What did you expect would happen?

– I don't know.

– Nobody expects the expected to actually occur.

She lit up. Her smoking reminded him of Naomi. Cigarette after cigarette.

– Did you go to university?

– Purdue. And McGill for graduate school.

– You could be a professor.

– They pay shit now. If you're starting. There's nothing more proletarianized than the teaching profession.

– Really?

– I wouldn't get out of bed in the morning for what they pay.

It was Dave's turn now, so he left the room. They stared at each other as he came out and Dave went in, stooped over like an old man looking for snails.

– He's a nice guy, your brother, said Charlotte to Dave.

– He hates me.

– No he doesn't.

– We don't get along.

– How come?

– I don't know. He was a wonderful kid, my brother. We were close when we were young. Things didn't work out for him after Dad died. And he had the brains, you know; he had the brains. But Cain slew Abel.

– Who's Cain and who's Abel?

– He's Cain. Killing me with his idiocy. I've helped him out. I've bailed him out so many times. And now he resents me. My success. I wish sometimes I hadn't been so lucky. Sometimes I think it would be better if we all had the same. Even-Steven.

– The dream of a rich man.

– Maybe it's guilt. But I think even I would be happier. Like when we were kids.

– Do you want to go back to those days?

– I don't know.

– Don't you?

– Too much resentment has built up. You know, we had a terrible fight before coming here. A physical fight. First time. My first fight ever actually. That's why my back is buggered. Can you do something about it?

– What was the fight about what?

– About an exhibition game.

– I'm disappointed in you. Family has to stick together.

Dave came out a while later, no longer stooping, but looking sad and guilty. He wanted to get home.

Something orgiastic had taken place, but they both looked sad. He saw that Dave was in love with Charlotte, and yet, in spite of himself, or because of himself, he would never have her.

– We'd better go, or else plug in the car.

– I love that girl, Dave said, as he closed the front door. My back feels great.

– I'm not going back to work, Dave.

– Do what the fuck you want.

But Dave didn't say this in a bad way. His voice was exhausted and understanding, almost, but not, tender.

– What are you going to do?

– I don't know.

– Do you want some money? Try again?

– No. I'm out of the financial markets, that's for sure.

– You could've left in style. You made monkeys out of those guys.

– That was Dennis. I lost it all back. As Dad used to say: *Oisge-flikt und aheim geshikt.*

– You still have to do something.

– I know. Time's running out for me. Suddy says I can take a shift in his cab.

– That'd kill Ma.

– Maybe I could work for Dennis's Canadian Holocaust Foundation.

– The Jewish community would kill you. You don't fuck with the Holocaust.

– What then? Dave. Help me.

– Something that doesn't involve killing someone or getting yourself killed.

– I'm tired of failing, Dave.

– How can I help you?

– I'm tired of it.

– You're breaking my heart, Mooney.

– Sorry.

– Fuck sorry. You're killing me.

– I need some time.

– Take it then. Think things through. Take a month. A year. I'll back you.

– I just need time, Dave.

13

A few months later, the day Suddy died, Mooney woke earlier than usual, as he had left the drapes open, and the light came in white and easy. One could see it was a winter that would not go away ever.

The night before he dreamt that Larry Brickman was a huge snake that ate him. When he woke up he felt ashamed and knew he had done the right thing by not seeing Naomi again. That calmed him: odd that he had attained some peace by denying himself what he wanted.

Showered and dressed, he was ready to start his first day driving cab for Suddy. He waited quietly in the kitchen for Suddy's night-shift driver to come over and pick him up. He would then drop the kid off and continue for the day.

His decision to drive cab had depressed his mother. He prodded her to get out of bed and have breakfast with him on his first day. Meaghan had taken to sleeping in the big bed with her and sighed tremendously when he woke them.

– Ma.
– What?
– Come have breakfast with me.
– No.
– Why not?
– I'm ashamed.
– I'm driving a cab, not a rickshaw.
– Don't be flippant. I don't deserve it.
– It's a transitional thing. I just need to clear my head. Plan my next moves.
– It's not a transitional thing. Nothing's transitional with you.
– Everything's transitional with me.

– That's why you can't settle.

But Mooney was looking forward to driving cab. Gone were the frantic days: he was no longer anxious about sudden shifts in the financial markets or exponential losses that stopped his heart from beating for seconds at a time. All that forced bravado was over. The ambition had faded, promising dignity, and Naomi was gone too. The commonsensicalness of his new life calmed him and his head felt clear for the first time since his father died almost twenty years ago.

Of course he felt the shits that he had never helped Dennis with his museum, that he had broken a promise, but maybe now that he had regular hours and no anxiety, he would go down there and see what was happening. Maybe it was not too late to keep that promise.

After his last fare for the night he dropped the cab off early at Suddy's place. He found Suddy on the chesterfield, barefoot, with a big bowl of peanut shells on the carpet in front of him.

– I just ate a pound of peanuts, Suddy said. Do you want any?

– Nah.

– What are you doing back?

– I'm tired, Suddy. I don't think I can do this the rest of the night.

– This is the best time. After ten. Saturday night.

– I'm tired.

– I'll go.

– What are you bothering for, Suddy? You're rich now.

– I'm bored.

– You don't need to do this.

– I'm bored. I'll pick up a few fares. Don't worry about me.

– Call that other kid who drives for you.

– He's at a wedding. Actually, he's at his own wedding. I gave him the night off.

– Suddy, let's just go to the casino.

– I was there last night. And all afternoon. I'll drive you home and then go get a couple of fares. I'm feeling spry.

– It's a cold night.

– It'll snow tonight, you'll see.

Suddy dropped him off at his mother's and waved goodbye. It was the last time he saw him because Suddy's last fare was fatal.

He had driven up to a bungalow to pick up a fare and honked, then honked again. No one came out so he got out of the cab. The cold made him shiver.

He took mincing steps through the snow up the walk of people who obviously didn't know how to shovel snow. He banged on the front metal door and rung the bell. All of a sudden out came this woman barefoot, full blast, almost knocking him over the rail into a snowdrift as she pushed past him. She made a beeline to the cab and got in and locked her door. He descended the steps slowly after her.

– Hurry. Just drive.

Suddy looked at her in the rear-view mirror and saw her eye had been closed by an enormous black bruise. Her plump lower lip had been split raw. Hair too black not to be dyed, and a roll of fat over her belt, Suddy told himself she was a hooker.

– Take me to emergency, she said.
– Which one?
– Does it matter?
He drove.
– Can't you drive any faster?
– It's my cab.
– Aren't you too old to drive a cab?
– Almost.
– Christ.
– What happened to you, anyway?
– Bad night, she said.
– What happened?
– Are you blind?
– I wouldn't be driving a cab if I were blind.
– I wasn't being literal, she said.
– Who did this to you?
– Those guys in the house. They beat me up and raped me.
– In that order?
– Are you an idiot?

Suddy continued driving north to the hospital, not as cautiously as the icy conditions advised.

– And they didn't even pay me.

Suddy hit the brakes and the car swirled like a curling stone until it was on the other side of the road, now going south.

– Why did you turn around?
– To get your money.
– Are you fucking crazy?
– They had no right. Maybe we should call the police.
– Are you kidding me?
– Let's go back. Get your money.
– I'm not going back in there.
– I'll go. I'll get your money. How much do they owe you?
– One-fifty each. But they're not going to pay you. They'll kick the shit out of you.
– No, they won't. I'm going back there. Where do they live?
– Who?
– The rapists.
– At the place where you picked me up. Are you an idiot?
He drove like mad over ice and snow up to the house and parked the cab on a sick angle on a snow drift on the boulevard.
– Stay in the cab.
– You stay in the cab.
– I'm going to get your money.
– Forget the money. I don't want the money. I just want to go to emergency. My lip is killing me.
– Put some snow on it.
– Don't go in there.
He wasn't listening to her.
He got out and retraced his footprints in the snow all the way up the stairs and banged furiously on the front door. Two huge fuckers in underwear, drunk out of their minds, opened the door.
– What the fuck do you want?
– We didn't order a cab.
– You didn't pay her. Suddy shook with indignation.
– Who?
– The girl you had here.
– She didn't give us a bill.
The two drunks found this hilarious. One of them was boisterous, banging his fists against the wallpaper. The other was a bit more subdued, and you could talk to him.
– You should pay her what you owe her.
– For what?
– For her services.

– What services? We raped her.

– Yeah, we did all the work, said the wall-banger.

The house had been heated to sauna temperatures, and the TV was on. The wall-banger was on top of the chesterfield now, banging on a new wall, his feet slipping into the slots between the upholstered cushions. His aggressive banging made the whole house tremble.

– Just pay her.

– We're not going to pay her.

– Well, then, I'm taking your TV. And a pair of shoes she left.

– You can have her shoes, but you're not taking the TV. You couldn't even lift it.

– I could lift it. Where are the shoes?

Suddy walked into the living room and unplugged the flat screen. The sound petered out to a ping all of a sudden. The boisterous drunk on the chesterfield jumped off and landed in a crouch, like an action hero, his head bowed, lifting it slowly, rotating it, his eyebrows pulled down to his nostrils.

– Don't fucking move.

– I'm taking this, said Suddy.

– The fuck you are.

– Well, then pay her.

– We're not paying her. And plug the TV back in.

– I'm taking it.

– You can't even lift it.

– We'll see about that.

– We'll call the cops.

– Call the cops. But I'm taking the TV.

– You won't get out the door.

– We'll throw you through the window.

– Yeah, we'll throw you through the window. With the TV!

– It's double-glazed, said Suddy.

– That's your bad luck.

Suddy, his powerful chest puffed up with excitement, lifted up the flat screen and waddled with it towards the front door.

– Where are those shoes?

– Fuck the shoes!

The boisterous drunk pushed him and Suddy fell back on the chesterfield, the TV cartwheeling onto the carpet then falling screen-side down. The nutty guy grabbed Suddy's ankles and the other one grabbed the thick part of his arms, right under the armpits.

 – You're going through the window, the wall-banger said.

They threw him against the picture window and he made a sickening smack when he bounced off it and onto the broadloom, just missing the coffee table. Suddenly, Suddy felt he was in danger.

 – You're going through that window, the wall-banger said.

 – It's too thick, Suddy said, his hip killing him.

The two men were shouting something at each other, shaking their heads and giggling. Then they picked him up again the same way as before and heaved a lot harder. He bounced off the window and landed on the broadloom again. They picked him up a third time.

 – This mother's going through.

 – It's too thick.

 – This time he's going through.

 – Let's just throw him out the door. Into the snow.

 – He's going through the window. One last shot.

 – It's my window.

 – What makes it your window?

 – This is my house.

 – You're just renting. He's going through.

On the third try Suddy went through the window.

 – Finally, Suddy said.

He landed on the hard packed, windswept part of the snow. The glass had cut him and he lay bleeding out of his *gorgle*, dying quite quickly actually. His head was numb. The woman, who was still in Suddy's cab, called the police on her cell phone and ran out of the cab, into the stinging air, still in bare feet, her mouth opened in horror.

 – We're not paying you, bitch, one of the men shouted at her through the broken picture window.

 – You killed him!

 – We just threw him out the window.

 – Took three times.

 – We didn't kill him.

 – We're keeping the TV.

 – You killed him!

– Here's your shoes. Catch!

They each threw a shoe at her, which fell wide of the mark into snowdrifts on her right and left.

– Take care of Mooney, Suddy was saying.

– Who the fuck is Mooney? the wall-banger said, from behind the shattered glass.

To tell the truth, Suddy felt lazy, lying on the snow. Too lazy to get up, which was unethical in Suddy's books. And then he felt drowsy, which was not lazy, and therefore, not unethical. He didn't know if it was summer or winter. There was nothing in front of him but his own soul, which was rather kind, someone you could love, he thought.

It started snowing. Suddy knew it would snow that night. How fantastic it was to be right. So much depended on it. And it was exactly the kind of snowfall he had envisaged.

– Who the fuck is Mooney?

– Who gives a fuck? We threw him right through the window.

– On the third try.

– What does it matter? He went through, didn't he?

– We're going to have to put some cardboard on the window.

At first the snow was like sand, pecking at him like hens. Then the flakes got big and juicy. Police sirens sounded, and then, for Suddy, it was flat calm.

■ ■ ■

Suddy's burial and *shiva*, because of the autopsy, took place a week after his death. Since Candy was back in Palm Springs, Dave gave his house for the *shiva*, so a lot of Dave's friends and business associates had to attend, which made it a pretty big one, as *shivas* go, and because of Suddy's age it was a pretty tearless, almost relaxed affair, comparing. There were guys from the casino there, Suddy's buddies, guys with rugs among them, looking odd in their pointy yarmulkes.

Dave spared no expense, and there were huge bottles of rye and scotch at the bar. There were seven tables crammed with food.

They wanted to bury Suddy next to his brother Duddy, but they couldn't because someone else was buried next to Duddy, Harry Zukor's wife, all because Harry Zukor didn't have the foresight to buy a double plot. Mooney made sure that Suddy got an aisle, as he always remembered Suddy taking an aisle seat at synagogue so he could get out fast, and as often as possible, to have a smoke, especially when the rabbi started his speech.

Mooney thought it must have been the coldest day of the year. A windy morning on the plain blew into the cemetery. The tears rolled down his cheeks and into the corners of his mouth with a salty tang. Dave was bawling, too. Because of the cold it must have been the fastest burial ever, and suddenly Suddy was gone. Mrs. Kaufman stayed in the car with the heat on.

There was a young rabbi standing at the door, surrounded by rubber overboots. Small puddles of melted snow made Dave's marble vestibule floor slippery. He was holding a razor blade, slashing ties as the men filed in. An argument broke out between him and Sammy.

    — You're not cutting my tie; I just bought this tie.

    — You have to let me cut it.

    — Can't you just crease it?

    — Then you'll have to iron it.

    — I don't do the ironing.

    — I have to cut it.

    — Why?

    — As a sign of mourning.

    — I don't need a sign to show I'm mourning. I am mourning.

    — It's tradition.

    — Who says?

    — And where's your yarmulke?

    — I put it back at the cemetery. I put it back in the box. It wasn't mine. I don't steal yarmulkes.

    — It was a courtesy kippa. You could've kept it.

    — So why did they have the box out to collect them?

    — You don't have to put them back.

    — I thought you did when I saw the box.

The rabbi cut his tie with the razor blade at the second button.

    — You buggered the tie.

    — Take some of your speculation money and buy a new tie.

    — What's it your business?

The rabbi got hold of the next guy coming in and that ended the conversation. Sammy could have belted him one.

Mrs. Kaufman and her two sons sat alone in Dave's den, while the main core of the *shiva* murmured in the vast open-plan living-room–dining-room, balancing their plates of hot fish and drinks or pastry and tea cups, sitting on the edge of enormous sofa combos. Mooney was still pretty broken up, and Dave, too.

– Poor Suddy, Mrs. Kaufman said. I knew him when he lived on Manitoba Avenue. Him and his brother Duddy. With the shmark running down their noses. They didn't know how to wipe their own ass. I can't stay long, the dog is alone. Maybe you should call me a cab. Poor Suddy.

– I thought you couldn't stand Suddy, said Dave.

– I couldn't stand his brother Duddy either. All the Joffes. But still, he was a good man. Not my taste, but a good man, for a slob.

– Suddy wasn't so bad, said Dave.

– I'm not saying he was bad. He was a yokel. They came from a farm. In Saskatchewan. All the Joffes were yokels.

– They were Dad's cousins.

– Nobody has to know that.

– Who cares?

– We never let people know that the Joffes were related. Your father agreed. You shouldn't have been seeing so much of Suddy, Mooney. The whole city was talking.

Dave was irked by that.

– Just leave him alone! He's been going through a pretty rough time.

– Look who's defending him.

– You know he left all his money to Mooney, said Dave. Tons of money.

– And the taxi license.

– I don't want to hear about the taxi license. I thought he had a nephew in Toronto. He should get the taxi license.

– That's what everybody thought. It was an imaginary nephew. Or rather he had a nephew, but the nephew never wanted anything to do with him. So he was disinherited.

– That's the Joffes for you.

Dave and his mother sat immobile for a while with Mooney in the lightless den, comforting Mooney, hardly speaking now. The shock and manner of Suddy's death was starting to sink in, leav-

ing them feeling something they couldn't quite square. The wind
outside had died down and there was a feeling it might be a mel-
lower afternoon.

Their mother broke the silence in the den.

– I'm glad your father isn't here to see this, she said suddenly.
He couldn't have hacked it. I was the strong one.

– He liked Suddy.

– This would have killed him.

– That's moot now.

– He couldn't have hacked it. He always tried to look after
Suddy. Always wanted people to know Suddy was family. I had to
put my foot down. And he agreed.

– We've gone through this already.

– I had to be the strong one. But he was fond of Suddy.

– Suddy was fond of him, too.

– Everybody liked your father. I was the ogre.

– Give it a rest, said Mooney.

Mooney, pissed off and feeling he had run out of tears, left his
mother and Dave alone in the den and went out to explore. His
eyes felt raw and his throat ached. Dennis was there with Marilyn, who was pregnant, and they were holding hands. Dennis
was pretty broken up, but in a serene way. He looked surprisingly
good in a suit. Mooney told him so.

– Smart, you're not wearing a tie, said Mooney.

– I know what can happen at these things.

– No, I mean you look smart without a tie.

– Marilyn has me dressing like an Iranian diplomat.

– You look cool, Dennis.

– So how come you've never come down to see me. See the
Foundation.

– I'll come by.

– What are you going to do with the money Suddy left you?
Want to invest it?

– Get back in the maw of the market?

– Very Suddyesque.

– Nah. I'm out. I'll drive cab for a while. Think over my
options.

More people came into the house bearing tortes and kugels and
lasagnas and casseroles. Naomi walked in with Larry Brickman;

she hadn't brought anything. She and Larry split off after Larry was castrated at the tie and she wandered over to the den, with those charming motions of hers. She stood in the doorframe, peering into the dark room, motionless. Mrs. Kaufman caught sight of her and felt imposed upon and raised a hackle, turning her head away. Dave saw her too and they entered into a screaming whisper match.

– It's Naomi, said Dave.

– I know who it is. What I don't know is what she's doing here.

– You don't have to talk to her.

– She ruined Mooney's life.

– No, she didn't.

– Now she wants a private minute.

– So?

– Why are you taking her side? After the breakup she never so much as said she was sorry.

– You wouldn't have talked to her anyway.

– Still, she could have said she was sorry.

– How?

– Was her dialling finger broken?

– She wanted to see you.

– She could have brought something. Look, she came empty-handed.

– Maybe she put it in the kitchen.

– I'm sure she came empty-handed. I know her.

– Be nice.

– Years of married life down the toilet. I don't like her. I'd like to tell her off, the *shtik drek*. She didn't even bring this much.

Mrs. Kaufman pinched her fingers together to indicate how little 'this much' meant.

– We have lots of food.

– Thanks to you. To your kindness.

Naomi drew a breath and marched into the den. Dave stood up, shook her hand, and let her sit beside his mother. It had been a long time, and the two women embraced with emotion.

– I wish it had worked out for you two. You were such a beautiful girl, and he loved you so much. I'm sorry if he ever caused you problems. He didn't have an easy life then. He couldn't find himself.

– I know. But I think . . .

– I wanted to see a baby from you two. From the two of you.

Mooney could see Naomi with his mother in the den from where he was standing with the Eisenteeth clique, far off to one side of the living room, by the coffee cakes.

Oz, looking shittier than ever, had a large glass of rye in his fist. Richie Michaels had placed it in his palm just ten minutes ago, in lieu of conversation.

– Hey, don't go away, he said to Oz, I want to talk to you later.

He had the slickest way of sloughing people off.

Dennis was still holding hands with Marilyn, right in front of Sammy.

Sammy was there alone, as Anna had refused to come for many reasons. Firstly, she couldn't stand Dave Kaufman and was worried that Mrs. Kaufman would have ignored her in front of everybody because she knew that Suddy was a cousin to Mrs. Kaufman, the way she knew all the Kaufman shit. Secondly, she had been ostracizing Marilyn since her daughter had announced her pregnancy and brought Dennis to the house. She told her he was too old for her.

– Right, Marilyn said sarcastically.

– He's too old for you, Anna said.

– Right, said Marilyn even more sarcastically. You married someone a lot older too.

– But . . .

– But what?

– But nothing.

– I know what you want to say about Dennis, mother.

– How do you know what I want to say? Are you psychic?

– I know what you want to say.

– I said what I wanted to say. He's too old for you.

– Right. Too old.

– That's what I said.

– There's something else you want to say, mother.

– I'm not saying anything. I'm not even talking to you.

Sammy's line on Dennis was that Marilyn had done a lot worse in the past. But truth be told, he didn't give a shit anymore what his kids did. They could go fuck themselves, and they and he'd

probably be better off for it. Lying in bed one night he told Anna
that they should stop worrying so much about the kids. Which
was like asking someone to stop eating for the rest of their life.

– Let's just do what the *goyim* do, said Sammy.

– What do the *goyim* do?

– They let them sink or swim. In some cases, they drown
them.

– We can't do that.

– Why not?

– We're better than that.

– Not true.

– I'm going to save her.

– By not talking to her?

– I'm her mother.

– I'm her father.

– A father is just a man inside. A mother has to be a father and
a mother and a lawyer and doctor.

– Just talk to her.

– When she listens to me.

The *shiva* was growing more relaxed. There was some muffled
laughter here and there, taut faces were softening. Death is a party,
Mooney thought, and poor is Suddy six feet under.

– You know, I'm more scared of going to a *briss* than a *shiva*,
said Sammy.

– You're fucking with me. You prefer a *shiva* to a *briss*? asked
Dennis.

– In all honesty? Yes. I'm squeamish; what can I say.

– In this city that's all there is, *shiva*s and *briss*es, and what's in
between, said Oz.

– Incidentally, the rapists killed him, said Sammy, wielding the
word rapists as if they were a political party.

– What do you mean rapists? asked Oz. Were they trying to
rape Suddy?

– It wasn't a homosexual crime, said Sammy.

– How did they kill him? asked Oz.

– They threw him through a window. Three times. Didn't they?
said Sammy.

– Yes, said Mooney. How did you know?

– The whole city knows.

– What I'd like to know, Marilyn said, was how could they throw him through the window three times?

– The first two times he didn't go through, said Sammy.

– That's right, said Mooney.

– Cut himself and bled to death. Cut his *gorgle* open, said Sammy.

– How do you know this, Sammy?

– The whole city knows.

– He's right, said Mooney.

– How do you know?

– I talked to the witness, said Mooney.

– How?

– Just like that. I contacted her.

– She was a hooker.

– Part time.

– It's this economy, said Oz.

– What I'd like to know was what Suddy was doing there in the first place? asked Sammy. With all the money, why was he driving cab.

– With this economy.

– It relaxed him, said Mooney.

– I mean why did he confront the rapists? said Sammy.

– He was trying to get her money?

– Whose money?

– The hooker's money. The money the rapists owed her.

– If they raped her, why did they owe her money?

– Was she raped?

– She was beaten up pretty badly, said Mooney, when I saw her.

– What was Suddy doing there in the first place?

– He drove the cab that night. It's my fault in a way. I dropped the cab off and I didn't stop him from working that night. Millions in his cash-out, and he wanted to drive cab that night.

– But what was he doing there?

– He picked up this fare, said Mooney. A prostitute who had been raped by these two guys, who then wouldn't pay her and threw her out of their house. Without her shoes. She called a cab and Suddy picked her up. He was on the way to the hospital with her when she told him what happened. But when he heard that they hadn't paid her, he went insane. He went back with her, demanded her money, and they threw him through the window. End of story.

– They used to throw Suddy out the window in elementary school, said Sammy. Back in the Depression.

– Bizarre.

– The big kids would open the window and just throw him out. Onto the snow or grass, didn't matter. He was that small.

– Poor Suddy.

– He'd be back in a flash; and they'd throw him out again.

– And that's how he died. End of story.

– It'll all come out in the inquest, said Oz.

– You're right, said Sammy, using Oz's finger of truth.

– I'm right, said Oz, using the finger of truth right back at him.

– Poor Suddy.

Someone put music on the stereo system.

– Should there be music at a *shiva*? asked Sammy. We haven't even said Kaddish.

– If it's not inappropriate, said Mooney.

– I don't get invited to many of these things, said Oz. I wouldn't know.

– You say that like it's a bad thing.

– You don't need an invitation, Oz.

– Now you do.

– You don't. You just show up.

– No. I hear they're restricting them. There are bouncers now. These are swanky affairs, said Oz. I bet you this one put Dave out at least five thou.

– What's come over Dave lately?

– Where do you get your information?

– The liquor alone and flowers I'd say cost three grand, said Oz.

– What about the other two?

– Staff and service.

– Staff is service.

The mild afternoon sun reflected off the snow. Dave had stowed his mother in a cab and sent her home. After Sammy and the

Rabbi led the Kaddish some people moved off to the entertainment room to watch the hockey game. Others were still drinking, and Dave moved around talking to people. He saw Naomi sitting alone in the den, with a dark yellow light coming off the snow through the windows.

– You want a light on?

– I'm good.

– Where's Larry?

– He went home. Hockey game.

– He could've watched it here.

– He wanted to watch it at home. .

– How come you're still here?

– I wanted to talk to Mooney.

– He told me you were seeing each other, Dave said.

– He broke it off. Months ago.

– Why?

– It's all or nothing with him.

– Double or nothing.

There was an awkward silence for a moment. He had forgotten completely how charming Naomi was and thought of something to keep the conversation going.

– Do you want me to get you anything?

– I'm good.

– Alright.

– I'm going to watch the game now.

– Alright.

– You're sure you're okay?

– I'm good. I'm just going to wait here for Mooney.

Dave left and Naomi sat alone in the dark, relaxed in that charming way of hers. There was hardly any light coming in from outside now, just a slip of silver lying on the sill. Mooney, having avoided Naomi since he first talked to her in the very spot where she was still sitting, saw how dreamy she looked and went inside and sat down next to her.

– Larry's gone?

– He went home to watch the game. Sorry about Suddy.

– He didn't deserve to die that way. It's made me feel very lost. I can't stop crying.

– You'll get over it.

– It's still early days.

– You sure cried a lot at the gravesite.

– I had a lot to get out of me. I've been crying for days. Like a horse.

– I've missed you.

– I've missed you. You look gorgeous.

– Thanks.

– No, really.

– Alright.

– How's Larry?

– Larry's great.

– I heard you were in Miami. The two of you.

– Yeah.

– How was that?

– Great. Miami was great.

– All that art deco.

– Yeah.

– And the Cuban food.

– Good.

– You were okay there?

– I was good.

– That's good.

– I heard Suddy left you a lot of money.

– How did you know?

– The whole city knows. How much was it?

– A lot.

– How much is a lot?

– Figure it out: he made three thousand percent on a hundred-fifty-thousand stake. Plus a taxi license and a taxi.

– Do you know what you're going to do with it? Are you getting back into the market?

– No. That's over.

– Good decision.

– Just saying it is like having a full body cast taken off. I think Oz knew what he was talking about. It wasn't right.

– You know what they say: behind every great fortune is a crime.

– Balzac?

– Balzac. What are you going to do?

– No idea. Just bumble along, as usual. Maybe I'll help Dennis out.

– We both know that's not true.

– But it's good that it's out there, as an option, the Dennis thing.

– Are we going to see each other? she asked.

– Nah. No more exes.

– And you're still in love with someone else?

– Right. And you're carrying my baby.

– Right.

– None of anything was true. I'm sorry.

– Yeah, sorry, she said.

– It was all fiction. Fictional money, fictional relationship. Just fiction.

– You're such a fuck-up, Mooney.

– There's something I'm not doing right. I don't know what it is. I can't seem to get it right. And I'm running out of time. I need something real. And it's my own fault I can't find it.

– Don't beat yourself up.

– I don't.

– That's your problem.

As the maids were clearing the dishes, after the hockey fans and the Eisenteethers and Naomi and everyone else had left, Mooney wandered round Dave's big empty house, wondering whether to go home or not. Once the maids left, the mini-manse fell into total darkness and silence.

The wind started whistling and howling again and when he looked out the window he swore he could see how cold it was getting. Being in Dave's monster house just magnified the sense of how violent the cold and wind were outside. The bigger the house, the emptier it can get, thought Mooney. With Candy in Palm Springs, and his kid and his family always following Candy around, it would always be this empty. And to think Dave and Candy had once had a hell of a fight because Candy thought it was too small.

He heard Dave in the den, crying. He followed the sobs and saw Dave on the sofa. His eyes glowed in the dark they were that red. It felt gorgeous to see Dave so down. Really gorgeous.

Mooney felt exhausted but flooded with relief and goodwill. He didn't understand shit, though.

– What's wrong?

– I need help.

– How can I help you, Dave?

– Fuck off.

– Come on.

– Just fuck off and go home already, Mooney.

– What's wrong?

– Just fuck off.

– You feel bad about Suddy?

– What?

– For treating Suddy like crap all these years. You never invited him to the *briss*.

– What? Oh that. Who was I going to seat him with?

– Yeah, you treated him like crap.

– No, I didn't.

– The way you treated Dad. Like crap.

– I didn't treat Suddy like crap.

– Whenever he'd come visit, he'd say to you: 'Where's my kiss?'

– That's right.

– But you wouldn't kiss him.

– You did the kissing.

– Suddy was lonely.

– He chose the life he lived.

– You liked Suddy, didn't you?

– Actually, I did.

– I knew it.

– I did. I did like Suddy.

– So why didn't you give him that kiss?

– It was you. It was you who never let me get close to Suddy.

– Me?

– Fuck off, Mooney. Just go home. Or better yet, take the money Suddy left you and buy a house for fuck's sake. Don't *intershtip* me.

– You'll be okay if I go?

– Just fuck off.

– Can I help you?

– No.

– How can I help you?

– Fuck off.

– Suddy used to say you were a good kid.

– That's not helping. Just fuck off, Mooney, for the umpteenth time.

Mooney felt he was getting close to something.

– How can I help you? he said again to Dave.

– Don't be such a suckhole.

– I'm not a suckhole.

– You always flaunted your relationship with Suddy, driving him here and there. And that big performance at the funeral. You blocked me from getting close to him. From getting close to Dad. You know why I never gave Suddy that kiss when he said 'Where's my kiss'? Because you were sucking up to him. You never left any room.

– You were a miserable kid.

– And you were a suck.

Now Mooney didn't feel so great. His face clouded. Dave stood up, threatening, his eyes red, his chest pounding with heartache.

– I'd just like to knock you down, said Dave. Cripple you.

– Go ahead. Knock me down. Would that put the world back in order?

– I think it would.

– Go ahead then.

Dave wiped his eyes and took a swing at Mooney. Mooney went down hard on the rug.

– I knew him, too. Dave said.

– Who?

– Suddy.

– What are you talking about?

– I knew him before he died, said Dave in a very hard Suddy way.

– Certainly!

That made them both piss themselves.